Sanibel Dreams

A Shellseeker Beach Novel
Book One

HOPE HOLLOWAY

Hope Holloway

Shellseeker Beach Book 1

Sanibel Dreams

Introduction to Shellseeker Beach

Come to Shellseeker Beach and fall in love with a cast of unforgettable characters who face life's challenges with humor, heart, and hope. For lovers of riveting and inspirational sagas about sisters, secrets, romance, mothers, and daughters...and the moments that make life worth living.

Sanibel Dreams - Book 1
Sanibel Treasures - Book 2
Sanibel Mornings – Book 3
Sanibel Sisters – Book 4
Sanibel Tides – Book 5
Sanibel Sunsets – Book 6
Sanibel Moonlight – Book 7

For release dates, excerpts, news, and more, sign up to receive Hope Holloway's newsletter! Or visit www.hopeholloway.com and follow Hope on Facebook and BookBub!

Prologue

Even before she opened her eyes, Teddy reached for Dutch, but he was gone. The cool sheets told her he'd been up and out for a while.

So it hadn't been a dream. He'd left their bed. That couldn't be good.

She rolled over to see the sliding glass doors wide open to a rare cloudy sky, allowing in wind-whipped air and the melancholy song of the seagulls.

It was as if all of Shellseeker Beach knew Dutch Vanderveen's time had come.

Sliding out of bed, she stepped onto the balcony and spotted him, way past the sea grass, sitting on the very end of the boardwalk, his head bowed. Without changing or even getting a cup of tea, Teddy marched down to the beach, surprised when he didn't turn around at the sound of her bare feet on the wood.

"Are you praying?" she asked.

His broad shoulders shook with a snort. "I don't believe in God. Or the devil."

"I know." She sat next to him and dropped her head on his shoulder.

"But if I'm wrong?" he asked. "Then the chances that

I'm going to meet one or the other today are pretty damn high."

Today? Really?

She took a deep breath and closed her fingers over the crystal that hung around her neck, not bothering to argue. When he'd stopped wearing one of his own, she knew he was giving up the fight.

She could feel Dutch's energy waning fast. At a few points in the night, she thought he might be gone. "Are you sure?" she asked on a whisper.

"Oh, hell, Theodora Blessing. I'm not sure of anything." He leaned into her. "'Cept that I love you."

She sighed. "I love you, too."

"And that my peripheral vision is gone and I'm weak."

But he didn't sound weak. Dutch never did. Even as he knocked on death's door, his voice was a deep baritone, warm and rumbling from his big chest like he was still in the cockpit of a 747.

This is your captain speaking.

"Why don't I make some lemon balm and jasmine tea?" she suggested. "It helped your vision the other day."

"For the love of all that's holy, woman, no more freaking tea."

"I'm trying to help."

"And you have." He put an apologetic arm around her. "You have given me seven hundred and four extra days. Did you know that?"

She hadn't counted, but wasn't surprised he had. "And each of them has been lovely."

"I landed on this Florida beach with six to eight weeks, max. Then you worked your Theo magic." He nestled his nose in her hair as the heavy breeze lifted her curls, his pet name for her tickling her ear. "My little silver-haired witch. How can I ever thank you?"

"I'm not a witch, and it wasn't magic." She inched back to look at him. "And you have thanked me by loving me. By staying with me and being my...my family."

She wanted to say "husband" but Dutch and Teddy never lied to each other, only the outside world.

"Everyone's your family, Theo. That's what you do. You make families. You pick up strays and lost souls and wanderers and...dying men. You shower them with tea and sympathy, give them a home, offer up your heart, and..." His voice cracked and he dropped his head with a sob.

"Dutch!" He never cried. Never. She almost couldn't stand the impact of it.

He lifted his head and looked at her, his silver-blue eyes as stormy as the sky behind him. "I'm so sorry."

"Don't." She rubbed his back in the soothing circular motion he loved. "Never be sorry."

"Messy, messy life," he murmured. "Great takeoff... hard landing. And so much turbulence until I met you at damn near eighty years old."

She just stroked his back, knowing he needed her touch and comfort more than answers right now. No reason to offer wisdom or guidance to this great pilot who'd charted his own course and followed it, for better or worse.

"And now...it's time," he said. "I'm not going to be here tomorrow. I'm not getting seven hundred and *five* days."

"We don't know that, Dutch, and your energy—"

"Stop it," he ground out. "My energy, my ass. What about my will?"

She blinked at him, stunned at the words. His *will*? His will to live or...the other kind? Because every time the subject came up, his answer had been firm. His will was written, his estate would go to his closest living heir.

And what she does with it...is up to her.

She'd heard it all before, and when she'd gently ask for more details or suggest he make an effort to reach out to the daughter he rarely spoke to, he'd go silent. And in Teddy's never-ending effort to give him peace, to heal and not hurt, she let that silence slide. So, really, they were both to blame.

After a long moment, he huffed out a breath. "It's the guilt that's killing me more than the stupid tumor, you know?"

"Let it go. Guilt just sucks your good energy and—"

"And makes you realize what a mess you've made."

She couldn't argue that. "But now isn't the time—"

"No, Theo. It's not the time. I should have done something years ago. Months ago, even. But I cannot right this plane now," he said gruffly. "And I can't guarantee you...anything. You know it's all done already."

She didn't know anything, because if she even whispered the word "will" he frequently disappeared for the whole day to brood, returning in a foul mood.

"Dutch," she sighed. "We can call an attorney and change whatever you want to change legally. You know how important it is to—"

"I can't do that!" he insisted.

Can't or won't? Was his daughter that important to him, or was this guilt he felt driving the decision? He'd all but ignored Eliza for the two years Teddy had known him, and she got the feeling it had always been that way. So now he was leaving his daughter, a veritable stranger, everything...regardless of the fact that Teddy's heart, soul, and bloodline was tied to this land he owned.

Frustration rolled through her, but she knew better than to let that negative energy waft off her and onto him. He was sensitive, like she was, and if he picked that up, it would increase his cortisol and that made the tumor grow. One of the ways she'd kept him alive for two extra years past the date the doctors gave him was by surrounding him with serenity.

In return, he'd loved her like no man she'd ever known. With all his confidence and humor and brashness. All his chaotic Dutch affection and attention that made her feel whole and alive and needed. And at seventy years old, that had been a rare and unexpected gift for Teddy.

He pushed up and started to walk away, leaving her to stare at him with heartache and confusion.

"Dutch..."

But he was already halfway to the surf, crossing the shell-laden sand with a surprising amount of purpose, slowing when he reached the gunmetal gray Gulf of Mexico.

She took a slow, steadying breath and followed him. But just as she reached him, he turned, his eyes red-rimmed and wet.

"I'm so ashamed," he admitted on a jagged whisper. "I'm so damned ashamed of my life and my mistakes and my bad choices and lousy..." His voice caught and he held his hands out, swaying.

"Dutch!"

He brushed her off with a moan, stumbling. "I'm so *ashamed!*" he roared, louder than the churned-up surf behind him. "I'm a selfish bastard who's lived every single day for *me*. For the next adventure. The next woman. The next flight. The next horizon. Now it's nothing but...wreckage."

She made another effort to go to him, but he spun around, the movement bringing him to his knees.

Crying out again, she looked around for help, but on a rare blustery day like this, the beach was empty as far as she could see in either direction.

Dutch fell completely then, hitting the sand with a grunt.

Instantly, she was on him, turning him over, tears blinding her as she said his name over and over again.

He opened his eyes, but looked past her, to the sky. His favorite destination.

"Dutch, please, let me—"

"Birdie," he whispered, his expression distant.

She glanced overhead to where a seagull swooped

and fluttered and headed toward the water, knowing the childish word was probably the result of a tumor that pressed on some tender memory in his brain. A tumor that no amount of tea and crystals could eliminate.

"Dutch, if I can get you inside and call—"

He gripped her arm, but he had no strength in his fingers. "Maybe...Eliza...can..."

Eliza can what? Forgive? Understand? Not care? She had no idea what his distant daughter would do. And right now, as she held the man she loved in her arms and felt him fade away, she didn't care.

"Please, Dutch, please—"

"She could help you...forgive me..."

"Don't die on me, Dutch!"

He stared past her at another seagull, into the sky where he'd spent so many hours, the life fading from his old eyes.

"Birdie." He breathed the word, his last.

Chapter One

Eliza

Six Months Later

The ferry from Key West to Sanibel Island was...a party barge?

Eliza handed in her ticket and crossed the rubber-covered gangway onto the triple-decker boat, which was already wall-to-cash bar with tourists.

She hadn't expected it to be this crowded in June, but no one seemed to mind the heat. She'd foolishly pictured an elegant ferry like the kind that cruised into Martha's Vineyard or Nantucket. Which was stupid, because she was in Florida and the throng at the dock in Key West was nothing but a sea of beach coverups and cargo shorts.

And she glided on board in a gauzy sundress.

Rolling her eyes at her natural tendency to *not* fit in, she settled on a bench for the start of the three-plus-hour ride up the coast. All around her, the passengers snapped pictures of the occasional dolphin that leaped from the deep blue waters, and marveled at the verdant Everglades that formed the coastline. Everyone on board the *Gulf*

Coast Express laughed, drank, soaked up the June sunshine, and left their troubles behind.

Everyone except Eliza Whitney.

For this newly widowed, recently fired, deeply heart-broken solo traveler, troubles weren't left behind. They were stuffed in her overnight bag, pressing on her heart, threatening to spring a few tears from behind her sunglasses. She wasn't here to bask in the sun, suck down umbrella drinks, or check out the scenery. This ferry was a fast and easy way to get from the Keys, where she was staying with friends, to Sanibel Island, where she was headed to meet her father's widow.

Even her purpose for being on board wasn't fun, which was another reason to feel severely out of place in this crowd.

After a bit, she got up and shouldered her way through the tourists, climbing to the top deck. It was less crowded, thanks to the wind, which whipped her hair. Fishing a ballcap out of her bag, she tugged it on, pulling her shoulder-length strands through the back.

She found a space where she could hold on to the railing and stare at the blue-on-blue horizon, asking herself the question that had plagued her since her husband died four months ago.

What in the name of all that was holy was she going to do with the rest of her life?

When there was nothing but silence in her head, she clung to the railing as the big boat cut through the glassy, smooth waters of the Gulf of Mexico, still feeling so frightfully out of place. But wasn't that always the case with her? Hadn't she spent most of her life in situations where she felt she didn't fit in?

When would she open her eyes some morning and think, *Ahh, this is where I belong?* Because, so far, it hadn't happened.

When she was not even ten years old, her divorced mother had remarried, moving them in with a man who had three much older kids and an established home. A nice man, a nice family, and a nice house. But Eliza didn't belong there. An outsider from day one, she left at eighteen without looking back.

For the next few years, she'd starved in New York, trying to make it as a singer and dancer on Broadway. No matter how hard she tried, how much she practiced, or how desperately she wanted to hit the big time, the back row of the chorus was the best she could do, always one beat out of step with everyone else.

Then Ben Whitney came along, swept her off her dancing feet, and when she landed, she was living in Los Angeles as the young wife of a boutique movie studio head. Canyon Studios made "wholesome" entertainment, so even that didn't mesh well with the rest of Tinseltown. She'd made a few friends, had two children, and lived a full life as a stay-at-home mom.

And then, when Olivia and Dane grew into independent teenagers, she decided to strike out again professionally. At forty, with Ben's urging, she launched her first real career as a talent agent at All Artists Representatives, hoping to use her nurturing skills to guide wanna-be stars to fame and fortune. Except most of those people didn't need a mama, they needed a shark.

Eliza was no more of a shark than that dolphin currently entertaining the passengers on this boat.

She kept the job for thirteen years, mostly because she was married to a studio head, and also because she'd snagged one of their most high-profile clients, who refused to work with anyone but her. Still, she never felt at home in that Century City office.

Finally, she entered the most recent chapter of her life—nursing her husband through his long and losing battle with pancreatic cancer. Had she been a good nurse? Maybe, but so many of those dark days ended in a teary breakdown in the bathtub at midnight. The last weeks of hospice had been so agonizing that she felt more relief than grief when Ben passed four months ago.

After that wore off, grief made its presence known. Along with guilt—had she done enough?—and fear and worry and this sense that it didn't matter where she went, she'd be lost and out of place.

Then the high-profile client retired, and AAR gave Eliza her walking papers. Free—and lost—she'd accepted an invitation from that same client to spend a few weeks at his guest house in the Keys. She'd hoped the respite would help her figure out what she should do with the rest of her life, but it hadn't.

All those weeks did was delay the inevitable return to LA, to an empty nest and an empty life and an empty bed. Where she would battle bouts of insomnia, waking up after a recurring dream of walking along the edge of the sea, toes in the sand, a flowery skirt flipping around her ankles, a woman at her side.

The woman in her dream was family, she knew, but it wasn't her daughter, Olivia, or her mother, gone these past four years. But *family*. And every time she turned to see who it was, the woman's face melted into nothing, the way things did in dreams, and she woke up with the fragrance of something beautiful filling her nose. The first few times she actually wondered if she'd left a scented candle burning, the smell was so strong.

In fact, she'd had the dream again last night, and it had sealed her decision to take this boat up the coast to Sanibel. The woman she was going to meet wasn't family, not exactly, but she was...related. Loosely. By marriage. Maybe she would have the answers to—

Her thoughts were interrupted by the digital melody of "Memory" from *Cats*, heralding a call from one of her favorite people, who was most definitely family.

She pulled out her phone and tapped the screen with a picture of a gorgeous brunette and the name Livvie Bug with a pink heart. Although Olivia lived in Seattle and spent most waking moments at work, her daughter was one of the great constants in Eliza's life. A day rarely passed when they didn't talk, especially now during what they both called The Year of Craptastic Changes.

"Hey, Livvie Bug," she said, using the term of endearment she'd hung on her baby girl almost thirty years ago when she brought her home from the hospital. "You're up early. It's only eight out there."

"Have you met me?" Olivia cracked. "I've been to the

gym, cleaned this apartment, and already premade my dinners and put them in Tupperware."

Eliza laughed. "Slacker."

"What about you?" she asked. "It sounds windy in Coconut Key."

"Sorry." Eliza cupped her hand over the mic in the phone. "I'm actually not in the Keys anymore. I'm on a party barge. Except in my case? It's a pity-party barge."

"Mom! You're not throwing Dad's ashes somewhere without me, are you? Because I'll kill you if you are."

"And then you'd have to throw my ashes somewhere," Eliza deadpanned right back. "No, honey, I left them in L.A." She flinched. "Does that make me a terrible widow? Should I be carrying them around in my purse or something, talking to him instead of myself?"

"Only if you've lost your mind. Where are you going on the pity-party barge?"

"Fort Myers."

"Which means nothing to this West Coast woman."

"It's a town on the Gulf of Mexico with a bridge that will take me to—brace yourself, now—Sanibel Island."

Olivia gasped. "You're going? Seriously? What happened?"

She wasn't exactly sure where the turning point was, but maybe it *was* that dream. But no matter how much she loved and trusted Olivia, she wasn't telling her that. Then she'd *know* Eliza had lost it.

"That woman, Theodora Blessing? She will not stop texting me and asking me to come and help settle my father's affairs." Eliza rolled her eyes at the words.

"Although the only 'affairs' Dutch Vanderveen had were with stewardesses."

"Um, they're called flight attendants now."

"Not by him. Anyway, yes, I'm taking a ferry up here because it is way faster than driving from the Lower Keys. When I get to Fort Myers, I'll rent a car and drive to Sanibel Island and finally meet the woman my father was married to for...a year? Two? I don't even know, because he couldn't be bothered to invite me to his wedding."

"He didn't come to yours, right?"

"He didn't come to a lot of things. There was always another trip for him, another place he had to be, another flight for Captain Aloysius Vanderveen." And while that was sad, Eliza had long ago accepted that truth about her larger-than-life, live-to-excess father.

"What changed your mind?" Olivia asked. "Last time we talked about it, you had no desire to meet this lady. I mean, you weren't exactly close to Dutch."

So true. At best, Eliza had a detached relationship with her now departed father. They spoke, they saw each other every few years, sometimes even less frequently than that. But they never *connected*. She never thought of him as Dad, not since he walked out of her life more than four decades ago. After that, he was just Dutch, the old Air Force call sign that she guessed was a nod to his family ancestry, or just easier to say and spell than Aloysius. Whatever name he used, he was always too busy flying somewhere to be a father to her. She'd stopped wishing he would be long ago.

"I think going up to Sanibel was in the back of my mind ever since I decided to visit the Keys, knowing I'd already be in Florida. And..." Eliza dug a little deeper and easily found the truth. "I feel guilty for missing his memorial service."

"Six months ago? Lose the guilt, Mom. You were in the thick of hospice with Dad when Dutch died. There was no reasonable way for you to go to Dutch's funeral."

Yes, but Dutch *was* her father. A lousy one, but the only one she'd ever had. She should have paid her last respects, so that's what she was doing now.

Not that she ever *respected* him when he was alive. Until the day she'd died, Eliza's mother had insisted that Dutch had been a lying, cheating, womanizing commercial pilot who Mary Ann referred to as "Satan" after he moved out when Eliza was eight. And for the next forty-five years, he'd done little to change that opinion. In fact, he'd practically disappeared off the face of the Earth two years ago.

"I wonder what this Theodora is like," Olivia mused.

"Well, she goes by Teddy, never changed her last name to Vanderveen, and lives in a place called Shellseeker Beach. That is the sum total of what I know about her."

"If nothing else, it should be interesting. Maybe you'll find out something cool about old Dutch. He was always a hoot when he showed up."

Except that he so rarely showed up.

"How long are you staying?" Olivia asked.

"I brought a change of travel clothes, a rolled-up

jersey maxi dress, and enough underwear for two days. So, not a long trip, and I haven't even told her I'm coming. I still might change my mind. If I can't stand her, I can get back on the ferry later this afternoon and be in the Keys by sunset."

"Don't change your mind, Mom," Olivia said. "You've gone this far and who knows? Maybe Dutch left you a fortune like in the movies."

She snorted. "Knowing that man? I'd be lucky to get his Pan Am wings and a copy of *The High and the Mighty*. He always told me I should read that book."

"Well, good luck in...what's this place called again? Shellshocker Beach? I hope it's full of happy surprises."

She laughed softly. "Me, too, Livvie Bug."

"And don't forget to sing, Mommy."

She smiled at the sweet reminder to sing, because what Olivia really meant was, "Don't forget to live."

"I'll try," she promised.

After they said goodbye, Eliza felt a little better. Olivia always had that effect on her.

When the boat docked in Fort Myers, she found her way to a car rental agency that catered to tourists arriving on the ferry. By the time she got to the front of the line, a candy-apple red Mustang convertible that cost more than she wanted to spend was the only vehicle available that wasn't a minivan or SUV.

When she touched the button and the roof slid into a snazzy compartment behind the back seat, replaced by blue, blue sky, Eliza felt like some kind of sports car-driving imposter. She wasn't a convertible person. With the sun on her face and the wind in her hair, she pulled out her phone and made an impulsive decision.

Tapping the screen, she found the Bluetooth and started up her favorite playlist, a simple backing track of show tunes, perfect for singing her heart out. The first few notes of "Somewhere" from *West Side Story* filled the air. And her heart.

Ben loved when she'd sing this song in the shower. It always made him climb in with her. Smiling at the memory, she listened to the opening chords slipping into the first stanza. And then, Eliza cleared her throat, opened her mouth, and...and...and...

Nothing.

Nope. She just wasn't ready to sing. Not yet. She could hear the words in her head, though.

There's a place for us. Somewhere—

With a soft grunt, she silenced the music. Not yet. She just couldn't do it yet.

But maybe someday...*somewhere.*

ELIZA REVVED the Mustang's engine to the top of the bridge—called a causeway, she noted—that connected this barrier island to the mainland, and got her first real look at Sanibel Island.

Surrounded by sun-dappled water, it stretched for more than ten miles, with a distinct weathered lighthouse at one end and nothing but shades of emerald green to the horizon.

As she reached land, everything seemed to transform from decent-sized city to charming small town. There were stop signs instead of traffic lights, a mom-and-pop grocery where one would expect a supermarket, and brightly colored restaurants with the specials painted on surf boards instead of fast-food chains or strip malls.

Residential neighborhoods were tucked into canal-lined streets along the main avenue that cut through lush foliage. She passed City Hall, a good-sized library, and many signs for a wildlife refuge with the precious name of Ding Darling.

Not a sign in sight for Shellseeker Beach, which didn't show up on her GPS.

So before she got to a small bridge to another island called Captiva, Eliza turned around and retraced her route, re-examining every sign. Just as she reached for her phone to call Teddy and give up on the element of surprise, she spied the welcome center and impulsively swung into the lot. Surely someone in here would know how to find this local beach.

She parked and took off the baseball cap, taking a deep inhale of the freshest air she'd ever smelled, redolent with a scent that was somehow both sweet and salty. Like honeysuckle and mint mixed with the sunshine beaming down from a blinding blue sky.

Was that the elusive fragrance she breathed in her dream?

Not quite, but the thought gave her some goose-bumps as she headed for the tidy stone building. Pulling the glass door open, she entered a blissfully air-conditioned reception area surrounded by racks of flyers, booklets, and brochures.

Behind a desk, a woman tapped on a computer keyboard without looking up. She kept her head down so that all Eliza could see were deep, dark roots sliding into yellow hair cut into a bad pageboy.

"Um, hello?" Eliza took a step closer.

With a sigh, the woman finally abandoned the keyboard and peered over glasses perched on her nose. "Yes?"

"I have a strange question," she said.

"They all do," the woman answered dryly, then gestured toward a row of free-standing shelves packed with tourism brochures. "The answer is there. Find it."

Eliza drew back and looked around. "Oh, sorry," she muttered under her breath. "Did I stumble into the *unwelcome* center?"

"And we got ourselves a comedian, Patty," the woman called out as she adjusted her glasses to get a good look at Eliza. "I'm not here to make friends and win votes, hon. I stock the flyers, answer the phones, and make sure no one breaks a rule. My husband's the mayor, my son's the head of the city council, and my daughter-in-law runs the historical preservation committee. That earns me the privilege of sitting in this seat and making sure the tourists can find their way to the wildlife refuge or the shell museum where you can see an actual junonia, because, trust me, you won't find one on the beach, even though everyone thinks they will."

"Well, I don't know what a junonia is—"

"The rarest of all seashells."

"And I saw the signs for Ding Darling. Is that really the name of a sanctuary?"

"Ding was JN Darling's nickname. You should go there and watch the birds. Goodbye."

Eliza actually laughed. Was Attila the Sanibellian for real? "I'm trying to find my way to Shellseeker Beach."

"That's a local name. It's officially called Mid-Gulf. What are you looking for?"

"A woman named Teddy Blessing."

Now the woman took her glasses off and inspected Eliza like she was an actual criminal.

"Hilton?" she asked.

"Blessing," Eliza corrected. "Theodora Blessing. I don't have an address, but..."

She ignored the questions, shaking her head, openly scrutinizing Eliza. "No, no, not Hilton or Marriott. Your clothes are too expensive. Ritz-Carlton? Ever since the word got out that Dutch died, those pigs have sniffed around Shellseeker so hard you'd expect them to come up with truffles."

Eliza frowned, completely confused.

"I'm going to go with Baldwin Hotels," the woman continued. "Upscale, expensive, and I understand they are hungry. Which you must be, since you look like you've never been in the same room as a cheeseburger." She leaned over the counter, narrowed her eyes, and flipped her hand over imaginary hair. "Good color job, though. Red without being that godawful purple they wear today. What's it called?"

Eliza reached for a strand of her hair that, after weeks in the Keys, had definitely gone from auburn to strawberry-blond. "I call it natural."

"*Right.* Did you hear that, Patty?"

No one answered, so Eliza pressed one more time, figuring she was dealing with the local lunatic. "Shellseeker Beach?"

"Yeah, yeah. But listen, whatever big chain sent you, I'm gonna warn you flat out. No amount of greasing the palms will get the laws changed. You can buy that dump on the beach, and you can put your logo on the sign, but no bigger than four inches. And you cannot build an eyesore in its place. We have rules for a reason. So, whatever cash you guys are waving around, we're hoping Teddy has the guts to say no. Being a new widow and all..." She crossed her arms. "Don't you try and take advantage of her, now."

"I have no plans to," she said, wondering how to get an answer. Maybe at *this* information center, you had to give some to get some. "I'm Teddy's stepdaughter," she offered.

"What?" Her eyes widened. "You're Dutch's daughter?"

Another woman popped out from a doorway Eliza hadn't noticed, a stack of glossy magazines in her hands. "Are you *really?*"

"Yes, I am," Eliza confirmed, bracing for whatever reaction that might bring.

The expression on the woman behind the desk

suddenly changed. Her features softened as she came around the desk with outstretched arms.

"You have my deepest sympathies," she crooned. "What a terrible loss it was."

The eavesdropper, Patty, tossed her magazines on the counter and darted out, and suddenly Eliza was in the middle of an unwanted group hug.

"Oh...well, thank you," Eliza said, standing stiffly as they squeezed.

"There was no one quite like Dutch," Patty said. "He made us laugh."

"The man lived like every day was a gift," the woman from behind the desk said.

Eliza stiffened a little more, trying to ease out of their touch.

"I'm Penny, by the way," she said. "Lucky Penny, your father used to call me." She bit her lip like it pained her to say it. "He always had to give a nickname, huh? What did he call you?"

Eliza frowned and thought about it. "I don't remember."

"Well, I'm sure he had one for you," the other woman said. "I'm Patience. Your father said I was named that because I have to put up with my sister." She pointed at Penny. "An *un*welcome center." She hooted softly. "Isn't that like something Dutch would say?"

"Exactly," Penny agreed, but then she narrowed her eyes, scrutinizing Eliza. "Why weren't you at his memorial service? I know I didn't see you there."

Why lie? "My husband was in hospice at the time."

"Hospice?" Patty looked horrified. "Is he…"

She nodded. "Four months ago."

"Oh, dear." Patty covered her mouth. "You poor, poor thing. Your daddy *and* your husband? That's not fair. So not fair."

But Penny looked askance, as though a dying husband simply wasn't a strong enough excuse for missing the memorial service of her gift-sharing, nick-name-giving father.

"Teddy can heal you," Penny announced, the words surprising Eliza.

"Oh, she will!" Patty agreed. "She's a healer, you know. What that woman can't fix with her collection of crystals, she'll do with a cup of homegrown tea and a hug. Look what she did for Dutch!"

What did she do for Dutch?

"Are you moving in with her?" Patty asked.

Moving in? She wasn't even sure she'd spend the night. "I'm just visiting."

"From?" they asked in sisterly unison.

"I live in Los Angeles."

Penny's eyes tapered to distrustful slits. "How *odd* that Dutch never mentioned anything about a daughter in Los Angeles."

"Oh, you know Dutch," Patty said. "He never talked about himself. He made everyone feel so special."

Everyone? Not Eliza.

"Does Teddy even know you're coming?" Penny asked, crossing her arms again, as if she wasn't going to believe one more word that came out of Eliza's mouth.

"I wanted to surprise her," Eliza said.

"That's so nice." Patty pressed praying hands against her lips.

"You're not just giving us a load of hooey, are you?" Penny demanded. "Those hotel people can get very creative trying to get a piece of this island, and the piece they want is Shellseeker Beach. There are millions and millions of dollars at stake on that property."

"Oh, Penny!" Patty clucked. "She wouldn't walk in here and pretend to be Dutch Vanderveen's daughter if she was with a hotel chain! Your imagination is one for the books."

"Wouldn't be the first person who tried to get around the system."

"Pay no attention to her," Patty said, grabbing something from a stack of brochures on the counter. "She's our resident rule maker."

"And where would we be without rules?" Penny scoffed. "We'd be another tourist ghetto with high-rises on the beach and Burger Kings on every corner. No siree, hun. Not on Sanibel Island. We have *standards*."

"Look here..." Patty snapped open a colorful, hand illustrated map. "What's your name again, sweetie?"

"Eliza. Eliza Whitney."

"Okay, Eliza. You see this big thing shaped like a shrimp's head? That's Sanibel Island. This fat part near the mainland is where you'll find the lighthouse; this is the causeway you came over. Here's where we are, and way up here is Captiva, our sister island."

"Bring your money," Penny muttered.

Patty just shook her head. "Okay, we're here. You head west—Sanibel is one of the rare barrier islands that runs east to west and doesn't hug the coast. That's why we get our amazing seashells. We're the seashell capital of the world, did you know?"

"Patty," Penny whispered with a warning look as she returned to her station behind the desk.

"Right, sorry. Okay, you go down here where it says Mid-Gulf. Look for Roosevelt Road, which is the name of the street the cottages are on. Shellseeker Cottages. There are seven of them, as you probably know, and of course, the main house that Teddy's grandfather built way back when he homesteaded that beach, but it was rebuilt after the hurricane of—"

"Patty, the woman isn't here for a history lesson."

"I'm sorry." Patty's chubby cheeks grew pink as she took a breath. "I just love Sanibel history. My sister likes her rules, but if you want to know history? I'm your girl."

"Thanks. I'll remember that." Eliza smiled and reached for the map. "This is plenty of information, Patty. I'm sure I can find it now."

"Well, just remember you'll see the tea house first, which isn't really much more than a hut with a counter for tea she practically gives away, but all of the teas are grown in her garden, and that's the real draw. Teddy'll be there, more than likely."

"Great, I'll—"

"You'll love the gardens, which are quite the spread of flowers and herbs. Teddy's mother planted them way back in the 1950s. She was a master gardener who absolutely went to her grave believing that her flowers were growing on a Calusa Indian burial ground. Now, that tribe went extinct in the 1600s, so that's a stretch even for a history lover like me, but who knows? What Teddy grows will knock your—"

"Patience Joan Burkhouser," Penny ground out. "Let the woman go."

Patty giggled. "Sorry."

"It's fine," Eliza assured her as she refolded the map. "And fascinating. Thank you, Patty. And Penny."

Penny leaned over the counter. "Don't let Teddy sell the place, please. I know it's tempting, and those hotel companies are throwing money at the woman because they can't build on Sanibel and there's only so much beachfront property in the world. Buying old hotels and motels is the only way they can get a piece of our tourist action, which is quite healthy, thank you very much. All Teddy needs is good help. And I don't mean that blond trollop who cleans the rooms with a kid and no husband in sight, or the guy who rents the paddleboards."

"Connor Deeley," Patty said, fanning her face with pink-tipped fingers. "Too young for us gals, but a woman can look, right?"

"You really need help," Penny fired at her.

Eliza laughed softly at the sister act, nodding once more to both of them. "Thanks for the advice and information, ladies."

As she walked out, Eliza was only mildly surprised that Patty followed, taking her arm and pulling her closer, clearly not done rattling off her fun island facts.

"One more thing," she said in a hushed whisper, glancing over her shoulder as if her sister might swoop out any minute. "If you get to Sanibel Treasures, the shell shop, you've gone too far, even though it is technically on Shellseeker Beach and is part of Teddy's business. But do stop in and meet Roz and George, who run it. And that's where you'll find the original message in a bottle written by Theodore Roosevelt himself! You know he used to vacation here and Teddy's grandfather worked for him?"

"I didn't know that."

"Oh, yes!" Her eyes, as pale blue as her sister's, but much warmer, danced. "She's named after him, did you know that? Oh, of course you did! Teddy's your stepmother. And Dutch was your dad, you lucky dog. A man who was a fighter pilot in Vietnam, and then flying for Pan Am in the glory days! It must have been a dream to be raised by him."

But Eliza *hadn't* been raised by him. And she sure couldn't break this poor woman's hero worship and tell her that the "glory days" were basically long absences punctuated by broken promises.

She just smiled and lifted the map. "Thanks for your help, Patty."

"Oh, of course. Your father was so charming and funny." She pressed her hand to her chest.

"Thank you," Eliza said vaguely, finally escaping to the parking lot.

As she slid into the Mustang, she stared straight ahead and thought about everything she knew about her father.

Charming and funny.

Yes, he was. But he was also distant, distracted, and determined to be anywhere but home.

She took another deep breath of that fabulous air and hoped to God she didn't have to listen to a litany about St. Dutch when she got to Shellseeker Beach. Of course, people change. But not that much.

Chapter Two

Teddy

The relentless June sun pressed hard on the gardens, dampening Teddy's scalp under the sun hat she wore. As the slow summer season settled over Shellseeker Beach, the stretch of white sand with thousands of seashells was nearly deserted. There were a couple of die-hard tourists doing their best to master the "Sanibel Stoop" picking up shells, but even Deeley's paddleboard and kayak rental cabana was slow today.

The heat was probably keeping any customers away from the tea house, too. Only a few would straggle up from the beach in search of the best hibiscus iced tea in the state of Florida.

That meant it was a perfect time to garden. She took a basket, gloves, and some tools to tend to the flowers. Kneeling in front of a lemon-yellow purslane bush under the shade of an oak, she tossed off the hat and watched a few butterflies flutter over the red and orange popcorn balls of lantana.

The flowers comforted her. The tea she made from them her. But nothing ever really erased the low-grade worry. Lately, that had plagued her more than grief, nipping at the edges of her heart, a constant reminder that she had no idea how long until the hammer fell.

Any day now, she supposed. She had no idea how probate worked, except that the lawyer she called after Dutch had died said it could be six months or more. Well, it was officially "more" now, and she still had no idea what was going to happen with Dutch's estate.

Teddy shoved her trowel deep into the soil, turning it over the root, wishing she could do something other than wait, or send vague texts to Dutch's daughter, hoping she'd respond before she got that will in hand and signed Teddy's life away.

"Hello?"

She squinted up, blinded by the sunshine that backlit a woman in a knee-length cotton dress draped over a narrow frame. She couldn't make out her face behind big plastic sunglasses and a ball cap pulled low.

"Do you want some tea, dear? It's the honor system in the tea house if you want to help yourself. Leave whatever amount you like. But if you want a certain flavor, I'll help you."

"No, no tea. I'm looking for Teddy Blessing." Her voice sounded tentative, and vaguely familiar.

"You found her." She felt her shoulders slump. Another hotel spy? They sent them all the time, as guests usually. They tried to cozy up to Teddy, find out her price, her weakness, her breaking point.

Or worse, maybe this was the attorney she'd been dreading, come with paperwork and bad, bad news.

"I'm Eliza Whitney."

For a moment, she wasn't sure she'd heard right, and she shook her head to clear it. "Eliza. Dutch's daughter?"

"Yes, that's me."

"You're here?" Her voice cracked as it rose with surprise and hope. She came! She didn't send a lawyer. That had to be good, right?

"I'm sorry I didn't call, but I wasn't sure I could make it until the last minute..."

Teddy felt momentarily paralyzed, trying to get ahold of this news. She put one hand on her chest as a thousand thoughts went to war, not the least of which was, would Eliza see things her way? Did Eliza *have a heart*?

She tried to push up, but just couldn't do it because her legs were shaking. Instantly, Eliza reached out a hand to help her, and Teddy took it.

"Guess these old legs aren't what they used to be," she said, letting the taller, stronger woman help her to her feet. "And you..." She squeezed Eliza's hand, struck by the aura of uncertainty and distrust that seemed to emanate from her very skin.

All the colors mixed and muddied together, making Teddy remove her hand because it upset her. Sometimes her empathy was her own worst enemy.

"Well, this is a surprise," Teddy said on a nervous chuckle, wiping her brow with the back of her hand. "Hello, Eliza. It's lovely to finally meet you."

Eliza gave a tight smile, nodding. "And you, Teddy. I...yeah. Nice to meet you."

They stood for an awkward moment of silence, but

Teddy brushed some dirt from her hands and gestured toward the hut. "Why don't we have some iced tea? And talk. Or is it too hot out here for you? My house is just over there."

"Sure. Tea would be great." She laughed softly. "And so would air conditioning."

"Of course, yes. June on Sanibel. Let me just put this away and..." She glanced at the basket and tools. "And get tea. I mean, you haven't lived until you've had my hibiscus."

Darn it! She was rambling.

Of course she was. She knew next to nothing about Eliza Whitney, since Dutch rarely talked about her. She fell into that great big unknown called "his past" and he refused to go there. All he ever said was that Eliza's mother had kept them apart.

"Come, I'll get the tea. Or you can just stay in the shade and look at the view. Pretty, isn't it?"

Eliza turned and took in the stretch of sea oats and sand, all the way to the water. "Gorgeous," she agreed.

At the tea hut, Teddy calmed herself with good thoughts and about fifty ujjayi breaths. She poured two iced teas and returned to the shade to walk Eliza to the house. They crossed the gardens, leaving the tea house and outdoor tables unattended, but she didn't care.

The only thing that mattered was Eliza, and how best to present...the issue.

"Oh, is this one of the rental bungalows?" Eliza asked, pausing at one of the smaller, efficiency-sized cottages.

"One of seven cottages," Teddy told her. "All different sizes and colors, each named for a shell you can find on Sanibel Island. That's Sunray Venus, and all along this strip of land past my house you'll find Slipper Snail, Cantharus, Bay Scallop, Wentletrap, Lion's Paw, and, at the end, our queen cottage, Junonia."

"The rarest shell, right?" Eliza asked with a smile.

"Ah, you've done your homework," Teddy said.

"I swung by the welcome center and got a quick lesson from the sisters."

"Oh, dear," Teddy said with a laugh. "Penny and Patty. Now there are some Sanibel treasures. Let me guess—some history from Patty and a lesson in island protocol from Penny."

"Pretty much on the money," Eliza said on a chuckle. "But they got me here."

"You could have called," Teddy said softly. *And warned me*, she thought with a slow inhale. Then she would have prepared with some calming tea and a long meditation this morning. And maybe a shot of Dutch's secret stash of Chivas.

"I know," Eliza replied. "I wasn't sure..." Her voice trailed off and she let out her own sigh. "And I imagine this is as awkward for you as it is for me."

The confession loosened something in Teddy's heart, erasing some of her worry. Maybe Dutch's daughter did have a heart.

"Yes," Teddy agreed as she turned toward her house. "But it doesn't have to be."

"Patty threw a lot at me at once," Eliza said as she

looked up at the two-story beach house raised on stilts, her gaze traveling up the stairs to the covered decks that faced the beach. "Your father built this. Am I right?"

"Technically, my grandfather built a tiny house that originally sat here. My father rebuilt the next iteration," she said, leading her toward the stairs. "There've been a few storms that meant the place needed more work, and then I added on years ago." She pointed to the sturdy railings and sea-foam green shutters that hung on all the windows, feeling a wave of pride at how lovely and inviting her house was.

And how tentative her hold on it actually was.

When they climbed up the stairs to the main level, Teddy used the sliding glass doors to enter the house, welcoming Eliza into the cool air-conditioned living level.

"Oh, this is lovely," Eliza said, looking around. "So bright and cheery."

"Thank you. It's a comfortable home and...well, please, have a seat."

Biting back her nerves at the conversation she knew she was about to have, Teddy set the iced teas on the coffee table. Eliza followed her to the living room and perched on the edge of the pale blue sofa. She took off her sunglasses and set them on the table, nearly stealing Teddy's breath when she looked into gray-blue eyes.

Wow. The reddish hair wasn't Dutch's, but those eyes? They matched Dutch's distinctive eyes fleck for fleck.

An attractive woman in her early fifties, Eliza didn't have any of the pulled or stretched appearance of someone trying to fight time. Her skin was fresh, with only mascara and lip gloss for makeup, a smattering of freckles over the bridge of her nose, and soft lines around her eyes.

But Teddy was rarely interested in the outside of a person, and never more so than right now. What she zeroed in on was a person's essence, which she sensed by touching them or feeling the waves of emotion that rolled off them.

And something was sure rolling off Eliza. An undercurrent of uneasiness and the feeling that she'd like to be anywhere but here. Did that mean Eliza was about to drop a bombshell?

I've inherited this property and decided to sell...

She couldn't bear to hear the words, so Teddy delayed the inevitable with small talk. "Did you fly in from California, Eliza?"

"No, actually. I was in the Keys and took the ferry to Fort Myers."

"Oh," Teddy said, raising her brows. "The Keys? I didn't realize you were so close. Were you on vacation?"

"Not exactly." Eliza gave a humorless laugh. "As you know, my husband died four months ago, and I was just..."

"Regrouping," Teddy suggested when Eliza couldn't seem to find the word.

"Exactly." She took her own sip of tea, as if she needed to collect her thoughts more than to wet her whistle. "So, I found out the ferry was only a few hours' ride and decided I should come and see you." She gave a sad smile. "I know I'm late."

Decided she should come? Because a lawyer told her to?

"Better late, and all that," Teddy replied. "And, please, accept my deepest condolences on the loss of your husband. Sadly, I know exactly how you feel."

"I know you do, and I'm sorry for your loss as well." Eliza looked right at her, her expression softening.

"Considering how difficult it is to lose one's husband," Teddy said slowly, "I appreciate you coming all the way here."

But are you here to ruin my life? she mentally added.

"I should have come sooner," Eliza said, seemingly unaware of Teddy's inner turmoil. "I know I should have been here for the memorial service, but..." She shifted in her seat, absently touching the polished amethyst crystal on the table, running her fingers over the purple edges and smooth surface. "This is pretty."

So she was delaying it, too. Or maybe...she didn't know about the will.

"Hold it," Teddy said softly. "Quartz has exquisite healing energy."

Eliza gave her a skeptical smile and glanced around. "I see you like them."

"The one you're holding is amethyst, which is a protective stone and excellent for reducing stress." She reached into a bowl and scooped up a handful of smooth red stones. "This is jasper, a nurturing stone that will do amazing things to eliminate negative energy."

Eliza nodded, obviously amused but too polite to roll her eyes. Teddy didn't care. Dutch had been that way in the beginning as well, but after a month of wearing a long quartz pendant and feeling like a new man, he'd become a believer.

She fingered the single stone around her neck, remembering how he called the first one he wore his magic fake diamond.

While Eliza held the amethyst, Teddy gestured toward the expansive view. "Well, whatever brought you here, Eliza, I'm certain you won't regret visiting Shellseeker Beach. First-time visitors say it stays with them forever."

"It's a very special place," she agreed, although Teddy could tell she was just saying that. She set the stone down and looked at Teddy. "And so fascinating that your family has owned it for all these years."

Fascinating...and false. Maybe she didn't know? Could she be here just because Teddy had asked so many times? Did that mean there was a chance to let this woman see what Shellseeker Beach meant to Teddy before it was turned over to Dutch's sole heir?

On a sigh, sensing that Eliza would be somewhat open to the history, Teddy stood and walked toward the sliders, preparing to tell the story properly. She was connected to the very earth they were standing on, and hopefully Eliza would understand and respect that. Hopefully.

"My family owned all of the land from the tea house to the shell shop," she began, wondering if Eliza picked up the past tense. "Not the waterfront, which can't be privately owned in this state, but from the sea oat line back to Roosevelt Road, for a half mile in either direction. The land was homesteaded by my grandfather, John Blessing, way back in the 1920s. He was one of the original forty families that lived here on Sanibel, long before there was a bridge from the mainland."

"That's truly a native of the state," Eliza said.

"Well, the original natives were the Calusa Indians, who lived here hundreds of years ago." She smiled, turning from the view to look at Eliza. "They still do, in some sense. The gardens you walked through were planted by my mother, Delia. She firmly believed there was an ancient burial ground under her lush and potent flowers."

"I heard some of this from Patty," Eliza said, but looked as if she might not be too interested in the Calusa tribes.

Teddy was sorry for that, but it was important that Eliza know the land had a different kind of value to Teddy, something with far more weight than money.

"My father built the cottages in the 1950s," Teddy continued. "And, along with my mother, ran a very nice little tourism business after the causeway was built. I was born here and lived every day of my seventy-two years in this house."

"Oh, wow," Eliza whispered as the first real impact of the history hit her. "That's amazing."

Yes, it was. And heartbreaking to lose.

"My father built the tea house so my mother would

have a place to serve the medicinal teas she grew in her garden. I grow those same plants and make those same brews to this day. And they turned an old boathouse into a shell and souvenir shop that still runs as Sanibel Treasures, a landmark on the island."

"There can't be many places like that left in this country," Eliza mused. "It seems everything gets parceled off and sold, especially waterfront property."

"Well, that's exactly what happened."

Eliza frowned, fully focused on Teddy. "What do you mean?"

So, maybe she *didn't* know. Hope crawled up her chest.

"In the 1970s," Teddy said slowly, "money got very tight. Tourism slowed and things were not great. My dad sold the property to an investor, and our family continued on as managers."

"Oh. So how did you get it back?" Eliza asked, confused enough to confirm Teddy's suspicions. If she thought Teddy owned the property, then maybe she didn't yet know that Dutch had left it to her.

"I worked at Sanibel Treasures as a teenager," Teddy told her, delaying the inevitable revelation. "And I helped manage the Cottages for most of my life. The property changed hands two or three times over the years, but all the owners wisely kept us as the groundskeepers and managers. And then, about ten years ago..." She swallowed and came back to sit down next to Eliza, knowing she should be close to deliver this news. "Dutch bought it."

"Dutch owned this property?" Her voice rose in surprise. "I had no idea. I remember when he retired to Florida a few years ago. He said he had a place, and I pictured a little condo, but...wow. He bought this?"

"Yes, but he didn't live here until two years ago. Before that, like all the previous owners, he kept me on to manage it."

"Huh." Eliza reached for her tea, processing this. "I honestly didn't know he had that much money."

Goodness, she didn't know anything about her father. On some level, Teddy knew that. But when faced with that truth, it shocked her. And left her disappointed in Dutch, and in Eliza.

"He had piles of Pan Am stock and knew long before the rest of the world that the company was going down the drain," Teddy explained. "He sold it all for a tidy profit, invested very wisely, and ultimately put his money here."

"I never knew any of that, but then..." She angled her head. "I'm sure you know that Dutch and I had a distant relationship. My father always had somewhere more important to be. I guess that place was Shellseeker Beach."

Teddy thought of the times Dutch had talked about Eliza, which was rare, but when he did, guilt wafted off him. Although some of his last words were about her.

Maybe...Eliza...can...

But she didn't know what he thought Eliza might do.

"That place was *only* Shellseeker Beach in the end," Teddy whispered. "Because Dutch came here to die."

"Came here to..." More confusion clouded her eyes. "What do you mean?"

"I mean exactly that. Two years ago, your father was diagnosed with an inoperable brain tumor and given a month, maybe two, to live."

Eliza's jaw loosened and her eyes widened.

"He made the decision to spend those few remaining weeks alone, here at Shellseeker."

"But he lived two more years?"

Teddy gave a soft laugh. "Never underestimate the power of my tea, some crystals, and a really good reiki massage."

The humor was lost on Eliza, who just stared at her.

"I was able to help him," Teddy explained. "I know some healing techniques that my mother taught me, some holistic approaches, not, you know, traditional Western medicine. He'd exhausted those routes. But he never expected a tomorrow, and was always grateful when he woke up, as his was an illness that could take him at any time."

Eliza let out a breath she might have been holding a long time. "And you married him knowing that?"

Time for more truth. There really was no way around it.

"I didn't actually...marry him," she admitted softly. "He wanted to sleep in my room, with me, as we got... closer. I wanted..." She'd wanted to get married, but Dutch said no. It was far too soon to confess that to Eliza. "Anyway, we had a 'unification ceremony' and started to call each other husband and wife. But it wasn't a legal marriage."

Eliza sat quiet for a moment, then closed her eyes. "Even knowing he was dying...he couldn't contact me."

Of course, her pain had nothing to do with Dutch's marital status, but his shortcomings as a father. Teddy understood that, and leaned closer, putting one gentle hand on Eliza's arm.

"He did contact you, Eliza."

"Not very often," she fired back, drawing out of Teddy's touch. "And I don't remember any real big apologies for being an absentee father."

"He was certain your mother poisoned him in your mind, and he was too proud to beg. And you..." Teddy lifted her brow. "Didn't exactly make time to see him."

She looked down at her lap, a soft grunt in her throat. "I know. It was hard. And I was consumed with kids and work and my sick husband." On a sigh, she looked up at Teddy. "All excuses, of course. We're both to blame, which is very sad. I wish I'd seen him in the end, but then, I wish he'd have been around most of my life."

"Well, you're here now."

She offered a wistful smile. "I do so wish I'd known he was sick. I just carried a man through cancer and buried him. I know what you went through, Teddy." Her eyes filled. "It's so, so hard."

For a long minute, they just looked at each other, matching mists in their eyes.

"I'm glad you were there for him at the end," Eliza said quietly as she picked up her tea and lifted the glass in a sweet toast. "And happy that your beautiful property is back in your family."

Teddy took a long, slow breath. "Except it's not."

Eliza lowered the tea without drinking, her gaze pinned on Teddy. "Dutch didn't leave it to you?"

Her heart hammered with the knowledge that she couldn't avoid one last fact any longer. "Well, that's where things get a little confusing."

She frowned again. "How so?"

Teddy picked up one piece of jasper, pressing the stone into her palm, taking the strength she needed. "I haven't seen his will, but I know one exists. He said it did. I assume, based on what my attorney told me, that someone will be contacting you after it's through probate."

"Me?"

"You're his only living heir, Eliza."

She blinked. "So...that means...he left all of this to me?"

"That's what I assume, but I haven't seen the will. Have you?"

She shook her head. "No, and no one has contacted me. I haven't heard about a will. I had no idea..."

"It can take months for the death notice to be filed and move through the probate system, according to the attorney I contacted. But when it does..." Teddy had to fight the urge to kneel in front of this woman and beg. Instead, she slowly returned the jasper to the bowl and put her hand on Eliza's arm once again.

"When it does, what?" Eliza asked.

"I don't have the money to buy it, but Shellseeker Beach is in my blood. It's my life and legacy and the only world I've ever known. I don't want to lose it. I can't. I just...can't. All I can hope is that you agree."

Eliza didn't say a word, but dropped back on the sofa with a thud, clearly stunned.

Chapter Three

Eliza

Of all the things she'd heard about the mystifying, elusive, infamous Dutch Vanderveen in her life, the very last thing Eliza ever expected was that he'd left her a dime, let alone a seven-cottage resort on the beach in Florida.

Wait. What had those women in the welcome center said?

Millions and millions?

Of course this much beachfront property would be worth a holy ton, and now she *owned* it? The man her mother called Satan really had left her a fortune? Land that Hilton and Baldwin and Ritz-Carlton wanted so badly the locals knew about it?

When her head stopped buzzing and her heart rate slowed to something less than freak-out level, Eliza tried hard to think through anything and everything Teddy had said.

Shellseeker Beach is in my blood. It's my life and legacy. I don't want to lose it.

She stared at the woman across from her, somehow seeing her in a different light than she had when she arrived.

Her first impression was...loose. A petite yogi with a cloud of silver curls that tumbled past her shoulders, with blue eyes as glittery as one of her New Age crystals, and unexpected dimples that blended into remarkably few laugh lines when she smiled. She was loose and gentle and as pliable as the drapey top that hung over her black leggings.

But the more Eliza studied the soft lines on her face and her graceful, spare movements, she realized that this woman was centered and strong and unlikely to hand over her *life* and *legacy* without a fight.

"I have to say I'm very, very confused and shocked," Eliza admitted. "And I'm sure you can understand that I can't believe he left me anything, let alone..." She pressed her hands on her chest and huffed out a breath as she thought of the scope of this. "Are you *sure*?"

Teddy lifted a shoulder, the picture of uncertainty. "This is why I've been contacting you. I didn't want to tell you over the phone or leave you to find out from a lawyer you don't know. This is difficult. I know you probably want to think about what to do with the property, maybe get to know me, but I'm hoping and praying you'll be reasonable, Eliza."

"Of course I'm reasonable," she said. "I don't have all the facts and figures, but I have no intention of being unreasonable. No one's going to boot you out of house and home, Teddy."

Teddy looked at her, blue eyes widening. "If you sell to an outsider, chances are this property will be broken into parcels and destroyed."

Sell to an outsider for...millions and millions. Eliza had a secure life and a comfortable savings, but not *millions and millions*.

"How much land did you say again?" She honestly hadn't been paying attention when Teddy recited the long history of the place, but had been sizing her up, and trying to imagine her tall and broad father with this woman who was barely five foot four.

"Just seven cottages and the main house, the gardens and tea house, and a souvenir shop," Teddy said.

Just? "So you're talking about essentially a half mile—"

"A little more."

"Of prime beachfront property that includes seven rental units and two functioning businesses?" She almost blew out a whistle, because holy *Moses* that was some inheritance.

"Eliza." Teddy's voice was taut and her surprisingly smooth skin was pale as she whispered, "If one of those hotels gets their hands on it, they'll ruin it."

"Isn't there a law against building high-rises?" She was certain rule-following Penny had told her that.

"Yes, but they'll take the heart out of the place. They'll turn it into something commercial and cold. They'll destroy my gardens and raze the old shell shop and turn the cottages into...something without a soul. Wait until you see what we have here, Eliza. It's one of a kind and, really, sort of holy."

Yes. Indian burial grounds where they had unification ceremonies. Bungalows with souls and sacred gardens. She got that, but...good heavens. This was life-changing, and who needed a changed life more than Eliza?

Well, maybe Teddy, but she didn't know the woman. At all.

"I promise you, I don't want to be greedy," Eliza said softly. "Just realistic."

Teddy's eyes shuttered. "But my family is deeply connected to Shellseeker, Eliza.That's my reality."

Eliza squirmed, suddenly feeling like she was back in the AAR conference room trying to get baseline perks for her client, but some sneaky, money-hungry producer was trying to negotiate her out of everything.

"I'm just making sure I understand this clearly," Eliza said. "My father, who wasn't legally married to you, bought a property that was once, many years ago, owned by your family and has had several owners since then. But Dutch owned it last, then he died, and left it entirely to his only heir, who is me. Are you asking me to...give it to you?"

"I'm not asking anything, but I want you to know that this is my home...in spirit."

"In spirit?" She didn't want to scoff, and she respected the woman's history, but seriously. "He left it to me," Eliza whispered, the impact really hitting her. "And maybe he did that as a kind of restitution." Otherwise, wouldn't he have changed his will or legally married Teddy to give her a fighting chance at ownership?

Honestly, it sounded to Eliza like he really hadn't changed all that much.

But Teddy was obviously suffering through this conversation, and Eliza didn't want to make things worse, so she kept all that to herself.

"I was just hoping to give you perspective," Teddy said. "I do not have the energy or the resources for a legal battle."

"And I don't want one, Teddy, nor do I want to swoop in here and wreck your life," Eliza said, holding her gaze, because she meant that very much. "But if it's mine? Well, I guess I'll have to read the will, talk to a lawyer, and think it through."

Teddy looked scared and worried. "I understand."

Did she? "Maybe it wasn't about money," Eliza said. "Maybe Dutch left it to me for other reasons."

"I've thought of that," Teddy said, studying her with an intense gaze. "But you didn't come here for money, did you?"

"Of course not," Eliza agreed. "I certainly didn't know there was any—not this much, anyway—at stake."

"Then why did you come?" Teddy asked.

She'd just answered that question on the phone with Olivia, but somehow this moment deserved an even deeper level of honesty. Guilt for missing the memorial service wasn't the only reason she'd come.

"I came because I was lost and not sure where to go next," she admitted. "And truthfully, I wanted to ignore your calls and texts and just put them in that...that box where I've stuffed Dutch for my whole life. But it felt like since he died, I should finally stop doing that."

Teddy nodded, sadness in her expression. "So you want closure?"

"Maybe. I guess if I talked to a shrink, that's what they'd tell me," she said on a quick laugh. "I've held a life-long grudge against him, but I'm mature enough to know I bear some of the responsibility. I've been an adult for many years, and it was always just, I don't know. It was easier to *forget* about Dutch. I get that he didn't come to my wedding or graduations because nobody wanted him and my mother in the same room. But I tried, Teddy."

She shook her head, remembering just how many times she tried and how it hurt to be rejected by him. "I invited him to join us on a ski trip, and he declined. After my mother died, I asked if he wanted to come to L.A. for a movie premier at Ben's studio. Something fun and different. Nope. He was...busy. I even called him when Ben was first diagnosed, hoping he'd say, hey, why don't I come and see you? Yeah...no. That didn't happen."

Next to her, Teddy let out a soft whimper of sympathy and reached out again, putting two hands on one of Eliza's. This time, Eliza had no desire to jerk out of her warm touch.

"Eliza, you do have some healing to do."

"I'm fine." But even as she said the words, she knew she wasn't, or these old memories wouldn't nip at her heart.

"I have an idea." Teddy added some pressure. "Why don't you stay in Shellseeker Beach for a while? You need time to figure this out and I can help you."

What that woman can't fix with her collection of crystals, she'll do with a cup of homegrown tea and a hug.

Eliza smiled at the memory of Patty's words, and the offer Teddy was making.

"I can tell you about Dutch, the good things you don't know," Teddy continued her effort. "And I would so love to hear about your dear Ben."

The words were as soothing as her hands, and surprisingly welcome. Eliza could feel her heart folding in half as she gazed into the mesmerizing crystal blue eyes of the other woman.

"I do need to see that will and figure out what this inheritance entails," she said.

"We can do that together," she urged. "And, of course, whatever you decide, I will abide by that decision. You have my word. I'm just asking you to give this some time and get to know the...magic of Shellseeker Beach. Can you do that?"

There was no possible way to say no to that touch, that voice, or those eyes. Even if Eliza wanted to leave, she couldn't. And for some reason, she didn't want to.

"I can stay for a bit," Eliza said on a sigh.

As soon as she did, perhaps for the first time in days, maybe months, she felt a very tiny tendril of hope in her heart. The feeling was unexpected, and it nearly took her breath away.

"Oh, thank you." Teddy folded her in a hug that was so warm, Eliza felt it right down to her toes.

She glanced at the coffee table and remembered Patty's words.

Tea and crystals and New Age lunacy aside, Eliza had to admit she felt better than she had in a long time. Of course, maybe that was because she'd just found out she'd inherited a fortune.

TEDDY INSISTED that Eliza stay in the "queen" of the cottages, Junonia. Together, they'd gotten her bag from the car and taken a tour of the property, which was simply a slice of heaven no matter which way she cut it.

And to think she'd inherited it? Even more beautiful, though she didn't say that to Teddy, who was clearly struggling and trying to do the right thing. So was Eliza. The problem was simple: they were both right.

After walking from one end of Shellseeker Beach to the other, even getting a glimpse of the adorable shell shop from the outside, Teddy had left Eliza in the two-bedroom cottage, promising to get her for dinner later.

Like all of the bungalows on the property, Junonia was compact, with a wide, white-washed deck, complete with a few Adirondack chairs for gazing out at the beach. The cottage was brightly painted in shades of yellow and teal, with one double-glass slider door facing the beach as the only entrance.

Inside, comfy rattan furniture sat on white tile under giant paddle fans that moved the air and fluttered the sheer curtains that framed the sliding doors. Seashell art, lamps with sand-filled bases, and beach-themed pillows on rattan furniture added to the quintessential coastal décor. There was a kitchenette with a counter and stools, a living area, one sizeable bedroom with an ensuite, a second bedroom, plus a second bathroom.

The shiplap-covered walls looked freshly painted and every room was spotlessly clean, but nothing had been really updated or renovated in probably ten or fifteen years.

Whoever bought it next should put granite where there was Formica, change out the tile for wood-like laminate, and call it a "villa" instead of a "cottage." Then they could probably double whatever rate Teddy was charging.

But future upgrades weren't her problem, Eliza thought as she hung up the one dress she'd rolled into her bag and put her shorts, T-shirt, and nightclothes in a drawer. But those upgrades might be her...opportunity.

If this property was *really* hers? That would be...

A rough blow for poor Teddy.

She shook her head, not quite ready to think that through yet. Instead, she checked out the kitchenette, and found the fridge had been stocked with water bottles.

Taking one, she grabbed her phone and stepped out onto the porch, folding herself into a chair to take in the postcard-worthy beach view.

The surf, which was as calm as the Gulf had been in the Keys, wasn't terribly close. The sand and shore were about thirty or forty feet away, on the other side of a section of sea oats or grass, accessible by a long wooden walkway.

She'd go to the beach next, but first, she needed to talk to someone who could help her make sense of this.

Tapping her phone, she made a face when she got her daughter's voicemail.

"Hello, you've reached the cell phone of Olivia Whitney, senior buyer for Promenade Department Stores. Please leave a message and I will get back to you as soon as possible."

No doubt her laser-focused workaholic daughter was running through spreadsheets or perusing next season's merchandise even though it was Sunday.

Olivia had been playing "work lady" since she was a kid and could sit behind Ben's big mahogany desk in the library. And when she wasn't, she'd been shopping, so her job as a buyer was the ideal combination of things Olivia loved. Eliza just wished the company that had her daughter on the fast track to top management was based in L.A., not Seattle, because she sure missed her Livvie Bug.

"Hey, it's Mom," Eliza said into the speaker phone. "Well, it turns out you were right about Shellshocker Beach." She laughed, a little giddy at the very idea of what she had to share with Olivia. "I have news. Big news. Better news than I had last time I called. Call me when you can, Liv. Love you."

She set the phone down and picked up the water bottle, just as the sound of a tiny, high-pitched voice began singing...

Did she say "dollars to donuts" and...the best state fair?

Was someone singing a song from one of Eliza's favorite Broadway musicals?

She leaned forward, looking toward the sound and smiling at the childish voice, when suddenly its owner meandered down the stone path in front of the cottage. A little girl, five at the most, dancing along in a yellow bathing suit and a tutu—a legit, netted tutu—with a bright blond ponytail shooting straight up from the top of her head like a palm tree.

"*State Fair*," Eliza called to her. "A fabulous play. I was in it on Broadway. Okay, I was an understudy for the chorus, but still."

The child froze in horror, eyes wide, mouth open.

"Harper, where are you?"

At the shouted question, which sounded like it came from the next cottage, about fifty feet away, the little girl stopped again, staring over her shoulder at Eliza.

"Is that your mommy calling you?" Eliza asked.

She nodded, still looking like a tutu-wearing deer in headlights.

"Harper?" A woman stepped out of the next cottage, holding a dustpan and a broom. "I can hear you, but I can't see you!"

"She's right here," Eliza called back, standing up. "Entertaining me with show tunes."

"Oh!" The woman blinked, surprised to see her. "I didn't know someone checked into Junonia! I'll be right over to get the place in order."

"It's fine," Eliza said, but the woman was already

walking toward her, a ponytail the same color as her child's swinging, a smile as bright as the sun.

Wait. Was this the "trollop" who cleaned that Penny had so snidely commented about? Good heavens, what a misnomer for this fresh-faced young woman.

"Teddy usually texts me when we have someone check in without a reservation," she said as she reached the cottage. "Welcome to Shellseeker Beach!"

Before Eliza could explain, the little girl shot forward and threw her arms around the woman's legs, glancing up at Eliza with an expression of sheer terror.

"You have a future Broadway star on your hands," Eliza said, taking the single step down from the deck to greet them. "With a glorious voice, too. What's your name, sweetheart?"

She hid behind her mother and blinked.

"Tell the lady your name, honey."

She stared, silent.

"Whatever it is, I bet it ends up in lights," Eliza said, coming closer. "My name is Eliza."

"I'm Katie, the housekeeper," the young woman said. "Did you find everything you need? I can bring you more water and fresh towels."

"I'm fine, Katie." She stole another look at the singing angel. "But I do have to say that I love *State Fair*. Do you know anything from *Oklahoma*? It's another classic."

The child shook her head and buried her face deeper.

"Just that one," Katie said. "I found the DVD at a garage sale for fifty cents, and she got a little obsessed with the Ferris wheel on the front. Then it became her comfort movie and I think she's watched it forty times."

"Well, it's very comforting," Eliza said. "We have the same taste, so we can be friends. And friends do tell each other their names."

She whispered something inaudible.

"Harper," her mother clarified. "Her name is Harper and she's four, shy, and loves to sing."

"Hello, Harper. I love that name. Definitely a future star."

"Say thank you, Harper."

She mouthed the magic words, still tight behind her mother's legs, making them both chuckle.

"I usually do a little extra for arrivals," Katie said, looking behind Eliza at the cottage. "But I didn't know you were coming."

"I'm, um, a friend of the family." Sort of. But she didn't need to explain that to—

"Oh my gosh!" Katie gasped noisily. "You're *that* Eliza! Dutch's daughter!"

"Yes, I am." She gave a self-conscious smile, a little ashamed for not saying that right away, but she didn't know if the housekeeper knew Dutch or not.

"I didn't think you were going to come. Teddy and I have...wow. You're here." She patted her daughter's shoulder. "Do you know who this is, Harper? This lady is Uncle Dutch's daughter!"

Uncle Dutch? Somehow that just didn't fit in Eliza's brain. And she couldn't help but feel a twinge of jealousy. These strangers knew and loved her father, who didn't even send his *actual* grandchildren—who were close to this young housekeeper's age—a birthday card?

Harper looked unimpressed with her relationship to Dutch anyway.

"I'm so sorry for your loss," Katie said. "He was a great guy and just adored Harper."

"Thanks." She swallowed all the temptation to let these Dutch-lovers know that he hadn't adored his own child or grandchildren.

But then she remembered that Teddy said he came here with a terminal illness and no idea how long he'd be around. Maybe he wanted to be nice to these people so he got a few much-needed points in heaven. Maybe that's why he left the whole place to the daughter he rarely saw. Who knew?

"How long are you staying?" Katie asked.

"I'm not exactly sure yet."

"Well, it's not our prime season, but you'll love the beach. And summer in Sanibel means much lighter traffic and a chance to really enjoy the island."

"It's all so beautiful," she said, looking down at the little girl. "And can I guess by that tutu that you're also a dancer, Harper?"

She nodded and whispered, "Ballet."

"She's taking her first dance class," Katie explained. "Nothing too serious, but they're teaching her some basic positions."

"First position," Eliza said, sliding her bare feet so her toes were out, heels in.

"Look at that, Harper," Katie cooed. "This lady knows dance."

"Second position," Eliza added, stepping out.

Very slowly, Harper inched to the side, still clinging to her mother's legs, but clearly interested.

"Can you do third?" Eliza asked.

Enormous blue eyes looked up at her, then the child cautiously stepped to the side, and lined up her heels in front of each other, toes out.

"Very good!" Eliza exclaimed. "Look at that turn out. You, Miss Harper of Shellseeker Beach, are a natural."

She giggled and flushed and looked up at her mother, who grinned with pride, a hand on her little girl's shoulder.

"We better let you get back to the hard work of relaxing, Eliza," Katie said. "Sorry for the intrusion."

"Not at all." She crouched all the way down to get face-to-face with Harper. "I danced for many years, as you can see by my slightly crooked toes. Life is better when you dance. And sing."

She nodded, silent, but the slightest smile pulled.

"So, it was very nice to meet you, future star." Eliza held her hand out for a shake, which, after a moment's hesitation, she got.

"Why don't you tell Miss Eliza it was nice to meet her?" Katie suggested.

"Nice to meet you," she squeaked in a mouse voice, making Eliza smile and sigh.

Just then, her cell phone rang with a few notes of "Memory." Eliza pointed her thumb over her shoulder.

"From *Cats*. I told you I love musicals." She popped up. "And that's my daughter, who was just your size about five minutes ago." She smiled at Katie. "Enjoy her while she's young. It does go fast."

"That's what I hear," she said lightly, giving a wave as she walked her little girl back to the cottage she'd been cleaning.

Eliza returned to the chair where the phone sat on the armrest, humming to the music it played and smiling at the name on the screen.

"Hello, my Livvie Bug."

"Mom? You sound so happy!"

"You know what? I am. I think the Year of Craptastic Changes has taken a turn for the surprising."

Chapter Four

Olivia

Olivia gazed out from the window of her high-rise in Bellevue, the panoramic view across Lake Washington lost on her as she unpacked what her mother had just told her.

"That is un-flipping-believable, Mom," she said, tucking her bare feet under her and taking a sip of coffee. "There *has* to be a catch."

"The catch is I haven't seen the will. Neither has she. I'm his only living heir, although that's no guarantee I'm on that document. It's Sunday, so I'll make some calls tomorrow."

"And in the meantime?"

"Well, the view isn't bad, and Teddy's nice. I'm having dinner with her tonight."

"What's she like?" Olivia asked, settling deeper into her couch for a true gossip fest with Mom. "I mean, really. Don't give me 'nice' when I want details."

"Um...lots of tea. And crystals. Kind of New Age, you know?"

"Oh, God save me from the sage burners."

"Yes, she is, but not in a weird way," Mom said. "She's kind. And there's something about her that's real and, I don't know, warm? Like she really cares and wants to help."

"What she wants is the pile of money you are sitting on," Olivia said. "Don't be naïve, Mom."

"I'm not. But the property has been in her family for a hundred years."

"And it belonged to *your* father who was not *her* husband."

Mom let out a loud sigh, sounding super conflicted, which Olivia didn't think she should be at all. No matter how super soft-hearted her mother was—especially now, when that heart was still broken from losing Dad—she didn't owe this lady a thing.

"So, are you finally relaxing on your Sunday, or do you have nineteen more things to overachieve?" Mom asked.

It was Olivia's turn for a noisy sigh.

"Is everything okay?" Mom asked when Olivia took too long to answer.

"Yeah, it's fine. New boss, you know? And he's a shark."

"Oh, that's right! He started this week. Alex, right? How is he?"

"Yeah, Alex Brody. New merch department head and a total snake." Olivia closed her eyes at the thought of how much she already despised the guy who couldn't find a single thing good to say about her work. He sure loved Jason's ideas, though, especially once he heard that the other senior buyer had a Harvard MBA.

"A snake? In what way?" Mom asked.

"In the way that he's from Saks and wants his own team and I'm afraid I'm not going to make his short-list."

"Livvie, that's insane. You're on everyone's list. Doesn't that head honcho Nadia just love everything you do?"

"She does, but there's a layer between Nadia and me and his name is Alex Brody. I waited a year for a promotion, and, wham, my old boss leaves and a new one comes in who doesn't know me from...Jason."

"Oh, yeah, Harvard."

Olivia smiled, loving her mother for keeping up with office politics. "That's the one, but don't worry about it, Mom. Plus, if you get a few million for this beach resort, maybe I'll quit and you and I can take a year to travel the world and buy Euro merch that we can sell in our own store. How's that sound?"

"Like your dream, not mine. Not to mention, do you really want to travel with your old, widowed mother?"

"Old? I hate it when you call yourself old. You're only fifty-three, which is the new thirty. And when you're a multi-millionairess? You'll be one hot commodity, Elizabeth Mary Whitney."

She snorted. "You're the hot commodity. And I still think what you really need is—"

"If you say a man, I'm hanging up."

"A trip to Florida!" Mom finished on a laugh, which made Olivia smile. It sure felt good to banter again, after all these months of mourning.

"No thanks. Too many alligators. Have you seen one yet?" Olivia asked.

"No, but I met a four-year-old singing 'State Fair.'"

"Your personal crack," she said on a snort. "Kids and musicals. Please don't start on how you want to be a grandmother."

"So you didn't load that new dating app, I take it."

Loaded it, skimmed some candidates, and deleted it after five minutes. "Please. Who has time for that while I'm crawling my way to the top of the org chart? Better hit up your son, the genius AI engineer. Dane could program you a robot grandchild."

Once again, her mother laughed softly. "I miss you and Dane so much. And..." Her voice trailed off and so did the lightness in her voice.

"And Dad," Olivia supplied. "Don't dance around your grief, Mom. It still hurts, and it's allowed to hurt, and we just have to...hurt."

"I know. I keep wanting to get back to normal, but then I remember there is no normal."

"Still waking up crying?" Olivia asked gently, thinking of the sad confession her mother had made a few weeks ago.

"Not as often. It sneaks up on me now and then, but I'll figure some way through the grief."

"A couple of *million* ways?" Olivia teased.

But Mom didn't laugh. "Money won't bring him back, Liv." Her voice cracked just enough to make Olivia's heart twist. "If it did, I'd sell this place so fast poor Teddy would throw a crystal at me on her way out."

"Yeah, I get that. Money doesn't buy happiness."

"And, uh, neither does a new title on the office door."

"Oof," Olivia grunted. "Talk about throwing projectiles that hurt."

"I don't want to hurt you, Livvie. I'm just saying Dad didn't lay there on that hospice bed and say he wished he'd spent more time at work."

Olivia pressed her fingers to her lips, not wanting Mom to hear in case the sob threatening slipped out. God, she missed her funny, brilliant father. "What *did* he say?"

"That he loved you. And Dane. And me. And..."

And out that sob came at the same time as her mother's. "Oh, Mom. I hate that he's gone."

"I do, too, baby."

For a long, long moment they both fought silent tears, the way they had so many times since Dad died. Even before. It was a long, hard road from that first diagnosis to today. Sometimes it seemed like no matter what they talked about, it came back to Dad's illness, then his death, and now their grief.

"We'll get through this, Liv," her mother whispered. "One call at a time."

"I know, Mom. There's no limit of calls, or time that you can't make one."

"You're the best, Livvie. No one understands me like you." Mom gave a sad sigh. "So, I guess after taking all that personal time for Dad's funeral you don't have any vacation stored up."

Olivia tamped down a punch of guilt. Her mother needed her, and, worse, she had plenty of vacation days in the bank. But she couldn't risk taking it. Not with a brand-new boss and a major promotion on the line.

"The timing is awful, Mom." But then, when wasn't it? If she got the promotion, she wouldn't leave because she'd need to prove herself worthy.

She closed her eyes as she felt that corporate ladder sway under her.

"No worries," Mom said with false brightness that made it worse. "I'll get chummy with Teddy and find some seashells."

"Just don't let this New Age Teddy Bear talk you out of your fortune," Olivia said.

"My fortune. Wow. I can't wrap my head around it. Dutch didn't even make my wedding. Why would he leave me a property worth millions?"

"Guilt," Olivia said without hesitation. "He probably wanted to get himself through the pearly gates. I mean, if half the things Grandma Mary Ann said about him were true, St. Peter laughed and pointed the other way."

"Yeah, I had the same thought," Eliza said on a soft laugh, still hearing the echo of her mother's complaints. "And, hey, if it all works out and I do end up with a pot of gold, you can name your first baby Dutch."

"You, Mommy dearest, are relentless," Olivia said with an eye roll.

"But you love me."

"So, so much. Now, go get those millions. Europe is waiting for us."

Chapter Five

Teddy

After the delivery guy from Bailey's had dropped off the food and she'd set up a buffet table, Teddy went out to the second-story deck, rolled out her mat and took lotus pose to meditate. As the sun inched closer to the Gulf of Mexico, she scanned her body for stress points—which basically started at her head and got worse on the way down.

By the time she reached her heart, she quit the mental scan and tried to figure out why she couldn't find peace today. Probably because Eliza was here, and brought with her more questions than answers.

What did she expect? That Dutch's estranged daughter would tip her head, slip into a smile, and say, "Of course you can have Shellseeker, Teddy! No problem!"

But he'd said...

Maybe...Eliza...can...

Can what? Was that what he was trying to accomplish when he left her everything? Or did he mean she would forgive Dutch? Or that Teddy should?

That morning when Dutch died seemed so far away

sometimes. Teddy didn't dwell on it, but liked to spend her meditation hours thinking about the laughter, the love, the sweet days that two old people got to share when one was seventy and single for decades, and the other was closer to eighty and dying.

The halcyon days of Dutch and Teddy had been brief, but they were over. Now, she *had* to save Shellseeker Beach. For her family. Not the one buried all around Sanibel, not the one who preceded her here, or the three little babies her womb couldn't keep. Not even for Dutch, or the memory of him.

She had to save Shellseeker Beach for the family she had *now*.

"Teddy! Are you here, dear?"

That family, she thought at the sound of Roselyn Turner's voice. Young, old, black, white, from near and far. The family she'd created herself. That's who needed Shellseeker Beach. That's who, someday, should inherit it. Her fam—

"Teddy?"

The impatience in Roz's voice was loud and clear, making Teddy push out of her pose and lean over the railing.

"You're early, Roz!" She blew a kiss to Roz and George, taking a deep breath for centering. Tonight wasn't just a typical "Teddy party" that she loved to throw for her friends and the people who kept Shellseeker Cottages and Sanibel Treasures running. This was a way to show Eliza what mattered.

"George is hungry, as if that's a surprise. Can we just go in?"

"Absolutely! I'll be right down."

She slipped into the bedroom, past Dutch's "wall of fame" photos to the mirror over the dresser. There, she fluffed her silver curls and smoothed the fabric of the black top she wore over cream-colored leggings. With one quick adjustment to the crystal quartz that hung over her chest, knowing it would give her strength, peace, and good energy tonight, she slipped into sparkly flipflops and headed downstairs.

As she did, she took a deep breath and centered herself, tamping down a pang of grief because Dutch had loved these parties. He'd tell stories and pat backs and smoke cigars with George and Deeley when he thought Teddy wasn't looking.

No more stories and cigars. No more battling Dutch to give him one more day of life. Teddy had a different mission now, and saving this property was all that mattered.

At the top of the stairs, she looked down to see George already sniffing around the buffet, and Roz right behind him, making sure he didn't help himself to a cold shrimp before the party started.

She couldn't help smiling at the couple she'd met darn near ten years ago when they walked into Sanibel Treasures and flipped out over the store they now managed for her. Roz was deep into what she called her "turban years," covering her luxurious natural 'fro with a colorful headpiece that always matched her flowing caftan. George was as bald as the proverbial cue ball, his espresso-colored dome shiny even from this distance. He carried an extra thirty pounds that just made him squishy and wonderful...but made Roz watch every bite he ate.

Just before Teddy opened her mouth to greet them, she saw Roz grip George's arm and lean in to say something.

"Don't tell her yet," she whispered, not realizing the acoustics of the open second floor carried her voice right up to the landing.

"She'd want to know."

"But the prodigal daughter has come back. You don't throw a bucket of cold water on our friend on a night like this."

Gripping the handrail, Teddy came down the stairs slowly, her mind skipping over all the possibilities of this conversation, none of them good.

"A bucket of cold water?" she asked, and they both whipped around to see her. "What's the matter? Is there something wrong at the store?"

"Teddy!" Roz cruised closer, her arms outstretched, the hem of her flowy dress fluttering over the floor. "This is a beautiful spread. Thank you for including us."

Teddy froze, tipped her head, and narrowed her eyes. "What bucket of cold water, Roselyn Turner?"

Roz let out a sigh, her shoulders hunching. "You weren't supposed to hear that."

"But I did." Sorry, but she wasn't in the mood to play games or keep secrets.

Roz looked over her shoulder at George, who tried to

hide the fact that he was chewing. At her glare, he looked suitably guilty. "Shrimp's five calories, Roz."

"And a ton of cholesterol." She turned to Teddy and sighed. "His blood work wasn't great. Again."

"Oh, George," Teddy said, giving him a look of genuine sympathy. "I know how hard you've been trying. Are you drinking the dandelion root tea? It will help."

"It tastes like a pile of dung, Teddy," he said.

"Well, it was fertilized in that," she replied, coming closer. "Is this what you don't want to tell me about? Your bad cholesterol?"

"No," Roz finally said. "Asia's been put on bed rest with pre-eclampsia."

"Oh, no. She's what, thirty weeks?"

"Thirty-two," Roz said. "Two months left and, as you know, determined to do this alone."

Facing thirty-five as a strong, independent, and firmly single woman, Asia had chosen to have a baby on her own. While she was surrounded by good friends and her brother's family, the pregnancy had been a challenge.

"She'll be fine, but it's scary, you know?" Roz said, her dark eyes giving away her maternal concerns.

"Honey, no one knows like a woman who..." She stopped herself, instantly catching her mistake.

"Had three miscarriages," Roz finished for her.

"Well, no need to dwell on things that happened fifty years ago," Teddy said quickly. "For one thing, mine were early on, and medicine is marvelous..." She eyed her friend, seeing worry etched on her normally smiling face.

"Roz, I'm sure Asia could use her mother."

"I don't think she wants me breathing down her neck. Plus, there's the store."

"The store will survive," George said. "And if you could just let her live her life and not try to control it, Roz, she'd probably welcome the help."

"You should go up to her," Teddy said. "If I have to run the store, I will."

"Run it into the ground, you mean," Roz teased. *Maybe* teased.

"I can."

"The last time you ran the store you gave away more than you sold," Roz said. "Fine for your tea house, where you literally grow the product in the ground. Give away your tea for free, Teddy. But we've had Sanibel Treasures profitable for a long time and you could wreck that in one over-generous summer."

Teddy laughed, knowing her weakness behind the cash register. "I wouldn't give away anything."

"You'd give away *everything*," Roz fired back. "Anyway, things are too in flux with Eliza here and..." She let her voice trail off, then lifted her brows. "Have you broached the subject of Dutch's will?"

George came closer. "We're dying to know, Ted."

"The subject has been broached, yes."

"What did she say?" Roz asked.

Teddy just shook her head, not wanting to have this conversation now. "Let's not talk about it tonight. Let's just make our guest feel welcome."

"But did she give you any idea what she'll do?" George pressed.

"She had no idea there was a will," Teddy said. "No one has even called her yet."

"Probate can take forever," Roz moaned with an eyeroll. "My dad's was interminable."

"This one is definitely dragging out, but I don't want bad energy in this room tonight. Just joy. Which means that you..." She elbowed George. "Go get a shrimp. And you..." She turned to Roz with a defiant look. "Start planning a trip to Ohio to see your pregnant daughter."

"Maybe," she conceded. As George walked away to the buffet, Roz leaned closer. "I'm just as worried about him," she whispered. "He's seventy-four and when I think about Dutch..."

Teddy gave a sympathetic nod. "Maybe a trip isn't enough. Maybe it's time for you two to pack it in."

"Retire?" Roz's eyes grew to the size of coffee-colored saucers as she spat out the word. "Shut your mouth, Theodora!"

"All right, but I'm serious about a trip to see Asia. Help her and be there when the baby's born."

"And have Sanibel Treasures go under from mismanagement?"

But Teddy knew that was just an excuse. Roz and Asia were both strong-willed, stubborn women who went head-to-head more than they were arm-in-arm.

"I can run the store," Teddy said and laughed at Roz's doubtful look. "Or find somebody. Or..." She closed her eyes as she thought of the real possibility of what might happen. "Or the new owner of Shellseeker will."

"You think that will be Eliza?" Roz asked.

"Or the hotel corporation she sells it to."

"Perish the thought!" George called from the buffet, proving that his cholesterol might be off, but his hearing was perfect. "'Cause they'll have to pry my Teddy Roosevelt message in a bottle from my cold, dead hands first."

Teddy chuckled, a wave of affection for the two of them rolling over her.

Heavy footsteps on the stairs pulled them from the conversation and announced the arrival of another member of their small group.

"That's Deeley," Teddy said. "Katie and Harper are on their way and Eliza will be here any minute."

Roz gave her one more nudge. "I didn't want to tell you about Asia. I knew you'd want me to leave."

"Want you to leave? Are you crazy? I merely want you to be there for your daughter if she needs you. Anyway, you can't keep a secret from me."

"True."

"We'll figure it out," Teddy assured her friend. "I trust the answer will appear to me."

Roz rolled her eyes. "You can't rub a crystal and save the world and everyone in it, Ted."

Teddy smiled and closed her fingers over the one hanging around her neck. "I can try," she said lightly.

Just then, Connor Deeley pushed open the slider and walked in. With one look at his six-foot-plus frame, his muscular body, and the long sun-bleached waves that brushed his shoulders, Teddy felt better.

"Deeley." She reached her arms out and let him pull

her into his broad chest for a hug, using the only name he ever answered to. She couldn't ever remember a person calling him Connor.

"Mama T."

She smiled at the nickname he'd given her on that dark day when he finally opened the cottage door that he'd been locked behind for two weeks, and let her in. She could still picture that wounded warrior who was hiding from his pain in Shellseeker Beach. Two years later, the scars on his soul remained, but they were fading more every day.

"You okay?" He inched back and frowned at her. "You feel shaky."

"I'm fine," she assured him, pleased that sometimes he was as empathetic as she was. "How were the rentals today?"

"Not bad for June," he said, plucking a shrimp from the plate Roz had already made for him.

"Oh, *he* gets shrimp," George muttered.

"He's thirty-two years old," Roz countered.

"Thirty-three," Deeley corrected as he popped one in his mouth.

"And built like a Mack truck." Roz lifted a brow and gave a noisy pat to Deeley's impressive abs, currently covered by his T-shirt. "He paddleboards, kayaks, runs the beach, fixes roof tiles, hauls palm tree trunks, and...oh, everything." She gazed up at him, her dark eyes full of unabashed adoration. "He *needs* his shrimp."

They all laughed, especially Deeley, who pointed his

shrimp tail at George. "Gotta find me a woman who looks at me the way yours does, brother."

George took a shrimp from Deeley's plate and ate it with his face close to Roz's. "And I gotta find me one who feeds me like she feeds you."

"Aunt Teddy!" The high-pitched voice, along with two tiny hands slapping at the glass door impatiently, stole their attention. "We made cookies!"

"Cookies?" Deeley's eyes widened as he shared a look with George. "Oh, now those are all yours," he whispered.

"If they're anything like the last time, I'll pass."

"Stop it, you two," Teddy chided as she slipped by them to help Harper open the door. "You brought cookies?" she asked animatedly through the glass.

"Also known as forty-four-caliber muzzleloaders," Deeley cracked.

Teddy shot him a warning look. "She's trying to be a good mom."

"She's a great mom," he said. "But the two of them need a TV show called *The Bad Baking Sisters*."

Laughing, Teddy pushed open the slider, reaching down to hug the little girl who practically leaped into her arms. Behind her, Katie carried a tray and a proud look.

"We made sugar cookies to welcome Eliza," Harper announced in her sweet little voice. "I decorated them!"

"How wonderful, girls." As she lowered Harper to the ground, she reached for the tray, not even glancing at what she knew would be a fairly hot mess of sugar and icing. "How did you find the time, Katie?"

"We had fun," she said, giving up the cookies and planting a kiss on Teddy's cheek. "Is the guest of honor here yet?"

"Not yet, but come on in and see everyone."

She heard them all exchange greetings, with Roz fussing over Harper's new sparkly shoes and Deeley teasing Katie just like Teddy imagined a big brother would.

As she set the tray of cookies on the counter, Teddy turned to the group, taking a minute to watch them laugh and talk.

Like a faint echo in her head, she heard Dutch's voice...

That's what you do...you make families...

Well, she'd made this one and she'd do whatever was necessary to keep it.

"Oh, Mama T. Looks like Eliza is here." Deeley peered out the sliders. "Dutch's daughter has red hair?" He turned with a skeptical look. "Really?"

"Maybe you should do a DNA test before she claims the place," Roz suggested.

Teddy blinked at them, then shook her head. "Wait until you see her eyes. It's like looking right into Dutch's."

No one spoke, as a wave of grief gripped them for a moment. They'd all looked into Dutch's eyes and, in his two short years here, he'd been a father and brother and friend to them.

Roz sighed. "Well, for that reason alone I'm looking forward to meeting her and telling her what a great man Dutch was."

Not to Eliza, Teddy thought. But she just smiled and walked to the door, inhaling the lovely energy permeating her house. As she did, she sent a plea to the universe that Eliza had not only Dutch's eyes, but the good heart that Teddy had managed to find.

Chapter Six

Eliza

"Dessert?" Katie rounded the table to offer Eliza a cookie—well, a flat piece of baked butter with pink icing globbed on top.

"This looks lovely," Eliza said, taking one and smiling at Harper. "Did you bake for us today?"

The child just smashed her face into her mother's legs, still as shy as when they'd first met. But only with Eliza. Harper had no problem chatting with Roz, or giggling when George did magic tricks by hiding pieces of jasper under paper cups. She was downright bold with Deeley, who was tall and tattooed and should intimidate a child, but they clearly had a bunch of inside jokes, the knock-knock kind that kids loved.

It wasn't just Teddy's friends who brought out Harper's personality. The love between the little girl and her "Aunt Teddy" was downright palpable, Eliza thought as she watched Teddy take Harper by the hand and lead her into the hall after dinner. Off they went, whispering conspiratorially while Deeley cleaned up the leftovers on the buffet.

"You don't have to eat it," Roz leaned across the table

after Katie headed back to the kitchen. "It's fine if you pretend and wrap it in a napkin."

"It's not so bad if you dip it in the Blue Lotus tea," George, sitting across from her, added with a smile, lifting his cup. "By the way, I have no idea what's in this tea concoction, but you'll sleep well tonight."

Eliza laughed softly. "It's sweet that Harper's learning to bake so young."

"Harper?" George lifted his brows. "Katie's the one trying to be Little Miss Homemaker, which does not come naturally to her despite the fact that she's a house-keeper. But we're all here to help her."

Learning to bake at, what? Twenty-four or -five? Eliza didn't know enough about the single mother to understand the comment.

"We're all the family they've got," Roz explained. "And what about you, dear? You've mentioned a son and a daughter. Where do they live? What do they do?"

"My oldest is Olivia. She's twenty-nine and currently one of the top buyers for Promenade, living just outside of Seattle, where the corporate headquarters are."

"Oh, I love Promenade," Roz cooed. "There aren't any down here in Florida, but up in Ohio? A great store with a fine eye for the mature woman, if you get my drift."

"Olivia buys for the women's apparel department, so I'll relay your compliment," Eliza said.

"And your son?"

"Dane is twenty-seven, an engineer for an AI startup

in Silicon Valley," she told them. "He's a brilliant nerd and this mother couldn't be more proud of both of them."

"Married? Grandchildren?" Roz pressed.

She shook her head. "Not yet. Neither one. And, as Teddy told you, they're both recovering from a big loss. We all are."

Roz put her hand on Eliza's, genuine sympathy in her eyes. "I can't imagine what you've been through." She slid a look at her husband. "I don't want to."

Eliza smiled her thanks. "I'm taking it one day at a time."

"No better place to put yourself back together than right here in Shellseeker Beach," Roz said. "Look at us."

Eliza frowned. "How long have you lived here?"

"Eight years? Nine?" She looked at George, who lowered his teacup.

"I got canned from a desk job ten years ago next month," he said.

"Oof." Eliza rolled her eyes. "I can relate."

"Best thing that ever happened to me," he added. "We came down here to lick our wounds and figure out what I was going to do for a job and...we never left."

"Really?" Eliza looked from one to the other. "You hear those stories, but I don't know if I ever met anyone who did that."

Roz laughed. "Well, you're in a roomful of stories like that."

"In our case, we walked into Sanibel Treasures about a week after Teddy's last manager quit," George said. "She was running the place—"

"And by running, I mean not charging anybody for anything," Roz interjected. "Teddy does not understand the concept of paying for a product. I mean, there's generous and then there's...dumb. Not that she is, but that woman would give you the shirt off her back and run up to her closet and find something else for you."

Eliza smiled as George leaned in to continue his story. "Well, I got one look at the Teddy Roosevelt stuff," George said, "and I 'bout cried with joy."

"He's a history buff," Roz explained. "And you probably heard that we have a piece of history at Sanibel Treasures."

She frowned, trying to remember something Patty at the welcome center had said. "A...message in a bottle?" she guessed.

"That Theodore Roosevelt wrote himself!" George exclaimed. "Teddy's grandfather found it in the water when he was pretty young, and returned it to the President, who vacationed here. And that great man rewarded him with a job. 'Course, he had to officially name the street out there Roosevelt Road, and then name his son Teddy, and his granddaughter." He chuckled. "Truly an amazing thing, that message in a bottle."

She had to smile at his enthusiasm. "I can't wait to see it."

"George has redesigned the store so there's a whole section on Sanibel history," Roz said.

"And Roz is one of the best shell artists on the island," George added, beaming at his wife.

"Not sure I know what a shell artist is," Eliza admitted.

"Anything decorated or created with a seashell," Roz said. "Give me a glue gun, a canvas, and whatever you can scrape up on a decent day down there..." She angled her head toward the beach. "And I'll make you something you can hang on your wall."

"And that's what you sell at Sanibel Treasures?"

"Along with all manner of junky crap that tourists call souvenirs," she said on a laugh. "You cannot believe what people think they want to take home from vacation, but I'm happy to sell it to them. But the real treasure in Treasures is what George has created."

Eliza looked from one to the other, feeling an unexpected punch of grief as she remembered what she and Ben used to call "relentless spouse promotion." Her throat closed up and she willed herself not to give in to the tears that threatened.

Roz put a sweet and understanding hand on her arm, obviously following Eliza's emotional path. "It'll get easier," she whispered. Her gaze shifted past Eliza. "And here's someone who wants to help."

Eliza turned to see little Harper, prodded by Teddy, holding a piece of yellow construction paper.

"This is for you, Miss Eliza," she said on a squeaky whisper. "It's our beach."

"Oh, Harper! Thank you." She took the paper and studied the rudimentary drawing, not quite sure she got "beach" out of it, but could read the name at the bottom, each letter painstakingly formed, including a clichéd backwards "r" that nearly ripped her heart out. "And you signed it for me." She pressed it to her heart. "I will treasure this forever. Thank you."

The little girl just smiled and slipped closer to Teddy, who wrapped an arm around her and kissed her head.

"She'll make you want grandchildren," Roz said to Eliza on a laugh.

"Oh, I already do," Eliza admitted, inching back from the table to look up at Teddy. "Thank you so much for dinner tonight."

"Stick around," she said, although the others were clearly picking up to end the evening. "I have something to show you."

"I would love that," Eliza said, curious and not in any rush to leave the gentle warmth that surrounded Teddy and her comfortable home.

It turned out that what Teddy wanted to show her was a gazebo on Shellseeker Beach that Teddy's father had built. To get there, they strolled along the beach in the moonlight that poured over the water and sand, making the thousands of shells glint and gleam.

"What is that scent?" Eliza asked as she took a deep, heady inhale of that same amazing smell she'd noticed the minute she'd arrived today.

"Sanibel has a fragrance all its own," Teddy said. "Flowers and salt air and even the Ding Darling refuge contributes to the distinct scent. Lots of people have tried to bottle it, but failed. Roz sells an essential oil called Sanibel Scent and people pay big bucks for it."

She paused, inhaling again. "I keep thinking I might have smelled it before," Eliza admitted.

"Oh? In California?"

"In a dream."

Teddy slowed her steps, smiling. "A dream? Now we're speaking my language. Tell me about it."

"Sure. In my dream, I'm walking on a beach with another woman, and she's related to me, but I don't know how. And everything smells so *good*. Literally, like goodness." Eliza smiled at her. "What do you make of that, oh great prophetess?"

Teddy chuckled a little, but then grew serious. "Well, my mother's theory about dreams was that they don't reflect you or your subconscious, as most people think, but they are more a window to the world. You're seeing something someone else is seeing at the same time, if you catch my drift."

"Maybe," Eliza said, not at all sure she understood. "Was your mother a Sanibel native, too?"

"No. Delia Blessing lived all over, including on a tea farm in Java where she worked as a governess when she was young. She came to Sanibel with a rich family way back in the 1940s, and met my father. She scandalized everyone by staying with him when the family got on the boat to leave. It was all very romantic," she said with awe in her voice.

"And your grandfather worked for Teddy Roosevelt, I learned tonight."

"He did, indeed, and he married Caroline Kinzie, who was part of the family that ran the very first ferry from the mainland out to the island. Then my dad, also Teddy, and Delia, built and started the businesses here..." She gestured toward the few lights of the Cottages. "And I was born here in 1950. I had a brother who passed away very young, and I was extremely close with my parents, and my uncle, who never married but built Sanibel Treasures from the old boathouse. Here we are, at the gazebo."

"Oh!" Eliza drew back at the sight of a classic eight-sided structure, painted white with a dark gabled roof latched to the posts with decorative corbels. She'd been so engrossed in the conversation and watching her steps in the shell-covered sand that she hadn't seen it.

But how could she miss it? The gazebo sat up like it was on a small rise in the sand, with a stone path leading to it and two steps up to get inside. Lit only by moonlight, it looked inviting and whimsical and utterly charming.

"This is wonderful," Eliza exclaimed as she stepped inside and turned. "It reminds me of that delightful I-am-sixteen scene in *The Sound of Music*."

"Go ahead, songstress. Give us a tune."

Oh, if only she could. "Not tonight. This is really pretty." Eliza walked to one of the benches and gazed out at the now black Gulf of Mexico. "I love how it's on higher ground and gives you such an incredible view."

"Because it's built on a Calusa Indian sacred mound," Teddy said.

"Do you know that for a fact?"

"My mother found a treasure trove of arrowheads out

here once, some hundreds and hundreds of years old. There are mounds like it all over Florida, some for burial, some just so they could have the advantage of being able to see an enemy coming, some were temples."

"And this one?" Eliza asked.

"We don't know what its purpose was, but if you spend enough time here, you'll know it's special. My mother found one arrowhead with an image of a crown carved into it, so she was convinced this was built for the Calusa king, called the Paramount. He was believed to have supernatural ties to the heavens."

Eliza smiled, stroking her hand over the scarred wooden railing, imagining a warrior chief standing on the mound, watching for enemies approaching...or gazing up at the stars. "Do you believe that's true?"

"I know that when I sit here at night, I can track the stars," Teddy said. "And no matter where I sit, depending on the time of year, I get a perfect sunset view, which is unusual on our east-west island. That's actually south." She pointed toward the Gulf. "So you have to look up the beach for a sunset most of the year. But one of the gazebo seats always faces the sunset and the stars."

"That's very cool," Eliza mused, settling on one of the benches that lined the octagonal walls.

"Even cooler?" Teddy grinned. "It's an honesty house."

"Excuse me?"

"People tell the truth when they're in here. It's inevitable. You'll see." She sighed and sat down near Eliza. "Dutch and I had our unification ceremony here.

And my parents were married here, too. My father built it for that ceremony, and then rebuilt it a few times after storms took it down."

"That's so sweet. It's perfect for weddings."

She nodded. "I've always hoped Katie might get married here someday. With Harper as her flower girl and..." Her voice cracked and she turned. "Anyway, I wanted you to see it."

And Eliza knew why—because this structure and its stories were another way for Teddy to drive home the intangible but monumental value of this property to the people who lived here.

"You've created a lovely family, Teddy."

"Someone told me the expression is 'found family,'" Teddy said. "I think that's perfect."

"Did everyone just kind of show up and stay? That's what Roz said."

"Each in their own way, and I'll let them tell you," she replied. "What matters is they are family, and they are all dependent on me, and on Shellseeker, for their lives."

"Livelihood," Eliza corrected.

"Lives." Teddy stared out toward the water, quiet for a long time before she said, "Shellseeker Beach is more than a strip of land on the Gulf, Eliza. It's home and heart to my found family."

"And now I've come to end it all." Eliza breathed the statement, wondering if that was part of the "honesty" Teddy was talking about.

"Maybe, maybe not," Teddy said. "It didn't end when

my father sold the property in the first place. My family stayed on to work. I suppose things could stay as they are, which would be one way to solve the problem. But if you choose to sell?"

In the moonlight, Eliza could see the sadness in Teddy's eyes.

"Change is never easy," Eliza finally said, not sure what else she could say.

Teddy let out a sad breath. "I've had enough change," she whispered. "Haven't you?"

The ache in her voice touched Eliza's heart. "Yeah, I have. And death is worse than just your garden-variety change. It's upheaval and agony and really, really hard. I had one of those unexpected grief punches tonight watching an exchange between George and Roz."

"Unexpected grief punch," Teddy repeated. "Good heavens, that's a perfect description. It's like you're just cruising along, minding your own business, and a memory or a song or the smell of something mundane reaches into your chest and..." She held her hand out and fisted it. "Squeezes the life out of your heart."

"Oh, that's an even better description," Eliza agreed. "And the squeeze brings the tears."

"And the tears make you angry and embarrassed."

"And ruin your mascara." Eliza dabbed her eyelids.

"And then your eyes get puffy," Teddy added with a soft laugh.

"And the cashier at the supermarket asks if you're okay." Eliza cringed, remembering the day that whole sequence of events took place.

"Oh, good heavens, the same thing happened to me." Teddy angled her head and smiled. "See? I told you it was an honesty house."

Was it? Grief could bring that out, too, Eliza thought. They just looked at each other, sharing a sad smile. Few people understood the cycle of mourning that crept up and took over months after the loved one was buried.

"I'm so sorry, Eliza," Teddy added on a whisper. "About Ben. And the loss of what you no doubt expected to be your golden years. I'm sorry."

Eliza's eyes stung at the words, the empathy—not sympathy, but true and genuine empathy—embracing her. "And I am, too."

Silent for a few heartbeats, they both gave in to the urge to give and get a tentative hug, the first time they'd hugged since Eliza had arrived. Which had only been that morning, but it already felt like a lifetime.

"I'm glad Dutch had you at the end," Eliza whispered. "I'm sure you were very good for him."

"Not good enough," Teddy said sadly. "But his dying words were about you."

Eliza sucked in a breath, drawing back, a little dizzy at that statement. "They were?"

"Yes. He mentioned your name just seconds before he passed."

"Really." She put her hand on her chest, surprised at how this news affected her. "What did he say?"

"Just...your name. A broken sentence."

She felt her shoulders sink, wishing there'd been more. "That's all?"

"He also said…" Teddy frowned, narrowing her eyes like she was holding something back. "What was his nickname for you?"

"If he had one, I don't remember it," Eliza admitted.

"I'm sure he had one," Teddy said. "He had a pet name for everyone. I was Theo from the day we met. He called Deeley Washboard for his abs, and Katie was Lady Katie and, oh, Little Harpsichord. What did he call you?"

"He called me…" She closed her eyes, digging into the past, trying to see him, trying to remember the big loud man who was her Daddy. But every single memory had been wiped clean by Mary Ann's unrelenting hatred for him.

She could see him standing in her bedroom door, that infernal flight bag at his side. Always, always, off to…somewhere.

Sorry, but I have to go…B…B…. "Something that began with a B," she whispered as the tendril from the past eluded her.

"I knew it! I knew it!" Teddy pressed her hands together and smiled at her. "Birdie. Am I right?"

Birdie? She closed her eyes again and tried to hear his voice. *Sorry, but I have to go…Birdie.*

No, that wasn't it. *Was* it?

"I don't think so," Eliza said. "That doesn't sound right. But maybe. He certainly didn't call me that as an adult." She gave a dry laugh and then leaned back, exhaustion slamming her. "And I think I'm going to call it a night, Teddy. Do you mind if I head in now?"

"Not at all," Teddy said. "But can you come over

tomorrow? For tea and more talking? I really like talking with you."

Eliza smiled. "Yes, I will." She reached for Teddy and gave her another hug, just as warm as the first one. "Thank you again for a lovely dinner. I'll see you in the morning."

As she walked in the moonlight back to her cottage, Eliza kept thinking about that nickname that began with a B, but it eluded her.

Chapter Seven

Teddy

Teddy made a decision while she meditated in a circle of pink quartz the next morning. When Eliza arrived, she was going to show her all the bins she'd packed full of Dutch's things.

But her meditation and planning were cut short because the tea hut had an unusual number of customers. Then a call from Katie to say she was running late because Harper could not get out of bed on time had Teddy stripping the beds in one of the cottages for an early arrival. A few minutes later, Roz called with a bank question from Treasures, and Deeley texted her that he was delayed by the tourists he'd taken on a sunrise kayak tour, so could she put a sign out at the cabana for him?

By the time she got it all done, Teddy was tired, sweaty, and hadn't even brewed anything special for Eliza.

But she found her sitting outside the tea house in the shade, wearing her baseball cap and reading her phone, calm and cool.

"Did you sleep well?" Teddy asked.

"Like a rock. Was it the Blue Lotus?"

"Yes!" Teddy gave a hoot of happiness. "How did you know?"

"George warned me. What's in that stuff? Home-grown Ambien?"

Teddy managed to look aghast. "Emphasis on the home-grown part. Plenty of passion flower and a touch of valerian. I see you got some iced hibiscus."

"I did. And so did about seven other people who, um, might not have paid. You really use the honor system? In this day and age?"

"Yes, and there's so little honor in the world today that sometimes I give it away for free. Ask me if I care." She let out a laugh and gestured for Eliza to get up. "Can you come to the house? I want to show you some stuff."

"More Dutch?" Eliza asked, holding back what sounded like a sigh.

"Yes, but only if you can take it." She could already feel some impatience rolling off Eliza. Maybe not impatience, but she'd had enough of her late father for the moment, Teddy could tell.

"I can, yes, but..." Eliza pushed the cap up to look into Teddy's eyes. "Can it wait? Last night was...a lot."

"Of course." Teddy sank onto the stone bench next to her. "You're grieving your husband and I'm trying to throw you into saying goodbye to your father. I am sorry, Eliza. There's only one good antidote for this."

"Thank you, but I think I've had enough tea."

"Tea?" Teddy trilled a laugh. "I was thinking a shopping trip to my favorite boutique. You surely didn't bring enough clothes if you were planning to stay one night."

Eliza's eyes lit up. "You're right, and I love shopping."

"Then let's go." Teddy stood and reached for her hand. "And please tell me we can take your snazzy rental with the top down."

"You got it."

Not very long after that, they were cruising down Periwinkle Way in the convertible.

"This is better than a Tibetan sound bath," Teddy announced, dropping her head back to look at the sky.

Eliza laughed. "I didn't even want this car, but it was this or a Kia Sorrento."

"You made a wise choice," Teddy said. "This is the best way to see Sanibel, side to side and the sky above. Over there is Bailey's Market, which catered our dinner last night. The Bailey family has been here longer than the Blessings. They've owned that store for four generations."

"But did any of them work for Theodore Roosevelt like your grandfather did?" Eliza asked.

"Not to my knowledge," she said.

"What kind of work did he do?"

"He did odd jobs and took care of Teddy's houseboat."

"Such a cool slice of history." Eliza thought about it, then looked harder at Teddy, more questions in her expression. "And what about your history, Teddy? Were you married before Dutch?"

"I was." She shifted in her seat, ready to share more of her story, secretly delighted to take down some walls with Eliza. "I was actually married to a very nice man named David Laurence."

Eliza looked a little surprised at this new revelation. "What happened?"

She lifted a shoulder, a bit apologetically. "He wanted children and I couldn't have them."

"That's a shame that you couldn't. I mean, assuming you wanted them."

"With every fiber of my being. And I could get pregnant, which I did, three times. But I lost them all before four months."

Eliza gave a sympathetic look. "I had a miscarriage before Dane, at seven weeks. And even that early, it was awful. I can't imagine three of them. I'm sorry."

Teddy smiled. "Another thing we have in common, Eliza. But David did remarry and have several children and I think a passel of grandchildren. I've lost touch with him over the years, but I'm happy that he got what he wanted."

"And there was no one else until Dutch?"

"No one serious. I had a few flings; I'm not going to lie. And there was my yogi, a Swedish stud named Hadrian."

Eliza threw her a smile. "Yeah?"

"Oh, yeah. I was about fifty. Really in my prime and this guy showed up and..." She chuckled softly. "Let's just say he opened my eyes...and the rest of me."

"What?" Eliza choked a laugh. "Theodora!"

"Well, it happened. He was here for about six months

and during that time, I learned...a lot. He brought my yoga practice to a new level—"

"I bet."

"And he was the one who educated me about crystals. And...the Kama Sutra."

One more look from Eliza, and they both laughed from the gut.

"Anyway, that's my love history. Not so exciting. And you? I'm guessing from the age of your children that you met Ben as a very young girl."

"I did, a twenty-one-year-old trying like crazy to make it on Broadway."

"Really?" Teddy sat up. "You were on Broadway?"

"On it like...I auditioned *on it* a lot. Had a few parts, made it to the chorus in some big musicals, but I could always sing better than I could dance."

"How did I not know this?" But the minute Teddy exclaimed that, she could have bitten her lip. Because Dutch didn't tell her about his daughter, and shame on him for that.

"It's okay."

But it wasn't. "Maybe you'll sing for me sometime."

"Maybe," she said, but she sounded a little less enthusiastic.

They'd reached Beachside Boutique, so Teddy showed her where to park, dropping the subject of their pasts as they walked toward the store.

"The owner, Sarah Beth, is a good friend and will give you a great discount. Which you will want, because

Sanibel isn't famous for great prices. There are always the outlets on the mainland, if you prefer."

"This is perfect. I just need some shorts and tops, a few dresses, and, oh, fresh underwear."

"She has some beautiful lingerie."

"That'll work," Eliza said. "And if I stay much longer, I could always go back down to the Keys and get my clothes. I left them at Nick Frye's beach house."

"Nick Frye? The actor?" Teddy's eyes popped. "You are full of surprises today!"

"He was my client, the biggest one I had. Well, I also had Pippa Jones."

"Never heard of her."

"No one over fifteen has, but she's a powerhouse."

"What's Nick Frye like?"

Eliza slowed her step and smiled, shaking her head. "Nothing like you'd imagine. And right now? He's a new daddy, a new husband, and just crazy content with his non-movie star life. Maybe I'll get him to bring my stuff up here and you can meet the whole family. He's the nicest guy on Earth."

"I love it when big stars are actually real people that you can like," Teddy said as she opened the door. "Come on, let's see what Sarah Beth has for you."

Inside, the store was almost empty but for a mother and daughter combing the sales rack. Sarah Beth Greenough, the owner for at least the last fifteen years, brightened as soon as Teddy walked in.

"Well, hello, there," she said, coming out from around

a glass counter that displayed all her jewelry. "And this must be the famous daughter of Dutch!"

Eliza looked surprised, but Teddy wasn't shocked. Patty and Penny knew, and that was as good as putting it on the front page of the local paper.

"It is, Sarah Beth. Meet Eliza Whitney."

"Eliza! Welcome to Sanibel."

After a quick hello, they chatted about clothes and what Eliza was looking for. Teddy plucked through some of the racks, not that interested in the clothes but enjoying the outing enormously.

"I was always so fond of your father, Eliza," Sarah Beth gushed. "He always bought Teddy turquoise jewelry from my collection. Such a joy to have in the store."

Poor Eliza. She must be sick of hearing how great Dutch was. Trying to stem the tide and protect her, Teddy snagged a pretty tea-length sundress that would look beautiful on Eliza.

"What about this?" she asked, stepping between the two women.

Eliza looked at it, then inched back, her eyes wide. "Yes. Where...how...that's just...wow."

"Do you like it?" Teddy asked, confused by the response.

"I've seen it before."

Really? The dress was so distinctive, with a pattern of oversized pink hibiscus flowers and a handkerchief hemline.

"You girls talk while I ring these two up." Sarah Beth stepped away to serve the mother and daughter.

"Do you own it already?" Teddy asked, holding up the dress.

"I don't but..." She took it from Teddy, looking at her, not the dress. "I have seen it before." She leaned closer to whisper, "In that dream I told you about. This is what I was wearing."

"No!" Chills danced up Teddy's spine, and her whole body just hummed with the rightness of this. "Then you better buy it."

"I'll try it on," she said, taking it to the dressing room. "Do you think that's weird?"

Teddy laughed. "I realize you haven't known me very long, but do you think I would think that's weird? I live for stuff like that."

She could hear Eliza chuckle in the dressing room. She was probably not a believer in prophetic dreams, but Teddy was. And this one...

She plopped into one of the guest chairs with a smile on her face. This one was something, wasn't it?

"What do you think?" Eliza asked, stepping out in the dress.

"Oh, that's stunning. Does it match your dream?"

"To a T." Eliza shook her head, fingering the flowers. "It's such a distinctive pattern with these big bright flowers on a cream background. How does something like that happen?"

Teddy shrugged. "I do not believe in coincidences, Eliza."

"A fact that doesn't surprise me," Eliza said on a laugh as she looked down at the skirt, but then a ding from her dressing room snagged her attention. "That's my phone," she said. "Hang on."

She disappeared with a swoosh of the silky fabric, leaving Teddy to close her eyes and think about the meaning of Eliza's dream.

"Yes, hello. Thank you for calling me back." Eliza's voice came from behind the dressing room curtain. "Did my message make sense?"

As she talked, Teddy got up, chatted for a moment with Sarah Beth, and then Eliza came out of the dressing room, carrying the sundress and wearing an even more puzzled expression.

"Everything okay?" Teddy asked.

"Yes, everything is fine. And I'd like to buy this dress." She smiled at Teddy. "My dream dress. Oh, and I need to scoop up some intimates and maybe some of those T-shirt and short sets on that table."

After she paid and they walked out, Teddy reached her hand out. "You got news," she said, and it wasn't a question. She could feel the vibrations rolling off Eliza.

"No news," she said. "I mean, that's the news—there isn't any."

"I'm confused," Teddy admitted.

"I had left a detailed message with my attorney who, before he called, did a deep dive with his partner, an estate specialist. No one has contacted me, and nothing has been filed that they can find. And if I'm the legal heir of Dutch's estate? We don't know that yet."

Teddy stared at her. "It's been over six months."

"Are you sure he had a will? Because if he doesn't have one, then that might be the holdup. There's a long process called intestacy, and it really could take time."

"And at the end of it?"

"His estate would go to his living, legal heir."

"Who would be you," Teddy said.

"Are you sure I'm his only living heir?"

"I'm not sure if he ever specified you by name, or I just assumed it," Teddy admitted. "It was always such a difficult and sore subject that either made him feel physically ill or sent him off on his own for hours and hours, making me worry half to death." She shook her head, frustration rising. "I guess I should look through his stuff again, but I never found anything."

"Can I look with you? Maybe together we can find a clue."

"Are you ready for more Dutch now?" Teddy asked.

She gave a definite nod. "I'm ready."

TEDDY TOOK Eliza right upstairs to her room when they got back, after a drive home that was considerably less lighthearted than on the way to their shopping expedition.

"He didn't come with much," Teddy said as they climbed the stairs. "He had a few suitcases, some personal effects, and some books."

"I'm surprised he didn't have more, after the life he lived."

"He said he threw a lot away after he got the diagnosis," Teddy told her. "He came with very little because he only expected to be alive for a month or two, max. But, I have some boxes that belonged to him in our closet. I have his clothes, which, I'm not ashamed to say, I haven't donated yet. Some are up here, and I think Katie put a box or two in a downstairs closet. Oh, and his top dresser drawer, which was his special keepsake place. I've kept that intact."

Eliza followed her into the bedroom, instantly drawn to the wall with eight or ten photos that Dutch had asked Teddy to hang when he moved in. "Are these all Dutch's?" she asked after a quick glance.

"Yes, they are," Teddy said. "He brought those pictures, and after it became apparent he wasn't going to die as quickly as he thought, he wanted to move in here with me. I thought it would feel more like his place, too, if I hung those. Now, I just...am used to them."

Eliza stepped closer, pressing her palms together at her lips, scanning what Dutch had called the Wall of Fame.

"It's chronological, from left to right," Teddy explained, pointing to a picture of Dutch in uniform, standing in front of his plane in Vietnam, the handwritten name "Dutch" clear on the helmet in his hand.

"He flew that F-105," Teddy said. "The plane was called a Thunderchief, but Dutch called it the Thud.

That's when he got the call sign Dutch and it never left him."

"I think I've seen that picture."

"That's possible. Dutch said he carted it around his whole life. And this one? His first day on the job at Pan Am. What a handsome man, really. Do you remember him like that?"

As Eliza stared at the picture of Dutch in his pilot's uniform, she rubbed her arms, but Teddy could see the chills that rose. "I remember the aviator sunglasses."

"His pride and joy," Teddy said, stepping to the dresser. "I have his last pair right here."

"That's the only way I remember him," Eliza continued, leaning in to look hard at the picture. "Coming in dressed like that, having been gone...forever." Her eyes shuttered. "He was never home. That's really my only memory of living with him until I was eight. Daddy was... in the air."

Teddy sighed, imagining that kind of schedule was hard on a kid. She pulled out the aviators and held them for a moment, making a decision. She should give these to Eliza. She should—

"Who is this with my father?"

Teddy turned to see which picture.

"Well, that's you, obviously. And your mother. You're what? Two in that picture, I'd guess, likely Easter from the basket you're holding. You can have it, Eliza and you can have—"

"No." She barely squeaked the word as her whole

body stiffened and she leaned a little closer, then Teddy could have sworn she swayed.

"Oh, dear." Teddy came closer, reaching out because she could practically taste Eliza's distress. "Is that a bad memory? Are you—"

"Who *is* that?" She ground out the words, her jaw so clenched, Teddy wasn't sure she understood.

"It's you and your mother and Dutch."

"It's...Dutch." She turned, all color gone from her face. "But that's not me and that for sure isn't my mother."

Teddy's eyes widened as the words hit her heart. "Are you sure? It's an old picture and faded, but—"

"That's *not* me and it *isn't* my mother," she repeated, louder and with a pinch of pain in her voice. "Who *is* that?"

Teddy put her hand to her mouth, her brain whirring. "Dutch said it was his wife and daughter."

Eliza reached to the wall like she might faint. "Did he use names?"

Did he? Teddy shook her head as if she could dislodge a memory out of it. "He told me your name. And Mary Ann, your mother."

"When he pointed to that picture?"

"I don't know," she confessed. "I just...assumed."

Her eyes flashing, Eliza practically lunged for the picture, yanking the frame off the wall with trembling hands. "Let me see it," she said in a shaky voice. "Let me..."

"I'll do it." She gave the sunglasses to Eliza and took

the picture to the bed, turning it over to get it out of the frame. "I know he said this was his wife..." She broke a nail pushing the tiny metal hook in the back, but just flinched without complaint. Her hands were shaking, too.

Finally, she got the cardboard back off, trying to remember anything Dutch had said about this picture. Absolutely anything. It had been in the simple cheap black frame when he brought it, and they'd never taken it out.

She lifted the cardboard backing out and stared at the back of the photo, seeing some handwriting on it.

"What does it say?" Eliza was next to her, shouldering closer to read the inscription written in faded blue ink.

Notre famille. Je t'aime, Camille Avril 1980

Who in God's name was—

"Camille!" Eliza exclaimed. "That was her name!"

"Whose name?"

"The stewardess he had an affair with! The one he left my mother for! A French floozy, my mother used to say, his...whore. Camille! I'd totally forgotten the name but..."

Teddy tried to comprehend what she was saying, rooting through her memories for any mention of a Camille. No, Dutch had never—

"His wife, you said?" Eliza backed up, clutching the glasses to her chin, eyes filled with tears. "Then that little girl must be my sister!"

Chapter Eight

Eliza

She never slept that night. For most of the endless hours between the time they'd found the picture and sunrise today, Eliza tossed, turned, cried, walked the beach at three a.m., and maybe prayed a little bit.

And she dug into the deepest, darkest holes of her childhood memories to piece together anything and everything her mother ever said about Dutch and...*her*.

It was always about the French woman. Always. Yes, Mary Ann had whined about "all of them"—meaning the young, attractive women who wore the Pan Am uniform and served up coffee, tea, and, according to her mother, whatever Dutch wanted.

But if Eliza burrowed deep enough into the recesses of her memory, there was something about...Camille.

She was certain that was her name. Camille. But what was her last name? Would she know it if she heard it? Had her mother ever said it?

Had Camille been the catalyst for the breakup, the reason for the late-night screaming battles? Or a child who looked to be two or three in April of 1980...about three years after her parents' divorce, four years after he moved out.

That little girl would be, what? In her forties now.

A sister...out there, somewhere.

Her heart twisted at the thought, and the realization that her mother might have known this and not told her. No. That would be too cruel. Maybe she didn't know. To her knowledge, her parents never so much as exchanged a word after their divorce, which was why any contact with Dutch was so rare while Eliza was a child and teenager.

She had to believe her mother didn't know, otherwise it was too heartbreaking to think Mary Ann had kept this information from Eliza. Dutch had, but nothing that man did surprised her. He hadn't even told Teddy and they lived together, slept in the same room with *that picture on the wall*.

What was *wrong* with him?

But her mother?

If she tried really hard to remember those fights between her parents, even as seen through the eyes of a child, there was something that made everything different. Something that had put Mary Ann Vanderveen over the edge. Something that defeated her.

Could it have been a child, or just a mistress that got too serious?

For the millionth time, Eliza looked at the picture, held it one way and another, and analyzed everything from the faded blue uniform her father wore to the green plaid skirt on the little girl.

So this was Camille. French, obviously, which made sense. She remembered her father flew to France frequently when she was little. And this must be who he stayed with on those weeks and weeks he was away.

Gorgeous. Black hair, stunning bones, a wide mouth, and a perfect figure. She wore a simple white blouse and skirt, which looked more like haute couture than a stewardess's uniform. But didn't those women wear Givenchy back in the day?

The little toddler clutching an Easter basket also had dark hair, up in a bow, and a big confident smile that reminded Eliza of Dutch.

And, again for the millionth time, she turned the picture over and read the words that had been a breeze to translate. They said, "Our family. I love you, Camille. April 1980."

Our family. His...with another woman.

And, of course, another question loomed. Was Camille, who he'd told Teddy was his wife, alive? Or had they divorced? If so, when? And what about the girl in that picture, who Eliza assumed was a daughter? Was she the "sole heir" he'd talked about to Teddy, and that was the reason Eliza never got contacted about a will? Were either or both of these women currently looking at a will in probate and about to arrive in Shellseeker Beach to claim it as their own?

Frustration and a fresh wave of pain rolled through Eliza as she took a cup of coffee out to the cottage deck. There, she sipped the brew and stared at the beach, inhaling the mix of coffee with that sweet and salty air, the scent she already associated with Sanibel.

Morning on Shellseeker Beach, she noticed, had a

wholly different feel than other times of day. Instead of the peach and plum colored sunset that had impressed her in the evening, or the stark white moon that accompanied her solo walk last night, the beach was fresh and bright today. The water was like diamond-studded turquoise with a soft, lapping surf that brought a new inventory of shells with every wave.

Taking another deep drink of coffee, she slid back to the problems weighing on her heart.

Now what? Something had to be done, some action, some investigation, some search for the truth. But how? Where to start? She knew nothing but a first name... Camille. And neither did Teddy, but they'd talked until late trying to figure it out.

Dutch had been deeply secretive about his past, she'd said, couching it as something he didn't want to dwell on while he was "at death's door." Damn him!

She ached to call Olivia and let her know that the shocks on Shellshocker Beach just kept coming, but it was only four in the morning on the West Coast. She couldn't call Dane, either, who only knew about the possible inheritance through Olivia. Eliza hadn't actually talked to him yet.

If only she had...*Ben*.

The familiar squeeze of grief almost brought her last sip of coffee back up. Oh, how she'd love to share this with her husband. He'd have so much to say, and ideas for where to go next.

But right now, all she had was Teddy, who was as perplexed as Eliza. Last night, over tears and tea, they'd

mulled over the possibilities, the questions, and the unde-
niable fact that without knowing if there was another
daughter, Eliza could hardly do *anything* about this land.

Who knew what Dutch's will said? She'd have to find
out, but her attorney had hit a dead end and suggested
she give it more time. Impatience crawled all over her and
she wanted to know *now*.

The first thing she'd decided, maybe during that
three a.m. walk on the beach on her way home from
Teddy's, was that she wasn't leaving Shellseeker Beach.
How could she? And she wasn't going back to Coconut
Key to get the clothes she'd left in two suitcases at Nick's
house when she thought this would be an overnight visit.

She'd buy what she needed, stay in this cottage or
another, or find a hotel, not that Teddy would let her do
that. She'd talk to people who knew Dutch, digging for a
clue. Maybe he told someone, anyone, a random person,
or a good friend.

Still holding her coffee, she stood and took a few steps
onto the sand, making her way down one of the boardwalks closer to the beach. There, past the tall grass that
waved in the breeze, she spotted a man strolling toward
the thatch-roofed cabana, instantly recognizing Connor
Deeley even from this distance.

Didn't someone make a joke at the party about
Deeley and Dutch drinking shots, smoking cigars, and
arguing over which was better, the Air Force or the
Navy?

What else had they discussed? Had liquor loosened
Dutch's tongue, maybe allowed him to share something

that fell into the "military bro code" about another daughter? Would Deeley break that code?

Maybe, considering the circumstances.

She made her way across the sand, her eye on the classic beach cabana. It was an inviting structure, covered in beach murals, and two service windows shaded by oversize hurricane shutters braced to the walls. Just outside by a standing sign listing rental prices, Deeley was hauling out paddleboards out to a rack, whistling loudly, looking like he'd stepped off Malibu Beach for a surfing movie with that long golden hair.

"Morning," she called.

He turned and his whole face brightened with a smile.

"Want to rent a board?" he asked. "I'll give you a discount and it's a great, glassy day for beginners."

"Not this beginner," she said. "Although it looks like fun and probably not that easy."

"Just takes some balance," he said, dropping a board into the display rack. "How's Shellseeker Beach treating you, Eliza?"

"It's...treating me."

At her tone, he eyed her with curiosity. "You sound like a woman who might need a nice long kayak ride. I promise you'll love it. No balance required."

"Not today, but thanks." She stepped under the shade of one of the raised shutters, peeking into the cabana to see the inside. "What a nice little business you have here."

"Don't tell anyone, but it's a goldmine."

"That's a secret?"

"Teddy and Dutch figured out some amazing payment system so that I keep almost everything we make, and the resort business doesn't get hit with enormous taxes."

So he was another person whose livelihood depended on the umbrella business that she may or may not inherit. "How long have you run this?"

"Well, since I got here, just under two years ago."

"You came right around the time Dutch did?" she asked, sitting on one of the benches outside the cabana while he continued lining up paddleboards for customers to choose.

"I was here before him, but not by much," he said.

"Don't tell me, you came for a vacation and never left?"

"I came for..." He closed his eyes and looked like he was carefully considering the answer. "After I got out of the Navy, I needed to, uh, decompress. I came here and..." For a long time, he stood very still, staring at the board in front of him, the thick, tattoo-covered biceps tensing as he held it with two hands.

"And liked it?" she prodded when the silence became uncomfortable.

"Well, Teddy worked her magic, you know?"

She didn't exactly know, but she was starting to understand. "And you stayed."

"I never considered leaving," he admitted. "And your dad was great, especially since every day he expected to die and didn't. Good man, Dutch. I liked him."

Didn't everyone? Even...Camille. With the reminder of why she'd come down here, Eliza leaned forward. "Did you spend a lot of time with him, then?"

"Oh, yeah. I didn't want to get into a big thing about it when we had dinner the other night, but I want you to know that he was a real help to me when I needed it. Teddy, of course, showered me with...whatever fairy dust she showers people with. Good stuff. And Dutch, being military, was great to talk to."

"I'm glad." A scooch jealous, but glad.

"Anyway, before long, I noticed this little shack down here. It was nothing like this, but it had been built by a previous owner and sort of abandoned. They gave me free rein to fix it. I had this idea for the grass roof and mural walls. I had a feeling rentals would make money on this beach, so they let me start this business."

"What did you do in the Navy?" she asked.

"Oh, you know. This and that. But I do like the water and the sun, so this is the perfect life for me." He turned and flashed a big smile that she imagined helped get him lots more customers every day. "Teddy and Dutch charmed the asses off the city council—who don't charm easily, I'll tell you—so I could build this thing. She turned a blind eye when I slept here before I had enough cash for rent. And Dutch invested in all the equipment so I could get started, then set up that sweet financial arrangement."

She inched back, impressed. "That's more than encouragement."

"Like I said, good man. And Teddy? Well, she's a

veritable saint and the grandmother everyone wants. Roz and George are pretty much the greatest humans alive, and we're tight. Katie's like a little sister." He grinned at her. "I guess you got all that at Teddy's little dinner party."

"I did, and it's nice. Dutch wasn't around much when I was a kid," she said. "He divorced my mother when I was really young."

He nodded, moving to the next board to hoist it into the rack.

"Did he ever talk about...his wife?" Or *wives*, as the case may be, but she didn't want to lead him along.

"Not so much," he said. "But he didn't spend a lot of time in the past like some old men do. He knew his days were numbered and he lived for the day he had, like no man I ever met. It was a helluva lesson for me."

She shifted on the bench, frustrated. She didn't want to hear about his encouragement and lessons anymore. She needed some clue, some direction. So she opted for the truth.

"I think he might have had another child, a daughter."

Deeley reacted with a blink of surprise. "Really? Like I said, he didn't talk much about his personal life or the past, except for Vietnam. We both shared some battle-field secrets, but nothing else."

She blew out a breath, knowing she'd most likely hit a dead end. "I don't know how I'm going to find out the truth," she said on a sigh. "Did he have any other friends he might have confided in?"

"Not that I know of, but I know someone who can definitely help you."

"Really? Someone who knew Dutch?"

He shook his head and pulled a cell phone from his pocket. "Miles Anderson is a PI who lives on Sanibel and specializes in missing relatives, closed adoptions, that kind of stuff. He was JAG..." He glanced at her. "A lawyer in the military. Incredibly smart, resourceful. Retired to Florida and started picking up extra cash doing private investigations. I'll text you his contact information."

"An investigator? That could help." She gave him her phone number and he tapped his screen.

"He's a good buddy of mine, so if you want me to grease the skids, I can tell him you're going to call. I won't tell him anything you've shared," he added. "I'll leave that up to you."

"That'd be great, thank you." She pushed up and smiled at him. "I think I'll call him today. It feels like something concrete that I can do."

He studied her for a few seconds, nodding. "You remind me of him, you know."

"Of Dutch?" She could barely see a resemblance, not in any of the pictures she'd seen. "I have my mother's coloring."

"I know, but there's something about you that seems strong. He didn't let life beat him down, no matter how much it sucked. And a brain tumor sucks."

"Sure does. And I might not have a terminal disease, but I do feel like life sure is trying to kick the stuffing out of me lately. So that would be a good quality to have right about now."

"Call Miles," he said, turning away from her as a family of three walked up to the cabana, laughing and talking. "I know he can help you find your sister."

Her sister. The cavalier way he said it made her heartbeat kick up a little.

Miles Anderson. Okay. It was a place to start to find... her sister.

Chapter Nine

Teddy

Teddy headed right out in the morning to find Eliza, but Junonia was empty. On the way back to her house, she spotted Katie cleaning Bay Scallop, so she popped into the small cottage. Katie must have taken one look at Teddy and guessed that something was very, very wrong.

It didn't take much for the details of yesterday's discovery to come pouring out.

"That picture really isn't her?" Katie had abandoned any effort to clean when Teddy started talking, and now they sat close on the rattan sofa in the main living area of the cottage. "I mean, I'd have to look closely at it again, but is she sure? The kid in that picture is only two or so."

"I know, but she knows what her own mother looked like. Anyway, it says, 'Our family. I love you, Camille,' with the date of 1980, when Eliza was eleven. In French, no less."

Katie pressed her fingers to her temples, processing this news. "So, he had another wife. Okay, that's not a shock that he was married and divorced more than once. But a child? One he never told you about? That means there's another heir, right? What's going to happen?"

"I don't know."

"How could he not tell you he'd been married more than once?" Katie asked.

Teddy shook her head at the question that had echoed in her head all sleepless night long.

She didn't even know him. *At all.*

The realization had wrecked her this morning. She hadn't had tea. She hadn't meditated. She hadn't even held a crystal. She reached for the one around her neck, moaning softly when she realized she'd forgotten to slide it on.

"I'm so out of sorts!"

"Of course you are," Katie cooed with a gentle touch. "This is stressful and concerning. And how does Eliza feel? She might have a sister! What's she going to do?"

"Nothing, until we figure out who that person is. If we can. And then we'll have to deal with two people who might have a claim on my land and this business."

Katie grunted, her eyes shuttering. "*Why* would Dutch not tell you any of this?"

"I don't know and, honestly, that's the hardest part."

"I bet it is," Katie said. "Especially for you, Teddy. You get people better than they get themselves."

"Not always, obviously." Not the one she thought she was closest to.

"Hello?" Eliza's voice floated in through the open sliders. "Teddy, is that you?"

"We're in here," Teddy called, jumping up, anxious to see her. They'd really had a good talk last night, even if it didn't result in any answers. She felt like Eliza was on her side, in some way, that this news of another woman and daughter had made them partners, not adversaries.

"Come on in and see Bay Scallop," she said, stepping to the cottage's wide-open sliders.

"Hi, Katie," Eliza said as she came in. "Are you working alone today? No little singing partner?"

Katie smiled at the question, clearly touched, like Teddy, by how much Eliza seemed to like Harper.

"She's at Vacation Bible School right now, which should mean I can clean the cottages twice as fast, but..." She gestured to Teddy. "We've lost twenty minutes talking."

"I told her about the picture," Teddy admitted.

Eliza sighed as she came into the living room to sit. "It's a conundrum, huh?"

"What are you going to do, Eliza?"

"Well, I have a first step," Eliza told them. "Deeley gave me the number of a man named Miles..." She narrowed her eyes, trying to remember his last name, and Katie and Teddy shared a look.

"Anderson," they said at exactly the same time.

"You know him? Yes, I guess this is a small island."

"We do," Teddy said. "He's a private investigator and very, very good." She slid a questioning glance to Katie. "Isn't he?"

She rolled her eyes. "Too good," she agreed. "But he also proved himself to be trustworthy and on the side of the angels, so, yeah."

Eliza frowned, obviously confused. "Am I missing something?"

Katie sighed. "Yeah. You're missing the reason I'm here and why we know this PI and..." She looked at Teddy. "She's sharing her story, so I can tell mine. I trust her."

Teddy nodded. "I think that's smart."

"And *she's* very intrigued," Eliza said with a smile. "Especially if it will help me know if I can trust this Miles Anderson. But please don't share anything that makes you uncomfortable."

"Everything about my past makes me uncomfortable," Katie confessed. "My parents kicked me out of the house when I was nineteen and pregnant with Harper."

"Oof," Eliza huffed. "That's rough."

"It was," she agreed, looking down at her lap for a moment, reminding Teddy how hard it was for Katie to share her story. "Anyway, it helps to know that my family is, um...how would you describe them, Teddy?"

"Loaded," Teddy supplied. "Like, they have four houses, two planes, and a net worth from a publishing empire with nine zeros, if you catch my drift."

Eliza's eyebrows rose. "Is that why George made a comment about being a homemaker not coming naturally to you?"

Katie laughed. "I don't think I *saw* a hamper until I was nineteen, let alone did my own laundry. I was raised by nannies and staff, never even knew there was such a thing as a budget, and, honestly, was kind of a spoiled brat."

"Not a brat," Teddy interjected. "You were a wealthy kid raised in an elite home."

"If 'elite' means cold, unhappy, and full of people who wanted to kill each other, then yeah, I was. And you're being nice, Teddy, but I was...entitled."

Teddy could feel the shame bubbling under Katie's surface and automatically reached for her, putting a gentle hand on her shoulder. "You're not now."

"So you came here?" Eliza asked, clearly intrigued.

"When they cut me off, I had nowhere to go, so I headed south toward sunshine."

"Wait. They really sent you off because you got pregnant?" Eliza looked dumbfounded. "This was 2018, right? Not...1918?"

"Years don't matter in the Bettencourt family. My stepmother, the coldest witch who ever lived, wanted me to get an abortion, and I refused. My father suggested I hole up in our chalet outside of Geneva and give the baby up for adoption."

"And you?" Eliza asked. "And the father?"

"I wanted my baby so much," Katie said on a sigh. "Her father is just...ugh. I don't even know what I was thinking, except that he was hot and...yeah. Hot. He worked as one of the groundskeepers at our Marblehead house. Not a bad guy, but...didn't belong in my family circle. However, I *wanted* that baby, although I couldn't tell you why."

"Maternal instinct?" Teddy suggested.

"I guess. I do frequently burst into tears just looking at her. I guess I knew deep inside, even at nineteen, that I wanted to be a mother."

"It's your calling," Teddy said softly.

Katie smiled at her. "If only Brianna, the evil step-mother, felt that way."

Teddy curled her lip at the mention of the woman's name. "Never met her, but still, I don't like that woman."

"*You* don't like her, Teddy," Katie agreed. "I literally hate her guts. But," she added with a finger in the air to underscore her point, "not quite as much as I despise her daughter, Jadyn, the stepsister from hell, who I still suspect was behind pushing for me to leave. Anyway, they threw money and legal documents at Harper's father, which he happily took and signed, then disappeared faster than you can say baby daddy."

"So what brought you here to Shellseeker?" Eliza asked.

"Fate. Good fortune. Teddy." She grinned at the other woman. "I left Boston with a thousand dollars in cash and a backpack. Trust me, for as spoiled as I was growing up, I got unspoiled in a hurry. And this wonderful person"—she leaned into Teddy—"came to my table at a diner where I was working as a waitress in Fort Myers."

"It was next door to the place where I got my car serviced," Teddy added, always happy to remember the day she met Katie. "This sweet, pregnant girl brought me lunch and we started talking."

"*You* started talking," Katie said. "You asked a bunch of questions that felt like you already knew the answers. And you told me Harper was a girl!"

"I got girl vibes," Teddy said.

"Long story short, Teddy brought me over here for

dinner that night, arranged for me to find a good doctor, and before I knew it, I had a job taking reservations and checking in guests."

"It was the height of our season, and I needed help," Teddy explained.

"She really needed another housekeeper, but wouldn't let me clean because she didn't want me on my feet or inhaling chemicals."

"It worked out," Teddy said, not wanting the heaps of praise, because who wouldn't help a darling single teenage mom?

"It worked out because you took me in and loved me..." Her voice cracked as she squeezed Teddy's hand. "And she even was with me at the hospital when Harper was born."

"I'll never forget that," Teddy whispered, the moment that little baby appeared still crystal clear in her memory. "I'd never seen a baby born in my whole life, and then...there was Harper. Life was never the same." Teddy blinked, only a little surprised that her eyes were damp.

"And then Dutch showed up," Katie continued. "And we all just...worked together, you know? He called me Lady Katie, because sometimes my inner rich girl crawls out and makes herself known."

"It's all part of what makes you *you*." Teddy put an arm around Katie's shoulders and pulled her closer. "You are my heart, little girl."

"Wow," Eliza whispered, leaning forward, rubbing her arms like she had chills, despite the sun and warmth pouring in through the sliding glass doors. "That is an amazing story."

"Oh! Miles." Katie laughed and clapped her hands. "I got so involved walking down memory lane that I forgot why I went there. About a year ago, maybe a little more, Miles Anderson found me. He'd been hired by an investigator working for my parents."

"They were looking for you?" Eliza asked.

"They were, and I don't want them to know where I am," she said. "I mean, I'm not hiding from them, but I just don't want to get sucked into the vortex of their life. Not to mention that I don't trust my stepmother as far as I could throw her. It would be just like her to announce that, 'Harper Bettencourt is coming home!' But only because it would make her look good to her rich friends. No, not taking that chance. This is our family, right here."

"Well, what happened when they found you?"

"Miles found me, and do not ask me how, because that man has uncanny ways of doing his research and he won't share. They knew I was somewhere in Florida, so my parents hired an investigator in Boston who tapped into his network all over the state. Anyway, Miles being Miles, he found me."

"So your parents know you're here?"

"No, they don't. I mean, I don't think they do. Miles came to me privately before he gave their investigator any information. He said he had no reason to believe I wasn't happy here. By the time that happened, I'd turned twenty-one, so definitely old enough not to have to tell my dad and stepmother where I am. I asked him not to, so all he reported was that I was healthy, happy, and had no desire to see them. Bottom line? Miles is a terrific investigator, and he's a stand-up guy."

"That's good to know, but wow," Eliza said, dropping back in her chair as she took all this in. "Katie, it took a lot of strength for you to do what you did."

"You have no idea," Teddy chimed in. "This young woman is a wonderful, hands-on mother who works harder than anyone I know."

"I finally figured out the whole cleaning thing," she said with a self-deprecating chuckle. "And mothering comes naturally. As you probably figured out, I'm not such a great cook but I am determined. You can't believe how many life skills rich kids don't have. Teddy literally taught me how to open a bank account and rent an apartment, which I have."

"I begged her to live with me, but..."

"I do need some semblance of independence," Katie explained. "I don't want to teach Harper to be dependent on anyone or anything. But, yeah, Harper has a room at Teddy's house, and we've spent many a night there."

"You should be very proud of yourself, Katie. And you..." Eliza looked at Teddy, warmth in her gray-blue eyes. "You sure do like to save people, don't you?"

She laughed. "It's my weakness."

"It's *your* calling," Eliza corrected.

"And don't change!" Katie exclaimed. "We love that about you. I've never been happier in my whole life."

"Except you don't *have* a life," Teddy lamented. "I can't get this girl to go out no matter how hard I try."

"Go out and what? Meet guys in a bar? Please. I have to be very picky, but you will be happy to know that I made friends with one of the other moms in Harper's Vacation Bible School, and she invited me to meet her friends at a book club. I'm going Friday night, if you'll babysit."

"Of course I will, but you won't meet a nice guy at book club."

"I don't want a nice guy. I just want some friends who have kids and know what I'm going through."

"Although there was that nice-looking pilot who stayed here a few weeks ago," Teddy said, still determined that Katie would find a good man.

"Cute Pilot Luke." Katie wiggled her eyebrows. "And, yes, that's how I put him in my phone."

"So you *did* give him your phone number?" Teddy asked.

"And, shocker, he hasn't used it yet. He probably has me in his phone as Single Mom With Baggage." She leaned forward, clearly uncomfortable with the subject. "I gotta get back to work. Sorry to bore you with my checkered past, Eliza, but I do think Miles is a good call."

Eliza nodded, but frowned as she looked at Katie. "Did you say your family is the Bettencourts?"

"Yes, and please tell me you don't know them."

"I know Charles Bettencourt, the venture capitalist. Any relation?"

"Uncle Charlie." She made a face. "My dad's brother. How do you know him?"

"He was an investor in my husband's studio and I had dinner with him and his...not his wife."

"His twenty-something gold-digger—er, I mean girl-friend." Her expression grew taut. "Please don't tell him—"

"Don't worry. I doubt I'll ever see the man again, and even if I did, I would never break your confidence."

Katie stood, going to Eliza's chair to reach for her hand. "You're good, Eliza," she said. "I'm happy you're here. We needed you here."

Eliza looked up, her eyes flickering with surprise, but before she could answer, Katie slipped away and scooped up her bucket.

"I'm off to clean the toilet!" She hoisted the bucket higher. "Take that, Brianna Bettencourt!" She laughed her way into the bathroom, leaving Eliza and Teddy to look at each other.

"You *are* needed here," Teddy whispered.

Eliza just smiled. "You run a remarkable resort, Teddy Blessing."

Teddy just laughed, knowing it was true.

Chapter Ten

Olivia

A sister? She had a long-lost aunt? Olivia listened to her mother's story with as much attention as she could give it, considering that while Mom talked, fourteen emails and two texts came in and it was barely eight in the morning.

And now her phone was ringing with a call from the Senior Vice President of Merchandise Planning, Nadia Gifford. *Herself.*

"I have to take this call, Mom," she said frantically. "Hold that thought. Or better yet, call me after you meet with Sherlock Holmes."

Mom snorted. "It's not a murder investigation, Livvie. Just a missing person. Maybe. Do you think—"

"I am so sorry, Mom. But Nadia Gifford cannot go to voicemail. Love you. Bye!" She tapped the desk phone and tried not to sound breathless. "Good morning, this is Olivia Whitney."

"*The* Olivia Whitney?" Nadia asked in her distinctively throaty voice that made her sound like a chain-smoking 1940s starlet. "The Olivia Whitney who insisted we test the whole Esmé Arnold line of women's wear in the Midwest stores? That Olivia Whitney?"

Olivia smiled into the phone because, dang, she knew the Esmé line was a winner. "That would be me, Ms. Gifford."

"Honey, you made us a fortune, and we're rolling out the entire line across the country for fall."

Olivia dropped back in her chair, enjoying the rush of success. "I thought the Esmé line would really appeal to the Promenade shopper," she said. "It's fresh, modern, and clean without belonging in the junior department."

"You're so right, Olivia," Nadia said. "And because we gave her that rollout? Esmé is designing an exclusive line for Promenade women's wear, and it is an astounding collection."

"Really?" Olivia practically fist pumped. Exclusives were the bread and butter of this business, and always meant they could crush the competition.

"Absolutely. And we will want a VP from your department on site for the launch in New York. I hope that will be you."

She hoped it would be her, too, but that call would be made by Alex Brody. "I'll talk to my boss, Ms. Gifford."

"That new guy? Brody?" She gave a little throat whimper. "Yeah, I met him at the management meeting in Santa Fe right when he came over from Saks. Very slick."

Slick was a compliment, but she wasn't about to say something bad about her boss. "And smart. I can't wait to tell him about the Esmé line."

"And make sure he knows who fought for that market test. Now, what are you thinking for next season's acces-

sories, Olivia? The Carveletto Collection of scarves from
Italy was downright lifeless and eighty percent of the stock
ended up on clearance. We can't let that happen again."

"No, we can't," Olivia agreed. "And you know, Ms.
Gifford—"

"Nadia," she corrected, making Olivia smile.

"Nadia. Color is everything, and I met with the
people from Jazzberry last week. Love. Total love for the
entire line, which pops with color."

"I like Jazzberry but haven't ever been able to market
and present their stuff. You have thoughts?"

"Oh, I do. Have you seen their winter collection?
The jewel tones are to die for, utterly rich and vibrant.
Not a steel or buttercream in sight."

"Thank the Lord," Nadia crooned. "I am so sick of
black, white, and boring old gray in winter."

"Then you will love the Jazzberry jewels. I have so
many ideas, too."

"Perfect! Why don't you send me samples and write
up a rollout plan? Can you do that?"

Not without getting approval from her boss. "Let me
talk to Alex on the timing and we'll get it to you before
you talk to the Jazzberry people," Olivia said.

"You rock, Olivia. Promenade is lucky we have you.
Gotta run."

She looked up to see Alex in her doorway, arms
crossed, a super smug look on his face.

"Me, too," she said. "And thank you so much for all
the kind words, Nadia."

"Well deserved."

"Oh, it's Nadia now?" Alex asked. "You two pals?"

"She's very cool," she said, doing her best to sound the same.

"She's the queen of merch," he said, coming in even though she hadn't invited him. "I heard about the Esmé Arnold line." He dropped into her guest chair. "Was that you who pushed that test so hard?"

"It was," she said, crossing her arms in a gesture that was both self-protective and maybe a little impatient. "Did you need something, Alex?"

"What was all that about Jazzberry?"

Something in the way he asked put her on guard. "We were just talking about their collection for next winter."

"What about it?"

"How...nice it is." She did not want to share her conversation, but Nadia was his boss, so... "She asked for a preliminary rollout plan with some fresh ideas, so I'm on that."

"Are you?"

"Assuming that fits in with your plans."

"Oh, by all means, do a rollout for Queen Nadia." He grinned. "Just be sure I see it first, okay?"

"Without a doubt." She waited a beat. "Is that all?"

"I just wanted to let you know you can take the Liz Claiborne meeting off your calendar for today."

"Did the rep cancel?" She tapped the open tablet on her desk to check her schedule, but the meeting with Gail was still there. "We set that up that months ago to do a preview of their winter casuals."

"No, Gail's coming with her team. But Jason will take the meeting."

She stared at him, trying not to react. Something told her he wanted a reaction, and she was not going to give it to him.

"Well, Alex, I realize you're new and you want to shake things up, but I've had the Claiborne account for two years. They won't be happy about a new buyer."

"They're fine," he said. "I already talked to Gail's boss. He was at the Promenade box at the Mariners game last night and I introduced him to Jason. We all agreed this is the right move."

Oh, did they? She knew Evan Roper. A total blowhard who she and Gail frequently gossiped about. Damn. Alex had *met* him? And Jason, no doubt waving his Harvard MBA diploma in the guy's face.

"Why would that be the right move?" she asked, not caring if the point-blank question was bad form. This was a crazy and unexpected change. Claiborne was a gem of an account, an anchor for the department, and she and Gail were buds. And that meant the whole buying process was smooth, profitable, and fun.

"Because you work too hard, Olivia," he said, enough condescension in his voice to put her on edge. "You're here at seven in the morning and haven't left before eight since I started. I've heard you're a regular on Sundays, too."

While he was at Mariners games in the company box with another buyer who was competing for the promotion she wanted. "And am I to understand that hard work is frowned upon now?"

"Burnout is frowned upon. I can't take the chance of you collapsing on the job with an account the size of Claiborne, kiddo."

Kiddo? Was he serious? "Collapsing on the job? What does that even mean?"

"Look," he said, leaning forward. "You're right, I am new. And I was hired to shake things up around here. I'm starting with some account restructuring. I'm putting Jason on the Liz Claiborne account and I'd like you to step in and handle general cruise wear."

"Cruise..." She shook her head, almost speechless. "Cruise wear isn't even a department in most of our stores. The buying is done locally."

He shrugged. "Maybe it can be moved to corporate for some discounts. I'm certain you'll work that same magic you did with Esmé." He pointed at her. "And don't stay so late, Olivia. A well-rounded life is healthy."

"I don't need—"

He cut her off by standing very slowly, placing both hands on her desk, looking hard at her. "Make something amazing happen with cruise wear, Olivia. I'm counting on you."

For a long moment, she just stared at him, feeling her pulse pound. Nothing amazing was ever going to happen with general cruise wear, and they both knew it. They also knew that there were three people in line for one merchandising promotion. And Nadia Gifford wasn't calling the other two directly to sing the praises of their product launch ideas.

Yes, Jason Bryn had his stinking Harvard B-school pedigree, and Marietta O'Neal had started with Promenade twenty years ago on the floor of the Dallas store. But neither of those people had her talent and everyone knew it.

"No need to call Gail," he said as he stepped toward the door. "Evan already let her know about the change." With that, he turned and walked out, leaving the door open so she could hear him tap on the door of the office beside hers.

"Jason, my friend," he said, all jovial and buddy-buddy. "How hungry are you?"

"Ready to eat the drywall, big man."

"Great. Let's get lunch and talk about Liz."

"Claiborne?"

"No, the Queen of England, you numbskull. Let's go."

Their laughter disappeared down the hall with their big, loud men's footsteps...men who didn't know squat about Liz or Esmé or even cruise wear, for that matter.

Suddenly she felt very, very powerless. And that wasn't a feeling Olivia Whitney liked at all.

She called her mother back, but got her voicemail. She hoped that meant she was well on her way to meeting with a PI who could find the missing sister. Or closing the deal on the multi-million-dollar resort that just landed in her lap.

After leaving a message, she opened up the Jazzberry file and got to work.

Chapter Eleven

Miles

By the time Elizabeth Mary Vanderveen Whitney arrived at his house on Seagrape Lane, Miles's curiosity was more than piqued. As he always did with a potential new client, he ran a cursory search on her prior to their meeting; nothing in-depth. But Miles Anderson didn't have to dig too deep to get a handle on people, and usually, within ten minutes, he had a pretty good idea of why they wanted to meet with him.

Not the case with Eliza Whitney.

Usually, his client had a cheating spouse, but this lady was a widow. Sometimes, it was a missing kid. But her kids were in plain sight, in San Jose and Seattle. Once in a while, it was an adoption issue—God, he loved having some sealed adoption records to crack—or an asset search. Her late husband held a large interest in a movie studio, so maybe he had a million hidden in the Cayman Islands and she wanted to find it. Not his specialty, but he had connections. And he'd want a percentage.

Maybe she'd given up a baby for adoption and wanted to track the kid down. That was possible, and much more up his alley.

Whatever it was, the trail of his clients' own lives

usually allowed him to guess what they were going to tell him before they walked in the door to his home office.

But this time, he didn't have a clue. Deeley had texted him a heads up, but he hadn't said anything beyond the fact that she was Dutch Vanderveen's daughter. That surprised him, because she hadn't been at the memorial service, based on the records he found on the funeral home's site. She hadn't posted a word about her father's passing on any social media—though she was a crappy Facebook user.

He narrowed his eyes at the picture of her standing next to that big star, Nick Frye, at some Hollywood shindig, described as his agent. A redhead, too. He wouldn't forget that, because they were his favorite.

So, she hobnobbed with the rich and famous, but Deeley said this was her first trip to Sanibel. That meant she hadn't come to see her father who, he learned when he did the Katie Bettencourt project, had come to Sanibel diagnosed with inoperable brain cancer. Who didn't visit their dying dad? Miles probably wasn't going to like her.

By the time she rang his doorbell that afternoon, he was real curious about what brought Elizabeth Mary to his home.

Tinkerbell was worked up, too, barking her fool head off as she waddled to the door, her stub knocking sideways, her paws slapping the ground at the possibility of an intruder.

"Easy, Tink," he said, taking a sly look out the sidelight to make sure it was her. Oh, yeah, it was her. Nice coppery hair and, jeez. Freckles. He liked freckles.

He rubbed a hand over his jaw, suddenly feeling every one of his fifty-six years. "Maybe I shoulda shaved."

Too late now. He opened the door and met a pair of gray-blue eyes that reminded him of Dutch, only prettier. So much prettier.

"Mr. Anderson?" she asked.

Instantly, Tink barked, trying to worm her pudgy body through his legs to get to the new arrival.

"Just Miles. And you are...Mrs. Whitney?"

"Just Eliza." She looked down and tipped her head. "And who's this?"

"Just Tinkerbell."

She laughed at the name—everyone did—which couldn't have been more off base for a pug/Frenchie/Boston terrier mix who was basically a fat, mushy, popeyed ball of saliva-dropping mutt with no regard for personal space.

"Come on in," he said. "She'll stop barking after a minute."

"Hello, Tinkerbell." She bent over and offered a hand to Tink, confident enough to show she knew her way around a dog, and long enough for him to see she was graceful—that made sense, since he knew she'd danced on Broadway—and that the hair color looked pretty damn natural in the unforgiving sunlight that shone behind her.

"Can I get you a cup of coffee?" he asked, gesturing for her to come all the way into the house.

"Oh, no, don't trouble yourself."

"No trouble, because it's always brewed here. I live on it, so are you sure?"

"Well, okay. I'll take one then." She took a few steps into the open living room, looking out to the pool and dock, nodding toward the sport fishing boat out there. "That looks nice."

"Very," he agreed. "Also my hole in the water where I throw money and time."

She smiled at the old joke, taking a few steps toward the windows. "*Miles Away*?" She read the name painted on the stern. "Clever."

"Thanks. It's a sweet ride and my reward for a hard day's work."

She looked beyond the dock to the wide canal beyond the boat. "You know, I really thought Sanibel was such a small island, but it's not."

"First time here?" So she *was* estranged from Dutch. He sure hoped *his* daughter would come see him if he was dying. The thought made him smile. Janie would not only come see him, she'd move in, help him run his business, and provide daily internet searches on the latest cures. And probably cut off his caffeine.

"It is my first time, yes." She looked back down at Tinkerbell, smiling at the dog, who was doing her best to lick Eliza's sandal-covered foot. "I don't know why, but I envisioned the island as being smaller."

"Come back in January," he said, rounding the kitchen counter to his always ready, always steaming coffee pot. "It feels miniscule when the snowbirds are packed in like sardines. How d'you take your coffee?"

"Black."

Ooh, he liked a woman who drank black coffee. It showed spine.

He stayed quiet while he poured, because if there was one thing he knew about people, it was that they talked too much when they were in a new situation. It was when he learned the most about his new clients, though this one seemed intent on scratching Tinkerbell's head.

"I have an office around the corner," he said, jutting his chin that way. "We can sit in there and talk."

"Thanks." She took the coffee he offered and followed him into the much dimmer hallway, but the brightness returned when he led her into the oversized space where he worked.

"Oh, my," she said. "You're serious about your computing."

He laughed at that, glancing at the desk that held three monitors and a laptop.

"One's for gaming when I don't have any work," he admitted.

"Gaming?" She gave a wry smile. "No offense, but you seem a little, um, mature for video games. I say that as the mother of a twenty-seven-year-old boy who was physically attached to his Xbox when he was a teenager."

He chuckled. "I have him by almost thirty years, and I bet I'd kick his butt in online *Call of Duty*. What can I say?" He gestured for her to sit on the sofa and took the only guest chair. "I'm a kid at heart."

Smiling, she took a seat. "That's a good quality, I

suppose." As she put her cup on the end table, she sighed and glanced around. "Not exactly what I was expecting."

"Looking for the walk-up with a frosted glass door and the words 'Private Investigator' painted on it?"

She laughed. "And a secretary in a short skirt with a beehive hairdo."

"Smoking Camels."

She shook her head, still laughing. "So you're not that kind of PI, I get it. You know, I've been on the set of *Magic Man*, a TV show where the lead is a PI. All my PI experience comes from fiction."

Of course, he knew the star of that show, Nick Frye, was her client. "Good show, but a total joke as far as an investigator's life is concerned. The magic tricks were cool, though." He grabbed a notebook from his desk, settling in to face her. "So, before we get into your situation, Eliza, let me just tell you that I'm not...inexpensive. You'll pay a fairly steep hourly fee for my services, but I am thorough and I am honest."

"But are you any good?" she asked with only a slight tease in her voice.

This was usually when he had to prove he was. "I can find out more about most people in a ten-minute online search than in an hour-long face-to-face conversation."

She took a sip of coffee, eyeing him over the rim.

"For instance, before you came, I took the liberty of dipping into some of my favorite databases that are not accessible to the public to find out a little about you."

She lowered the cup. "You did?"

"I know you were born in Brooklyn, but moved to

Long Island after your mother remarried. I also learned you skipped college, even though you had the grades for it, and then you lived in a not-so-nice area in New York City, and actually had bit parts in four Broadway productions, and more off Broadway."

Her eyes flickered. "Even more off-off Broadway, but..." She angled her head. "What else?"

"You didn't make much in those lean years."

"You know that?"

"I know you didn't have to file taxes, since you fell that far under minimum wage and probably didn't claim your money as...a waitress? I'm guessing on that one."

"Hostess at a nightclub," she filled in, a gleam that might be humor, might be admiration—but was definitely attractive—in her eyes.

"I know that you married Benjamin Whitney, who'd launched a family-friendly movie studio, and lost him recently. My sympathies."

She nodded. "Thank you. I'm not sure if I should be impressed or terrified."

"It depends. Do you have anything to hide?"

She studied him for a moment, holding his gaze with one that was exactly the color of the sky about an hour before a summer storm. "I actually made a lot as a hostess, but I never claimed a dime. Does that mean I have something to hide?"

"It means you're smart and were probably a good hostess. Something to hide is usually, you know, an affair, a baby you never told anyone about, a dead body in the basement."

She almost smiled, which he really wanted to see again, but then her expression softened. "Yeah, well, some of those are on the money. At least the first two. No dead bodies. I hope."

She had an affair and a secret baby? He didn't react, but waited for her to continue.

"Did you know my father, Dutch Vanderveen, a Sanibel resident?"

"I did. Not terribly well, but we lived on the same island. It might not seem small to you but trust me, there's basically one grocery store."

She smiled. "Well, he was eccentric."

"I got that impression."

"He claimed to have left a will, but so far, Teddy—do you know Teddy Blessing?"

"Everyone on this island knows Teddy."

"Well, Teddy hasn't found it. My attorney in L.A. hasn't found it in probate for New York or Florida, his only known places of residence."

"You want me to find his will?" Because that couldn't be too hard or require her to pay his exorbitant fees.

"I want you to find this woman." She opened a handbag and slid out a small picture, handing it to him.

"That's Dutch," he said, even before he looked very closely at the circa-1970s photo.

Dutch was easy to recognize. The man had been close to six-two, and though his hair had been white, and was black in this picture, he had a distinct face with movie star good looks that hadn't completely faded in his old age. "And my guess is that's not you, so you're not asking me to find your mother."

"That's not me. I don't know who that woman is, other than Camille. Turn it over."

He did, reading the inscription written around the Kodak logo. "Our family. I love you, Camille. April 1980." He looked up. "French mistress?"

"Except he told Teddy it was his wife and daughter."

Eesh. Wouldn't be the first bigamist he'd investigated. "So this little girl would be your half-sister."

"Yes." She sighed the word. "And I'd like to find her. For one thing, my father's estate is up in the air and without knowing who's in his will, I can't do anything with Shellseeker Cottages, the tea house, or Sanibel Treasures."

He looked at her, feeling a frown form. "Dutch owned all that? Teddy is like Sanibel royalty, and I thought her family homesteaded the property."

"I think that's what most people think, but apparently her father sold it many years ago; it's changed hands a few times. Dutch bought it last."

He let out a whistle. "Nice payday for somebody. You? Teddy? Or..." He waved the picture.

"I'm not interested in a payday, Mr. Anderson."

"Miles."

"If I have a sister, I want to meet her."

He nodded and looked down at the picture again. "What about your mother? Does she know—"

"She's been gone four years," she said. "But she did mention a Camille, and, to the best of my recollection, she was a stewardess for Pan Am. She wasn't the only one, but I believe she was the one who broke my parents up."

"What year did they divorce?"

"You can probably find the records, but I was maybe seven, so 1976 or 77."

He nodded, still examining the picture. "Teddy doesn't know anything? Doesn't have anything of Dutch's?"

"She does, but I haven't been through it all yet. Nothing she can remember that would be a clue, and he'd never mentioned this woman to her."

"Did he ever give you any clues that he had another family?"

She shook her head. "We weren't close. As a kid, I rarely heard from him because the relationship with my mother was very acrimonious. And even as I got older, there were years when I didn't hear from him. Sometimes I'd get a call or post card, and we saw each other infrequently. He was always distant, in every way."

He nodded, thinking about that. Kind of sad for her to have a man like Dutch as a father and be cut off from him.

"If I have a sister," she continued, "I want to know it. I want to know her. And I want to be fair about the property that's been in Teddy's family for many generations."

Ethical. He liked that.

He nodded, wrote a note, and looked up at her. "So that means we have a huge bargaining chip with the sister," he said. "If she wants to remain invisible or not talk to you, or her mother does, we could lure them out with the promise of an inheritance."

She made a face. "I hope it doesn't come to that."

"You never know. People are weird and they stay hidden for personal reasons, and sometimes they don't even know they are hidden. I'll need whatever you can give me as far as information about this woman."

"Camille. French. That's it."

He gave a soft laugh. "Okay, a challenge."

She reached down as Tink pawed the sofa. "Is she allowed up here?"

"Are you allowed on her sofa is a better question."

Smiling, she closed her hands around the dog to help her up. "Come up here, cutie pie."

"Careful," he said. "She's, uh, solid."

She laughed, grunting a little as she got the dog onto the seat. "No kidding." She offered her knuckles to Tink, who licked the daylights out of them, particularly fond of a sparkly wedding ring this widow still wore on her left hand.

So he should really stop admiring that natural hair.

"So, any idea at all where I should start?" he asked.

She stroked Tink's head as the dog nuzzled into her thigh. "Dutch probably had more than one mistress, if I'm to believe my mother."

He nodded. "Pan Am pilot, right?"

"Yes, which put him in touch with oodles of women, but she griped the most about the flight attendants. Do you think that's a uniform Camille has on?"

He studied the photograph again. "Could be. I can find out a lot from this picture."

"Good. That's good."

"Paris wasn't a Pan Am hub, as I recall," he said, thinking about the challenge ahead. "I'll need to check. But it would be easy enough to fly in and out of de Gaulle."

He made a note, then looked up at her, catching her scratching Tink's back and sharing some playful eye contact with the dog.

Don't like my dog, lady. 'Cause I already like you.

She shifted in her seat and picked up the coffee mug, then put it back down again, clearly not saying all that was on her mind.

"Anything else?" he urged.

"I really hesitate to ask this, but..." She leaned forward, looking him in the eye. "How well do you know Teddy Blessing?"

"Better than I knew Dutch. If I were a tea drinker, she'd be my go-to, but I like my coffee. Why?"

"Well, she obviously has a deep interest in Shellseeker Cottages and the ancillary businesses. In fact, she wants them back. I respect that and, like I said, I want to do the right thing. She is kind of hoping that I'll just... hand them over."

He lifted a brow. "Would you?"

"I don't know what I'm going to do. I don't have enough information, which is why I'm here."

"It's odd that he didn't leave a will with his wife."

"Well, Teddy wasn't legally his wife," she said. "He didn't marry her."

"Oh? Then you already know more than I do."

She looked down at Tink, who was gazing back with so much love in her bulging brown eyes that it was actually embarrassing.

"Anything else, Eliza?"

"No, just that..." She leaned down and snuggled the dog. "Just that I adore you," she said in a soft whisper.

Ah, man. Seriously? Life wasn't fair.

"Do you need a retainer or advance?" she asked before taking one more drink of coffee.

"Text me an email address and I'll send you a contract and the specifics. How long are you planning to stay on Sanibel Island?"

"I honestly don't know. I'm in no hurry to get home to a very empty house in Los Angeles. I'm learning a lot about my father, who I didn't know at all. I like Teddy, and..." She lifted a shoulder. "I'll stick around a little while."

He held her gaze one tiny second past what he should have, then instantly looked down at his notes. "I'll be in touch."

"Great. I look forward to that." When she stood, Tink barked.

"And so will my dog," he joked.

"Thank you, Miles." She extended her hand and they shook, which only made Tink bark more. "And thank you for all the attention, Miss Tinkerbell," she added with a light rub of Tink's head.

When she left and he closed the door behind her, he looked down at Tink, who'd already started moping.

"Let's not make fools of ourselves, okay?"

Tink just barked and flattened her round belly on the tile, looking out the glass panel like she would just have to wait for Red to come back. Guess they both would.

Chapter Twelve

Eliza

"Frozen? That's not on my backing track."

At the statement, Harper gave Eliza a look of total confusion. Of course a four-year-old didn't understand the concept of an instrumental-only track, but she *really* didn't understand a person unfamiliar with *Frozen*.

Eliza wouldn't give up. The child was too bright, too much fun, and finally coming out of her shell.

"But this"—Eliza held up her phone—"is like karaoke for Broadway tunes. If Rogers and Hammerstein wrote it, I've got it. *Oklahoma, Sound of Music, South Pacific.* Anything work for you?"

"*Frozen*."

Eliza laughed at her sweetly stubborn face. "I know you like musicals because I heard you singing *State Fair*. How about we learn a dance from that one, Harper?"

She shook her head and threw her arms up. "Let it go!" she yelled. But that was no speaking voice when she sang. The kid had pipes.

Curled on the sofa in her living room sipping tea, Teddy smiled at the exchange. "But Miss Eliza wants to teach the dance steps." She leaned forward to whisper, "She was a professional dancer in New York!"

Harper was only moderately impressed.

"Please do *Frozen*," she said, with praying hands that were so adorable it actually hurt.

Truth was, Eliza had done nothing but thoroughly enjoy Harper ever since Teddy called and invited her to spend the evening babysitting while Katie was at her book club.

"Can we at least watch the movie first?" Eliza asked on a laugh, but Harper shook her head and lifted her arms again, opening her mouth.

"Let it go, I know," Eliza stopped her before she belted it out again, leaning forward to take her hands. "But I don't know that song."

"Don't you have a little girl?" she asked.

"I do. Her name is Olivia, but she's not little. She was pre-*Frozen*."

"Oh." Her tiny, narrow shoulders dropped in disappointment.

"So, can we do, Our state fair is a great state fair..." she whispered the line and mimicked a marching dance to the tune, enough to make Harper's face brighten as she sang the next line, much louder.

"She's not even off-key," Eliza said to Teddy. "I'm sorry, but the talent agent in me kind of itches to get this girl out there."

"I doubt Katie would agree to that, but a private show in my living room would be nice."

Eliza pushed the coffee table with its breakable crystals out of the way and reaching for Harper's hand. "Shall we learn some steps, Harper?"

A cascade of giggles followed as she gave in, taking a very simple dance lesson, with Teddy clapping along and taking plenty of video. But it didn't take long to teach Harper, who had a freakishly sharp mind and remembered every step the first time she was taught. She was literally brimming with raw talent.

By the time Teddy announced it was bedtime, they had a short performance ready to give her mother the next day. Harper made it until nine, but her eyes were heavy, so Eliza went with Teddy to tuck her into a guest room that had enough toys and a table of crafts—many of them from *Frozen*—that Eliza imagined the kid was a regular.

"So," Teddy whispered as they came out of the bedroom back into the living area. "How about a good cup of tea for all your singing and dancing efforts?"

"I'd love one of those peppermint teas you made me. That was delicious."

"If I add a little extra bitter grass, you can expect some very exciting dreams," Teddy said. "Are you up for it?"

"Well, yeah. Maybe I'll finally see the face of the woman in my dream."

"Ah, yes. The mysterious family woman. Maybe it's the long-lost sister you want to find," Teddy suggested.

"Or maybe it's you," Eliza said softly.

A smile pulled at Teddy's lips. "Well, I'd like that.

You know, Eliza, I forgot about our whole messy situation while you taught Harper that dance."

"Music and dancing does make you forget," Eliza agreed.

"But why do you whisper when you want to sing? So Harper's voice is louder?"

"Because..." She tapped her throat as if that were the culprit and not her head. "I can't sing anymore. I essentially stopped when Ben got sick, and every once in a while I can let out a line or two, but..." Eliza settled on a bar stool to watch Teddy go through her rather elaborate tea-brewing ritual. "It's like I'm too sad to sing. Is that crazy?"

Teddy lifted both brows. "You're asking the wrong person, hon. Nothing is crazy to me. That makes perfect sense. What does it feel like when you try?"

"Like my voice has dried up. Oh, I can do a note or two, in the shower. And when I was in Coconut Key, I helped choreograph a high school musical, but I didn't have to sing much at all." She sighed, recognizing how deep the longing was, which only made it worse.

"What do you think is going on?" Teddy asked.

"Singing the way I used to—and the way Harper likes to—takes an emotional component. You have to feel the music and let it fill your whole being and..." She gave a tight smile. "There's a level of joy required and I'm just not there yet."

"I understand," Teddy said, and Eliza knew that wasn't lip service. She *did* understand. And she was a healer.

"Any advice?" Eliza asked.

"Yes. I would do a crystal bath with rose quartz and citrine. Maybe throw a garnet in there for regeneration. I'll send some home with you tonight. And you've inspired me to concoct a tea for joy and singing."

Eliza laughed. "There is such a thing?"

"Just you wait, young lady." Teddy poured some tap water into a glass electric kettle and set it on a burner.

"Water right out of the sink?" Eliza asked, pretending to be aghast. "Where's the joy in that?"

"This is for warming the pot." Then, Teddy pulled down an elegant cream-colored porcelain teapot from a shelf that housed about six of them, each one more beautiful than the next. "I'll use the filtered water for drinking, and joy. And singing."

She opened a metal tin, one of a dozen or so that lined the counter, each with handwritten and taped labels of their flower or herb. Taking a sniff, she closed her eyes. "I love that peppermint, too, but I think tonight I'm going to give you jasmine because it's soothing for your throat and oozing with antioxidants. It detoxes with phenolic compounds, and adds some very critical flavonoids to your body."

Eliza blinked. "That sounds far more scientific than woo-woo."

"How do you think I kept your father alive for an extra...seven hundred and four days?"

"You counted?"

"He did," she said, pressing a button under the kettle

and almost instantly some bubbles rose. "And every one of them mattered to him."

"Not enough to mention, you know, that other wife and daughter."

Teddy winced, then blew out a breath, using the back of her hand to swipe away a silver curl that fell over her face.

"He was such a dichotomy," she said. "Loud and brash and talkative, but at the same time secretive and protective of his past. There were subjects I couldn't broach, and others he wouldn't stop talking about. Loving Dutch was a rush, and a risk. But never boring."

Eliza nodded. "Love is always a risk, I suppose."

"And he needed to be healed, which, while rewarding, can be exhausting."

Eliza dropped her chin on her knuckles, staring at her. "How so?"

"Well..." Teddy started opening tins and laying them out in a row. "I'm an empath, you know."

She didn't actually know that, but had picked up hints in their conversations. Still, she stayed quiet while Teddy opened various tins and studied her loose tea like a chemist.

"And that's a blessing and a curse," she continued. "It's wonderful to get a very quick 'sense' of a person and what they need. It makes me a good judge of character. It also makes me a little distrustful of people."

"Is that the curse part?"

"No, the curse is that when I heal someone, when I

really lay my hands on them and send my energy to them, it drains me."

"Do you do that often?" Eliza asked.

"With someone who is deeply wounded, like Dutch, I did it every day until he was whole. With a lot of people, well..." She smiled as she mixed three different blends in a shallow bowl. "A long hug can be incredibly effective."

"But when you healed Dutch, you never learned why he was so deeply wounded?" Eliza inched forward, surprised at how much she wanted the answer to that question.

"Like I said, I knew some things, not others. It's not important that I understand the root of a wound to heal it," she added. "I'm not a psychiatrist, just a person who can deliver positive, healing energy, like my mother did."

Eliza thought about that, watching silently as Teddy poured out the pot-warming water, then filled the pot with her mixture of her loose teas. She added boiling filtered water and covered the whole thing with a tea cozy shaped like a kitten's head, ears and all.

"I'm surprised you don't have a cat," Eliza mused, looking at the oddity. "You strike me as a cat lady."

"I had three and lost them all in the last few years. Dutch wasn't a fan of cats. He's allergic. Did you know?"

"No," Eliza admitted. "File that under the many, many things I didn't know about my own father." She held up her hand to stave off any reminders of how she'd never contacted him. "My fault, I know." And at Teddy's sad look, Eliza's heart dropped. "Please tell me that my not seeing him wasn't one of his wounds."

Teddy swallowed, hesitating just enough for Eliza to know the answer. It was.

"Regrets are such a giant waste of energy," Teddy said, stroking the cozy as if to warm her hands, or maybe imagine it was one of those three cats she lost. "Why don't you save me the trouble of helping you through that, and do what Harper has been trying to get you to do all night: Let it go!"

She laughed and they talked about the tea some more, with Teddy carefully explaining the healing properties. When she finally offered Eliza a brewed cup, the simple liquid seemed far more potent than she'd ever imagined.

"How do I bathe with crystals?" Eliza asked after taking a sip.

"You literally put them in the bathwater with you. Add a little essence of eucalyptus and lemon balm. And a nice fragrant candle."

"Do you have one that has that Sanibel Scent?"

"I do. I'll go make you a goodie bag right now, so we don't forget." She came around the counter and put a hand on Eliza's shoulder, leaning in to add an unexpected kiss on the cheek. "We'll get you singing again, Eliza."

When Teddy walked out, she sipped the tea and let the flavonoids and antioxidants and detoxy things do their stuff. Yeah, maybe all that was true. But...

She reached up and touched the cheek Teddy had

kissed. She suspected that the real healing agent around here was Theodora Blessing herself.

❧

AFTER KATIE CAME HOME from her book club meeting, Eliza stepped out into the warm, coastal air to walk back to her cottage. A colorful reusable shopping bag hung heavy on her arm, weighed down with crystals, a candle, an aromatherapy kit, and...whatever else Teddy included in her bag of tricks.

Still feeling completely relaxed from the tea and company, she followed the now familiar path through the gardens, lit only by the moon and a few solar-powered lights that were strategically placed around the property.

Shellseeker Beach was quiet but for the distant soft splash of the water, close enough that she guessed it was high tide. In the moonlight, she caught sight of the gazebo, perched on its sandy rise like some kind of topper on a wedding cake. It really was the perfect place for nuptials and if she owned this place, she'd push for intimate destination weddings here.

Wait. She *did* own this place. Or might.

Drawn to the peace of the gazebo, she walked toward it, sighing at the *unfinishedness* of this whole situation, something she didn't relish.

She couldn't make plans if she didn't know about this property, or the mysterious Camille and...the half-sister she might or might not have. And if there was no sister?

Then she had inherited Shellseeker Beach, and she

was back to square one. What should she do? Sell it for a tidy profit that she would happily share with Teddy and her makeshift family? There was so much money at stake, there had to be a way to make everyone happy.

But if she *didn't* sell...she could make them even happier. She could give Teddy her legacy and her land, and go back to life as she knew it in California. She wouldn't need a job, and maybe she could sell the big house in Pacific Palisades and move...where? Seattle to be near Olivia, or northern California to settle near Dane. Maybe she'd wait and do volunteer work or maybe get another job or just hang out until Olivia or Dane got married and had kids. Then she would have little adorable grandchildren like Harper.

Or she could...stay.

She sucked in a soft breath when the word landed in her head. *Stay.*

Stay in Shellseeker Beach.

She'd be like one of them, sucked into the healing love of Teddy Blessing and suddenly part of her world.

What would that be like?

She set the heavy bag on one of the benches and took a long, slow walk around the inside of the gazebo, once again thinking of *The Sound of Music* set in the movie and the Broadway production, with Liesl and Rolf. She'd auditioned for the part of Liesl once, and had to learn every word and step, but didn't get it.

The lyrics came back to her, the opening lines echoing in her head in Rolf's voice, singing about a little girl on an empty stage.

She moved her foot in a half circle, dipping, remembering the way that director wanted her to play Liesl as naïve, even stupid.

But she hadn't, and that probably cost her the part. Eliza saw Liesl as a little bit canny, already knowing her own power around poor, helpless Rolf. When she proclaimed she needed someone older and wiser, she was playing with the boy, who, it turned out, deserved that and worse.

She closed her eyes and let herself be transported back to that New York stage, the notes playing while she cleared her throat. She opened her mouth, and...nothing came out.

With a soft grunt, she dropped onto the bench. It didn't matter that she couldn't sing, but it was just one more loss, like Ben. Something she'd loved and counted on and enjoyed every day of her life. There was nothing wrong with her, she just didn't want to dig to that singing place.

I am sixteen going on seventeen...

She shifted on the bench and bumped into the bag, nearly knocking it to the ground. She grabbed and saved it from the fall, but heard two crystals tap against each other. Reaching in to make sure she hadn't broken them, her fingers closed around the big pink crystal that Teddy had included.

Pulling out the fist-sized stone, she ran her fingers over the sharp edges, angling it so the moonlight shone on the pale pink color. Closing her eyes, she leaned back, and lifted the stone to her chest. Then she slid it up to her throat.

Once more, she took a deep breath and cleared her vocal cords.

"I am sixteen going on seventeen." She sucked in a little breath as her singing voice filled the gazebo, rich and real for that one line. She tried another. "I know that I'm naïve."

She stood slowly, holding the crystal tighter, not daring to sing more. It was a start. A small, simple, inconsequential start...but everything had to start somewhere, right?

Clutching the crystal in one hand, and the bag in the other, she rushed back to the cottage to draw herself a bath, humming every note she could remember from *The Sound of Music.*

Chapter Thirteen

Olivia

Olivia stared at the last page of her PowerPoint presentation for the Jazzberry rollout plan and couldn't wipe the smile from her face. Nadia Gifford, guru of merchandise planning, would love these ideas.

The only thing better than sending it would be delivering it in person. Olivia could knock this rollout out of the park, then Nadia would be calling Alex and insisting he make his best senior buyer a merchandising VP, which would place her feet firmly on the next rung of the Promenade corporate ladder.

"A girl can dream," she whispered as she saved the document and pulled her phone out when it rang with a call from her mother. "Hey, Mommy," she said playfully. "How's life in Shellshocker Beach?"

Her mother snorted. "I had no idea how right you'd be with that name. It's wonderful, actually."

She pulled the phone away and gave it a good look. Mom sounded *amazing*. "Wonderful, huh? Did you track down the will and become a multi-millionairess?"

"No, not yet. Nothing new on that front, but I taught a four-year-old a dance routine and learned all about the health benefits of tea and I took a crystal bath with lemon balm and candles and, Livvie, I sang a little bit! Just a little bit, but..." She let out a happy, happy sigh. "I do feel better."

"That's great, Mom."

"Oh, I'm going on a Vacation Bible School field trip to Ding Darling Wildlife Refuge today."

Olivia shook her head like she couldn't possibly have heard any of that right. "Say again?"

Her mother laughed, a musical, happy sound that Olivia hadn't heard in so long, it kind of took her breath away. "Long story, but trust me, it'll be amazing. Teddy has been talking about Ding Darling so much I can't wait to see it. And, oh! I went on a sunrise kayak trip which, I am telling you, is the way to start every day."

"That sounds terrific, but, really, no progress on that will? Or the picture? Remember, the sister you didn't know you had?"

"Well, I can't spend every day mooning about it, can I? I hired an investigator and my attorney's estate guy is on the job for five hundred dollars an hour. So, I'm having fun."

"I hear it in your voice," Olivia said.

"I love it here and I can see why it matters so much to Teddy. Her history is really remarkable. Her family goes back to before there was a bridge from the mainland to Sanibel. We went to this absolutely dreamy cemetery at the Chapel by the Sea and all of her family is buried there!"

Olivia closed her eyes and tried to focus on what her mother was saying, and not just that she made a trip to a cemetery sound like a day at the beach. Like if this Teddy person's family was so important... "You're not thinking about caving, are you?"

"Caving? There are no caves on Sanibel Island."

"Mom!"

Eliza laughed. "I know what you mean, Liv. I'm not caving to anything."

"Not the pressure to hand over a half mile of beachfront property that legally belongs to you, and maybe a half-sister you don't know if you have?" she pressed. "Eyes on the prize, Elizabeth Mary."

"Only if that prize really and truly belongs to me."

"You're Dutch's legal heir, Mom." And she seemed to keep forgetting that. What kind of spell was this New Age Teddy casting?

"We don't know who's going to inherit it yet, Livvie. And if I have a sister, well, that is more important to me than anything. I want to know her. Do I really want a resort in Florida? It's rooted in Teddy's life. Yes, it's tempting to stay here because I—"

"Stay?" She almost choked. "You're thinking about staying there? Or even considering handing over something worth seven figures—and the first figure isn't a one, I might add—to a virtual stranger?"

"She's not a stranger anymore. We have a great connection and a lot in common. She's really insightful and deep and funny and warm. I like her."

"Which is fine, you like her. Good. But, Mom, has it ever occurred to you that maybe she's playing you a little?

Trying to get you to go all gooey inside and hand over what Dutch wanted you to have?"

"I hope I'm never that cynical, Liv."

"Practical, not cynical," Olivia insisted. "You're in the thick of it there with darling Ding and seaside chapels and...what in God's name is a crystal bath? Mom, listen to yourself."

"I am, Livvie. I feel like I can sing here. Doesn't that mean anything to you?"

Yeah, if she were singing that she sold the property and made four million. But Olivia knew better than to push. The fact was, it did feel great to hear her mother so happy. She'd been wretchedly sad for months and months, and Olivia did not want to steal that from her.

"Well, you just enjoy the experience, Mom. It'll work out when someone finds the will or locates your long-lost sister." Both of which sounded a little out of the realm of reality, but she let it go. "I've got to get back to finishing a project right now."

"Is it the Jazz thing you mentioned?"

"Yes, and my rollout plan kicks serious butt." A tap on her door made Olivia swing around from the computer monitor to see Alex Brody standing in her doorway. "Gotta go now."

"Oh, and Livvie—"

"Will call you back." She tapped the call off and smiled at her boss. "Hey, Alex. What's up?"

"Just thought I'd check on the Jazzberry rollout. I need to look at that before you send it to Nadia."

Seriously? She'd been five minutes from hitting Send,

making sure they got it simultaneously. Now it was on the monitor behind her and—

"Is that it?"

"Oh, I'm still putting the finishing touches on it."

But he came around her desk and squinted. "A color wheel and jewels? Oh, I like that. I think—"

She reached out and touched the mouse, clearing the screen before he saw another thing. "Not ready for prime time," she ground out. "I promise you'll have it by the end of the day."

"Why don't you just send me what you have, and copy Jason."

She stared at him. *Why don't you drop dead*, she thought as she gave him a smile that she knew didn't reach her eyes. "Jason doesn't need it, and I still need to run some numbers so the spreadsheets make sense."

"Jason and I will make sense of them."

She flicked her hand to get him to back away from her desk, adding just enough of a glare that he obeyed. "Not yet. End of day. Did you have anything else to tell me?"

He dropped into her guest chair like she'd actually invited him, which she certainly did not. "I do have something to tell you."

She hoped to God it was that Gail went to her boss at Claiborne and insisted that Olivia be put back on the account.

"I'm doing a major department reorg that'll be announced next week."

Just the way he said it made her blood go cold. "Okay. Do you need help?"

He snorted softly with the not-so-subtle implication that if he did, it wouldn't be from her. "I got it all figured out, Olivia. It really doesn't affect you too much, but I'm moving Jason to a direct report to Nadia."

"He's promoted?"

"No, no. Not yet. I'll save those promotions for the next reorganization. There will be one, I promise. But I'm sliding Jason over to share women's apparel with you, and it makes sense for him to report to her because of the heavy merch involved."

"What about his accounts?" she asked.

"I'm hiring someone from my old job who just slams it in accessories. Like, whoa. You're going to love this woman. She's the brains behind the Saks bags and shoes, and I ask you, does anyone do it better than Saks?"

"Um...Promenade? Did you see what Marietta and I did for last spring's accessories? Highest profit in the company that season. Maybe you need to check out the numbers."

She reached for her tablet, but he held up his hand, and shook his head with disinterest. "It was very cute what you two did with the whole Kate Spade thing, which was, I agree, wildly profitable."

"Yes. So why change things?"

"Because Apple Farthington is a buyer and merchandiser with an eye like you've never seen before."

"Wait—her name is Apple?"

He angled his head and narrowed his eyes. "If you

haven't heard of her, you should. She discovered Lars Brennan and Blue November, two of the hottest handbag lines on the market."

Hot if you're in high school. "Not of any interest to the Promenade shopper," she said. "Our demographics do not support lines like that."

"They will when Apple is on board. So, get ready for change, my friend. It's good." He pointed to the computer screen. "Email that to me right now, please."

So he could share it with...Apple and Jason?

"Oh, I'm leaving tonight for a bunch of meetings with the top brass," he added. "Nadia will be there, of course, and we'll talk about Jazzberry. After that, I'm visiting a few stores so I can get a feel for departments in each city. I'll be meeting Apple in Chicago and taking her with me through the Midwest."

"Okay." Great, he'd be gone. That would be a nice break.

"I've asked Jason to handle any crises that come up if I can't jump on a call fast enough."

And that would not be a nice break. "Okay," she repeated, knowing that it wasn't worth it to fight. "Have a nice trip."

After he walked out, she turned back to the computer, opened her email, and addressed it to him. The last thing she needed was to go around him and get canned so Apple could move into this office.

But before she typed a word, her phone rang again. This time, it was her brother out in Silicon Valley. She'd briefed him on everything, and she knew he'd talked to Mom, too.

"Hey, fathead," she said when she picked up.

"I just talked to Mom," he replied without an ounce of humor. "She mentioned something about staying there? Is she for real?"

Olivia sighed deeply and instantly knew she had to defend their mother. It was always her role to take Mom's side with Dane, who was a great guy, but really thought he knew everything about everything. "She's still grieving, Dane."

"And sitting on a goldmine."

And Mom thought Olivia was the practical one. "She'll figure it out."

"Liv."

She stared at the screen, thinking. This time her know-it-all brother was likely right. "What should we do, Dane?"

"You have to ask?"

Of course. One of them had to go talk sense into her.

"Nose goes," she said, only half joking with the childhood game that meant whoever said it didn't have to do it. Only in this case, it wasn't, "Nose goes to get the chips from the pantry." It meant, "Nose goes *to Sanibel.*"

"Don't be ridiculous," Dane murmured.

"I know, your job is way more important than mine."

"No," he said. "You're way better with Mom."

She sighed. Right again. "I got this, bro."

They chatted for another minute or two, but before

she was off the phone, she'd already found a flight online. She opened up her email and started typing.

Alex,

Here's the Jazzberry rollout, as discussed. Since you'll be out and Jason is here to hold down the fort, please be advised that I'll be taking my long overdue vacation starting tomorrow and will be out of the office, and out of town, for a few days. I'll check messages and will be happy to answer any questions regarding this or any other buying issues.

Best,

Olivia

She texted her mom, and went into the hall to commiserate with Marietta, but Alex was already in her office delivering his bad news.

Chapter Fourteen

Eliza

E liza came home from the Ding Darling field trip soaked in sweat, slightly exhausted, and ready for some downtime in her cottage. Harper, however, was buzzing around Teddy's house nattering about the birds they'd seen and the alligator coloring book she'd gotten, and every once in a while she burst into giggles over the "scoop on poop" video they'd watched in the education center.

Katie was cleaning for another hour, since a party was coming in and taking four cottages, so hyped-up Harper was all theirs.

Once Eliza and Teddy got the child settled with crayons and a snack, they looked at each other and burst out laughing.

"So, this grandparenting thing is not for the faint of heart," Eliza joked.

"You were great with those kids."

"I love kids. Not a big fan of tracking ibis footprints, but hey, it was fun. And that wildlife refuge is unlike anything I've ever seen." Eliza stepped forward and reached for Teddy's hands. "But I think you need a shower, some tea, and to put your feet up."

"Am I looking all of my seventy-two years?" Teddy asked on a laugh.

"Not even close, but let me do this for you. Go, shower. I'll make you an amazing cup of tea. Any suggestions from that collection of yours?"

"Surprise me," Teddy said, pulling Eliza closer. "Which you have done every day since you got here."

Eliza smiled at her. "Olivia calls this place Shell-shocker Beach."

Teddy hooted. "I love her already, and am so excited she's coming. We'll shock her, all right. She'll never want to leave."

Eliza laughed and nudged Teddy upstairs. "She doesn't stray far from the office, I'm afraid. The fact that she's taking a few days off to come here surprised the heck out of me. Go shower, and I'll be up with tea in a bit."

"Oh, Eliza. I love..." She didn't finish but closed her eyes as if she was stopping herself from saying what she was going to. "I love having you here," she finished, blowing Eliza a kiss, then glancing at Harper, who was laying on the sofa coloring, her eyes heavy. "She's going to be out in ten minutes."

"I feel her," Eliza joked. "Go."

When Teddy went upstairs, Eliza headed into the kitchen and did her best to replicate the ritual she'd seen Teddy perform quite a few times. She went with straight lavender tea, because she seemed to remember that helped a person rest. She went through the warming and brewing with a little less flair, but she got the job done.

While the tea steeped, she walked back into the living area and, sure enough, Harper was out, rolled onto the sofa, crayon dropped to the floor. Eliza snagged a soft blanket from the back of a chair and covered her, moving the coloring book and picking up the crayon.

When the child looked snug and secure, she leaned over and put the lightest kiss on Harper's forehead, so fond of this little angel whose shyness lifted a little more with each passing moment.

Smiling, Eliza walked back to get the tea, pressing her hand against her heart because something twisted in her chest. She closed her eyes and gave in to the feeling. It was...not grief.

Oh, good heavens. *Not* grief.

There was no other way to describe it. For the first time in four months—even longer, since she'd known she was saying goodbye to Ben for several months before he actually died— the only real feeling in her heart, in her soul, had been bone-deep sadness.

But today, somewhere between the ibis tracking and that kiss on Harper's head, maybe while she was laughing with Teddy or eating ice cream—ice cream! When was the last time she'd even had it?—or during the bus ride with fifteen kids singing about Jesus at the top of their lungs...grief lifted.

It felt like she'd opened a window inside her heart, letting in air and light and hope.

She took a moment just to feel it, to pray it would last, then put some cookies on a tray with the tea and carried it upstairs to Teddy's room. She expected to hear the shower, but the bathroom door was wide open and Teddy wasn't in there. She wasn't on the bed, or the deck outside, either.

"Teddy?"

"In the closet."

"Oh, okay. I brought you the tea. Are you showered?"

"Come in here, Eliza. Please."

Frowning, she set the tray on the night table and headed to the open closet door, sending a glance to Dutch's photos on the wall, including the blank spot where one of another woman and another daughter had hung.

"Are you all right?" she asked, stepping to the doorway to find Teddy on the floor of a walk-in closet with an open plastic bin in front of her.

She looked up, an unreadable expression in her eyes. "I started thinking on the way upstairs that we got sidetracked when we found the picture and never looked through his things for more information or the will, or maybe more pictures. I certainly hadn't looked with an eye toward a different wife or another daughter."

"Okay." She came closer, tired from the day, but intrigued.

"I pulled down this bin." She pointed to a shelf overhead where two more bins were stored. "That's all his. Clothes, mostly, but this one had papers, books, and I really thought he had a journal or a pilot's logbook. When I packed this, I was in a fog. Want to look?"

Did she? As much as she wanted to know Dutch, or this mysterious "wife" and daughter, did she want to replace her first breath of non-grief air with a deep dive into Dutch's logbooks? "Now?"

"Maybe you don't want to know."

"Of course I want to know," she said, folding onto the floor next to her. "It's just...we're tired and...and..."

"It's hard for you," Teddy said, putting her ever-empathetic hand on Eliza's arm. "Part of you really wants to know, and to know your sister, of course. But when you're faced with Dutch's life, it's a constant reminder that you weren't really in it very much."

Eliza gave a slow smile. "Man, you're good, Theodora Blessing."

"Right?" She patted Eliza's hand. "Is Harper asleep?"

"She's Ding Darlinged out."

Teddy pushed up, remarkably agile for her age. "Then I have a way to make this a teeny tiny bit easier. A sip of something."

"Oh, your tea is right there. I went with lavender."

"Excellent choice." She disappeared out the door, leaving Eliza to look into the bin, lifting out a Marsh Wheeling cigar box to find newspaper clippings and a white handkerchief with the letters AV embroidered on the edge, wrapped around another pair of aviator glasses. Not the more modern ones that Teddy had in the dresser, these were...classic. Originals. Probably worn in Vietnam to keep the sun out of his eyes while he flew missions.

Setting them down carefully, she brought the handkerchief closer, inhaling a vague and distant scent of something that took her back...to that room...to that flight bag...

Sorry, but I have to go... What had he called her? There'd been a nickname, something like—

"I hit Dutch's secret stash."

Eliza looked up to see Teddy holding two shot glasses etched with the familiar circular Pan Am logo and filled with golden liquid. "In the middle of the day, Teddy?"

"After a field trip with four-year-olds?" Teddy rolled her eyes. "Sometimes, Chivas is more medicinal than lavender tea."

Eliza laughed softly, taking both glasses so Teddy could sit back down next to her. When she was settled, Teddy took one of the glasses and touched the rim to Eliza's.

"To Dutch?" Eliza guessed.

"Oh, please. I've toasted that man so many times he should be burnt by now." Another clink. "To answers that clear the path for both of us."

Eliza thought about that, angling her head, staring into Teddy's eyes, which were the color of the skies over Shellseeker Beach. "I'll drink to that, Theo."

"Dutch's nickname for me."

"I know," she said after she took a sip that stung her lips and numbed her throat. "I was just trying to remember his nickname for me." She perched the shot glass on the bin lid on the floor, lifting the handkerchief she still held. "The scent of this almost had me there."

Teddy leaned in and took a whiff. "The man loved his Old Spice."

"Is that what this is?" She pressed it to her nose and sniffed again. "It smells like my earliest years. And these?" She held up the aviators. "These would probably go on eBay for a thousand bucks."

"Yes, they were his during the war."

"I guessed that." She gently set the glasses on top of the handkerchief, took another sip of Chivas, and kept looking.

Eliza didn't believe in woo-woo or anything supernatural, nor did she believe in the spirits of long-dead Native Americans or that inanimate objects gave off "vibrations" or anything that Teddy definitely bought into.

But she couldn't deny that sitting in that closet, touching Dutch's things, she felt something...alive. The man had truly lived, and it had been a remarkable life. Shot down but survived in Vietnam, then he'd gone on to be one of the most respected and admired pilots who flew for Pan Am.

Suddenly, Eliza had the sharpest sensation of...frustration. She lifted an award for Pilot of the Year and groaned as it hit again.

"What is it?" Teddy asked, her attention on an old flight log she paged through. "Did you find something?"

"No, I'm just frustrated," she admitted.

"Not finding anything?"

"Not understanding him. Why would he leave something to me, assuming he did, but barely talk to me for all those years? Why would he live this amazing, award-winning life but keep the people that matter so far away? And why, why, *why* would he put me in such an untenable situation?"

"By leaving you his property?"

"By pitting me against you."

Teddy surprised her with a smile. "He wanted us to meet, I think. It worked."

But that didn't work for Eliza. "I'm glad I met you," she said. "But it would have been a whole lot better if you two had just come to L.A. and met my family, or invited us here for a family vacation, or just..." Her throat thickened. "He could have just called me. What *stopped* him?"

"Fear."

"Of what?" Eliza demanded, hating the tears that swam in her eyes.

"I honestly don't know," Teddy said, closing the logbook with that soft-eyed look she had when she was about to offer a healing, helping hand. "But I do know the only thing that paralyzed your father was fear, and that was because he simply wasn't afraid of very much at all. Not of death, not of flying, not of danger or bad people or...anything. He was fearless. But every once in a while, something scared him, and he folded."

"Like what?"

"Once, I had severe chest pains and was convinced I was having a heart attack. On the way to the hospital, I could sense his fear. I was fine, and as soon as he found that out, he denied he was afraid of anything. But I saw it with my own two eyes."

Eliza nodded, considering that. "I guess, but I don't know why he'd be afraid of me."

"I'm so sorry that I don't have answers, dear Eliza." She put her hand on Eliza's arm and, yes, the touch helped, but nothing could erase the ache in her chest. Nothing could fill the father-sized hole that...that had been burning near her heart since she was not even seven years old.

Since that day, that cold, rainy dawn when she opened her eyes and saw him standing in her doorway.

I gotta go, Boo-Boo. I don't know when I'll see you again.

She sucked in a breath. "Boo-Boo."

"Excuse me?"

"He called me Boo-Boo," she whispered, the memory almost too much to take. "I knew it began with a B."

Boo-Boo.

"Oh," Teddy sounded disappointed. "So not Birdie."

"Nope. Boo-Boo." She closed her eyes and, damn, there it was again. Sadness. But not for Ben. This time the ache in her heart was for the father she barely knew, and for the first time since she found out he'd died, she gave in to tears for Dutch.

Teddy enveloped her in an embrace, giving comfort that Eliza inhaled with her whole body, needing it with her whole soul.

After Eliza dried her tears, Teddy rose to leave the room and promised to come back with one more shot of Chivas. Eliza stood and brought down another box, this one with some old Pan Am uniforms and a few books.

At the bottom, she lifted out an old, worn copy of a novel, the dust jacket so tattered and torn that it barely stayed on the book.

The High and the Mighty, by Ernest K. Gann.

"Maybe I should read it after all, Dutch," she whispered, grazing her finger over the pictures of clouds and contrails drawn on the cover art.

She opened the book tentatively. The binding was so old she knew it could crack and separate with any force. Turning the first page, she looked for a publishing date, finding that the book had been released in 1953.

Had he owned this all those years? She turned the next page, sucking in a breath when she saw a woman's handwriting under the title.

Darling,

A first edition of your favorite book. For my favorite man. Je t'aime.

Camille.

And she was back.

She flipped a page, then another, frustrated and angry and sad and...who the heck was Camille, anyway? And did she have a daughter? And was she the reason her father ignored her all those years?

As she heard Teddy coming back, she lifted the book to ask her about it and when she did, a card slipped to the floor.

"Look at this, Teddy." She lifted the business card to read it while Teddy took the book. "A first edition of his favorite book, inscribed by Camille."

"Oh, *The High and the Mighty*? His favorite," Teddy said. "I think he made me watch the John Wayne movie ten times."

"Teddy. Look at this!" She held up the card, which was slightly oversized, with navy blue letters embossed on a pale blue card. "It's a business card from Jean-Philippe Margot." She looked up at Teddy. "Ever heard of him?"

"Never. Who is he?"

She read the title under his name. "*Avocat.*" Then it clicked. "Advocate? A lawyer?" Her voice rose. "This could help us."

"Call him!" Teddy demanded. "Call him right now and find out what he knows. I can't believe I missed that the first time through."

"You probably didn't open the book," Eliza said, running her thumb over the card. "And I do want to call him. What time is it in Paris?"

"It's evening or later, I think, but who cares? Where's your phone?"

She snagged it from her back pocket, making a face. "Country code for France?"

"Google it. Just call him, Eliza."

Eliza laughed at her desperation, kind of touched that she wanted answers, too. They might not be easy for her. This was Camille, who'd broken up her parents' marriage and might be another woman Dutch had once loved. She might be the new owner of Shellseeker Beach, for all they knew.

But still, Teddy wanted the truth, and Eliza found that as honorable as anything the woman did.

"I know a better way," Eliza said. "I'll take this to Miles Anderson and let him make the call. He's an investigator and I might set off alarm bells or something by calling."

"Alarm bells?"

"We don't know this woman. We don't know if she's dead or alive, or when she was last in touch with him. She might not want to answer our questions, but if Miles calls this Philippe guy? He might get somewhere."

"Aunt Teddy? Miss Eliza?" Harper's voice floated up, small and scared. Instantly Teddy pushed up.

"I'll go get her while you finish up."

"I'm done for now," Eliza said, looking at the business card. "And it's late, but I'll go see Miles tomorrow. Olivia doesn't get in until late afternoon."

"Do you want me to come with you?"

"More than anything," Eliza said, meaning it.

"We're in this together, aren't we?" Teddy asked, putting a hand on her shoulder.

"We sure are."

"Then we'll go together...Boo-Boo."

Eliza smiled, all her frustration replaced by hope. The card had given her that. Well, the card and Teddy.

Chapter Fifteen

Miles

S he'd called ahead, so this time, Miles had cleaned up a bit, shaved around his goatee, combed his hair, put on khakis instead of shorts. He wasn't sure why, except that now Eliza Whitney was a paying client. So, he was better prepared for her impact, but poor Tinker-bell damn near wet the floor, rolling over with joy when she saw who'd just rung the bell.

"Missed her, did you?" Miles chuckled as he opened the door, surprised to see the familiar face of Teddy Blessing next to her. "Oh, hello, Teddy."

"Miles." They shook hands and he gestured for them to come in, not even trying to talk over Tink's barking.

"There's my girl," Eliza said, bending down to rub Tink's belly, which made the dog's stubby tail knock back and forth. "You happy to see me again?"

"Understatement," Miles mumbled. "She doesn't love everyone," he added. "But when she does? You can't escape. Coffee, ladies? I'd offer tea, but Teddy would cry if I dropped a bag of Lipton in a cup."

They both laughed. "We've had plenty of tea today," Teddy assured him. "And thank you for letting us pop by on such short notice."

"It's fine." He gestured for them to come into the living room, since the office would be tight with three people, what with Tink trying to get next to Eliza and all. "What have you got for me?"

"First, do you have anything for us?" Eliza asked as she sat down on the leather sofa and, God bless her, made room for Tink.

He hoped she wouldn't ask that, because he didn't want to lie, but he was absolutely not ready to tell her about the trail he was following. Until he got to the end, he'd keep it to himself.

"Not much yet," he said, which wasn't a lie.

"Nothing on Camille?" she asked.

That he could answer with full confidence of the truth. "I'm tracing down every French Pan Am flight attendant with the first name of Camille who could have been flying at the same time as Dutch. So far, I've hit dead ends, though I did talk to one who knew *of* him, but didn't *know* him."

"Oh. That could take a while, huh?" Eliza's narrow shoulders slumped.

"It could take days or even weeks," he said. "But if I hit paydirt, then I'm done. That could happen at any moment."

"Then maybe I have some paydirt for you," she said, opening her bag to take out a blue business card, which he instantly recognized as European based on the size. "We found this in a book that I think Camille gave Dutch. Am I right that *avocat* means lawyer?"

He studied the card, instantly sensing that, yes, this

could shorten the trail, but he didn't want to get Eliza's hopes up. "Yes, you are correct." He looked up and met her gray-blue gaze. "Have you tried calling this number?"

"Actually, no. I thought you should."

"Good thinking," he said, setting the card on the coffee table between them.

"So, have you found anything at all?" Eliza asked.

"Yes," he told her, which wasn't the trail he was holding back. "I found a copy of the deed that states that the house at 143 Roosevelt Road, all seven Shellseeker Cottages, Shellseeker Tea Garden, Sanibel Treasures, plus the land between those places, is owned by Mr. Vanderveen, free and clear."

He saw Teddy flinch but she didn't say a word.

"Teddy," he asked. "Have you retained an attorney yet?"

"I have one I use, but this isn't his specialty. And Eliza has one in L.A."

He nodded, not wanting to muddy the waters until he dug a little deeper. "I'm doing my best to help you find this Camille, and her daughter, if she has one. There's no saying for sure and certain the little girl in the picture is Camille's daughter or, for that matter, Dutch's. Could be her niece or a neighbor she likes and the term 'family' on the back is just an expression. Could be a child from another relationship."

The two women shared a look, silent, but he got the impression they didn't think that was the case.

"All in all, I think you and Eliza are doing the right thing trying to find her, to avoid trouble down the line."

He looked at Eliza for a moment, fighting a smile because Tink was slathering all over her arm and she wasn't even fazed. "Are you starting to settle in, Eliza?" he asked. "Liking Sanibel?"

"Very much," she said, sliding a hand over Tink's head to gently stop the licking, but not the contact. "I even made it to Ding Darling."

"Then you've seen the land, but have you seen the water? I'd be happy to give you a tour on my boat sometime." The offer was out before he—a former lawyer who made a living choosing words carefully—could think it through. "I mean, Tink would love to show you around," he added on an awkward laugh. "That is, if she doesn't decide to leave with you."

Eliza smiled, leaning down to nuzzle Tink. "You mean if I don't take her. Thank you for the offer. My daughter's coming into town later today and she may get restless. Then we'll call you for a free excursion."

"Hardly free," he joked. "Thank you for prepaying the retainer."

"No problem. Just help us find Camille and..." She let out a sigh. "My half-sister, if she exists."

"I am doing my best, I promise. Should have something soon." He pushed up and the two ladies did the same, making Tink jump off the sofa and bark. "You have really made yourself a friend," he added.

"She's a doll." Eliza reached down and gave Tink one last pat. Instantly, the dog collapsed on the ground for a minute, then popped up, trotted to her toybox, and grabbed a torn and tattered stuffed animal. With the prize in her mouth, she returned to Eliza.

"For me?" Eliza asked, feigning joy and surprise.

"For you to throw," Miles told her.

"Catch?" Eliza bent over and retrieved the toy, not bothered by how wet it was, he noticed, then tossed it toward the door.

Tink took off, making them laugh, and waited there for Eliza, who seemed to sense that this was how the game was played. When she walked toward the door, Teddy put a light hand on his arm, pulling his attention.

"Should I?" she asked so softly he wasn't sure he heard her over Tink's barking.

"Should you..."

"Hire an attorney? I know you were one in your former life."

He regarded her for a long moment, considering his answer. "You could and you might win, but it would be very expensive and..." He glanced toward Eliza who was now sitting on the floor rubbing Tink's face with the stuffed animal and letting out peals of musical laughter.

"I'd wait, Teddy," he finally said. "See what I find out in the next few days." He was tempted to tell her about the trail, and share the fact that, if his gut instinct was correct, she had a bigger, badder fight on her hands. But not yet. No reason to worry them until he knew more. "And if and when you want to, I'll make recommendations."

"I don't want to," she said. "I don't want a legal battle. I'm optimistic Eliza and I can figure something out."

"Are you talking about a compromise? Maybe sharing the land or the profits or..."

She shook her head as if she knew she'd talked out of school. "I don't know. But I am hopeful, since I am already quite fond of Eliza."

He glanced at Eliza again, now getting a Tink face lick. "Get in line behind Tink," he said on a laugh as he watched his dog go to work.

When he turned back to Teddy, she was beaming at him like she knew something he didn't want her to know. Damn. He was probably drooling as bad as his dog.

He forgot old Teddy Blessing was kind of famous for reading people. He'd have to be careful, or she'd know that he thought Sanibel's latest arrival was very, very attractive. So, he just smiled and guided her toward the door.

Chapter Sixteen

Olivia

"**M**om, the real shocker of Shellshocker Beach is how gorgeous it is." Olivia wrapped her hands around a mug of coffee to help her severe case of jetlag.

And what the caffeine didn't do to wake up her brain, the view did. "Why have we never come here again?" she asked as she stared out the open sliders.

"Pretty sure we stayed up until two discussing that because it was eleven your time," her mother said from the tiny kitchenette where she was making her own coffee.

"Ah, yes. I remember now: Dutch Vanderveen. The elusive and enigmatic grandfather who, if Grandma Mary Ann was to be believed, was in cahoots with the devil. Now that you know him through this Teddy character, do you think your mother was right?"

"Please don't call her that, Olivia. Teddy is one of the loveliest people I've ever met."

"A lovely person who wants your inheritance."

"She said she'll abide by whatever I decide. Oof." Mom let out a grunt. "Where is this water coming from? Something is not right with this sink."

But Olivia didn't care about the sink. Something was

not right with this picture. "You're going to give it to her, aren't you?"

Ignoring the question, her mother crouched down and opened the cabinet under the sink to peer at the plumbing. "Crap. It's leaking."

"Mom!"

Very slowly, she stood, narrowing her eyes at Olivia. "I don't know what I'm going to do, honey. The very first order of business is to find the will, which still hasn't shown up in any state that my attorney has checked, which is weird. Next is to find the infamous Camille, to discover if she has a daughter—"

"Or a legal will."

Mom shrugged. "I suppose she could, but wouldn't that have come out by now? Wouldn't we know?"

"Why? If she claims his stuff, if she owns everything he has, why would you know before that moment when she marches onto this beach and says, 'So long, suckers.'"

"You think?"

Olivia dropped her head back. "I know. People are awful. Most people, in fact. But this Teddy char...but your friend, Teddy, is banking on you being not awful. People don't just give their multimillion-dollar inheritances away. Not normal, intelligent, sane people who like money."

"If I'm not named his heir, then this is all moot. In the meantime..." She wiped her hands, turning the faucet on and off, then shook her head. "I hope Teddy knows a plumber. I'm going to call her."

"Great. I'll just sit outside and stare at the beach. Color me happy."

Pushing back sheer white curtains, Olivia stepped out to a wide planked deck and drank in a view that seemed to go forever. Between this precious cottage and a deep blue and freakishly calm ocean—no, wait, that was the Gulf of Mexico—was about half a football field-length of soft sea grass blowing in the wind.

A wooden boardwalk led to the sand, where a few people meandered, more interested in their feet than the shockingly beautiful horizon.

Shellseekers, she guessed by the way they hunched over and picked things up from the sand.

She dropped onto a chair, scanning the beach, marveling that there were no high-rise condos, no tacky restaurants, nothing to impede the view. No wonder hotel chains wanted a piece of this action. She didn't know Florida at all, but she had to believe there were very few waterfront places this untouched.

The only thing on the beach was a darling thatch-roofed cabana with some paddleboards leaning against one side. As she studied the small structure, a man stepped out from inside, carrying another paddleboard.

She squinted, trying to get a better look, because from a distance...the view was...*whoa*. Built. With some ink. Long, surfer-blond hair. Did she mention built?

"Okay, we're good," Mom said, joining her on the porch and sliding into the other painfully cute Adirondack chair. "Yes, this place is stunning, but be warned, come noon, you'll be sweating your you-know-whats off."

She smiled at that. "It's a million miles from Seattle, and today, with what's going on at work, that makes me happy." She let out a noisy sigh. "What should I do? How should I handle this? Fight or back off and watch my hard work be overlooked?"

"I think you should let this Alex character"—she winked at Eliza—"run himself into the ground. He's Ned the New Guy, and they always want to shake things up. When he shakes, the cream will rise to the top, if I may mix the heck out of my metaphors."

Olivia gave a dry laugh. "Shaken cream gets lost in the coffee. Or spilled and wiped up by Apple. Who names their kid Apple? I can't."

"Who's the real competition? Apple or Jason?"

"Everyone's competition in the corporate world. After, what? Thirteen years at an agency, you know that."

Her mother let out a groan. "I hated that part of work," she said. "The clawing to the top. The backstabbing. The subtle digs. If one more person referred to me as 'Nick Frye's agent' or 'Pippa Jones's Mom's friend' I would have clawed their eyes out."

Olivia snorted. "Do they really think that the only reason you got Pippa was because you and her mom were friends who lived on the same street?"

"It kind of *was* the only reason I got Pippa as a client before she hit it big. Pippa is a major hot commodity now."

"She's seriously killing it, Mom. I do hope you have a piece of her career."

"All Artists Representatives has that piece," her

mother said dryly. "And I got a lovely severance package and a non-compete contract."

"Oh, why is it so hard?" Olivia moaned and dropped her head back again. "Why can't people just do their job and be kind and recognize talent when it stares them in the face?"

"That's not how the corporate world works, honey, and if recognition is what you want?" She lifted a brow. "You're in the wrong business."

"I'm in the right business," she said. "I know buying like I know my name and I can visualize a store footprint for sales better than anybody in merchandising, including Nadia Gifford herself. I am Promenade's secret weapon and Alex Brody would be so smart to just figure that out, promote me, and let me help him look good."

Mom shook her head. "You know it doesn't work that way. You help him look good until the powers that be realize where the real talent is. Then he'll keep you down so you don't step on his fingers as you march over him to the top."

"Fingers? Please. I'd like to step on his *head*. Nothing would give me more pleasure." She pulled out her phone and tapped it. "Of course, he hasn't responded to the Jazzberry plan and all he said about my vacation was, 'It's about time, kiddo.' Kiddo! Does he call Apple 'kiddo'?" She threw one hand in the air. "Something tells me no."

"You need some of Teddy's calming tea."

She looked skyward, not wanting to hear any more about Teddy. It was obvious her mother had gone to the dark side, and one of the reasons she was here was to get her to see straight. But it was too early for a persuasion campaign.

"I just need to think, Mom. I needed to get out of there, clear my head, and reconsider...everything. And I can't imagine a better place to do it." She raised her coffee mug. "We can thank old Dutch for bringing us to this little slice of paradise to get our heads back on correctly, huh?"

"I do think you'd be a lot happier at work if you had more in your life," Mom said, plucking at an imaginary loose thread on her shorts. "Don't you?"

"If by 'more in my life' you mean a serious relationship, a pending engagement, and a wedding for you to plan, then..."

"There is a darling gazebo on this property that would be an absolutely amazing place to get married. Teddy's father and mother married there and even Teddy and Dutch had their unification ceremony there."

Olivia just stared at her, truly worried. Maybe she should start talking sense into Mom this very minute. A unification ceremony? That was enough to hand over the inheritance?

"Really, Olivia, is there no one at all in your—"

She swiped the air with her free hand, stopping the words in their tracks. "Trust me, it's not for lack of trying, but the pickings are slim for a woman staring down the barrel of thirty who has done nothing but work her butt off."

"Are you going to all the right places to meet men?

The gym? The grocery store when single men shop? Church?"

Olivia laughed softly because...she'd heard it all. And done it all. And failed like she'd never failed at anything in her life. "I don't think men are attracted to women like me."

Her mother choked. "Gorgeous, blue-eyed brunettes who are smart, funny, and make more than they do? What is not to like?"

"That last part. I know men all say, 'Yay, women's lib, my wife makes bank,' but when it comes right down to it, they want to *provide*." She curled her lip. "I don't need a provider."

"I think they want a partner," her mom said. "Dad always said he couldn't make a decision without running it by me first."

Olivia sighed noisily. "Marriages like you and Dad had are rare, Mom. Like, I don't even think they happen anymore. Now people get prenups online as part of the wedding planning. There's no such thing as a happily ever after in this day and age."

"Honey, you're so jaded."

"I'm the voice of reason, as you frequently say," Olivia replied. "And look at you. Happiest marriage imaginable and he..." Her voice faded out. "Like, how unfair is that?"

Her mother flinched, which made Olivia instantly regret the comment.

"I'm sorry, Mom." Sadness, familiar and deep, ate at her, spurred on by a good amount of guilt for the reminder. "You're doing so well. You're happy. And if you do inherit and sell this place? Think of what you could do with that kind of money."

"Alone? What's to do?"

"Anything you want. Money buys freedom. Why do you think I work so hard?"

"You work so hard because you have tied your self-worth to your job title, and that's why Apple and Jason and Alex and all the office politics has you tangled in knots."

Was that true? Yes, probably, but she wasn't going to let her mother go down the road of Olivia's work ethic. "I wouldn't have to be tangled in anything if our family were independently wealthy."

"You'd still want to work," Mom replied.

"Maybe, but not at the whim of Alex Brody." She eyed her mother and remembered her conversation with Dane. She didn't come here solely to think about the next rung on her corporate ladder. "Please tell me that was the late hour and the wine speaking last night when you said you're having second thoughts about selling."

Her mother made a face that told Olivia all she needed to know. Eliza Whitney was about to cave.

"Mom!" She shot forward so fast her coffee spilled over the rim of her mug. "You had no relationship with the man, you met his pseudo-wife less than two weeks ago, and you are, by her own admission, his sole heir."

"Maybe. Don't forget Camille and company."

"Even if you have to split it with some stranger, it's a couple of million at least," Olivia said, hearing her own voice rise. "You can't walk away from a payday like that, not when you are out of a job and fifty-three."

"Oh, Olivia. I have money and our house. I'm fine financially. Not wealthy, but fine. You think like a businesswoman."

"Because I have an MBA from UCLA, thank you very much. It doesn't take an advanced degree to know your life would be improved by this money and your father left it to you, fair and square."

"It's more complicated than that," Mom said. "Teddy's not only built this business—a few of them—she's taken in people who need her; people who would otherwise be lost. She has saved them and helped them and given them new lives."

Olivia looked hard at her. "And you think she's going to do that for you?"

"You know, maybe."

Frustration rolled through her. "Oh, Mom. I get it. She makes you feel good. She makes nice tea. Oh, and everyone liked Dutch, so maybe he wasn't Satan after all." She leaned forward and looked directly into her mother's eyes, just a shade lighter than the ones she met in the mirror every day. "I'm so glad I came here to talk sense into you."

"I thought you came to take a much-needed vacation from Apple Tart."

Olivia laughed. "Good one."

"Oh, here comes Deeley with a toolbox. He's going to fix the sink."

Olivia peered past Mom, sucking in a soft breath. "Him?"

"He runs the beach rental and fixes things on the property for Teddy." She laughed softly and stood, eyeing Olivia. "And improves the scenery."

"No kidding." Olivia sat up straighter as he approached, kind of wishing she'd bothered with a hairbrush. Not that he had. His sun-bleached hair fluttered in the wind like he was on the cover of a romance novel called *Fifty Shades of Gold*. He wore nothing but swim shorts and six-pack abs, bare feet and tree-trunk thighs, and sunglasses that showed enough face to know it was as nice as the rest of him.

"Hey, Eliza," he called in a deep voice. "Heard that sink's acting up."

"It is."

As he got closer, he pushed his sunglasses up and Olivia saw whiskey-colored eyes that looked like they could make a woman drunk and want more.

"Hi, there," he said, adding a smile that took the whole package straight to eleven.

"Hi." She didn't move, which was probably smart, because she was wearing a tank top and sleep shorts.

"Oh, Connor Deeley, this is my daughter, Olivia, who's come from Seattle for a visit. Livvie, this is Deeley." Mom laughed. "Everyone calls you that, right?"

"Only if I like you." He threw another smile at Olivia. "Livvie, is it?"

"Only if I like you," she volleyed back, getting a quick chuckle in response.

They shared a beat of eye contact as he walked inside the cottage, making Olivia have to work to wipe the smile off her face.

Mom talked to him about the leaky sink while Olivia listened, hearing enough of a gentle twang in his voice, plus a few "ma'ams" that made her imagine he was a sweet Southern surfer who listened to country music when he wasn't renting paddleboards or fixing faucets. Lived at the beach. Never cut his hair. Probably got high six nights a week and had a scruffy dog named Bojangles.

Pretty much the polar opposite of every overachiever she'd ever dated or wanted to date.

She twisted in the chair to get another look at him through the sliders, seeing him in profile while he leaned over the sink.

No, the scenery at Shellseeker Beach was not bad at all.

"Why don't you get dressed and we'll go meet Teddy," Mom suggested when she came outside.

"What should I wear?"

"Not much," Surfer Dude called from the kitchen. Then he looked at her, smiling from underneath a long lock of hair that covered his face. "I mean, it's June in Florida and about to get hot as hell."

It *was* hot as hell.

"He's right, Liv. A bathing suit and coverup. We'll definitely want to hit the beach later."

"Do you paddleboard?" Deeley asked.

"I've never tried."

"It's easy. I'll give you a free lesson." He flashed a

deadly smile and her toes practically curled into little helpless balls of attraction.

Seriously? Five minutes in this place and the hippie plumber beach bum makes her hormones go haywire?

Must be the humidity.

Chapter Seventeen

Teddy

Even if she hadn't been introduced as Eliza's daughter, Teddy might have known that Olivia Whitney was Dutch's granddaughter. She shared the unique Vanderveen gray-blue eyes, maybe a tad darker than her mother's, and thick dark hair that fell in layers over her shoulders, the very color of Dutch's before it went pure white, based on his pictures. Her face was beautiful, with lovely bones like his, framing a wide mouth, and she had a long, lean, athletic build.

But it wasn't her physical appearance that tied the two generations together in Teddy's mind. It was her brain, which was sharp and fast, able to analyze and make a joke with the same effortlessness that Dutch showed. She had that undercurrent of...wanting more, the way her grandfather always wanted to fly higher or faster, or do whatever he did in the very best and biggest way he could.

None of that surprised her as much as the subtle buzz of resentment she picked up from Olivia's vibes. Without the benefit of time and exposure or understanding about the land, no doubt this ambitious young woman saw this potential inheritance as a life-changing opportunity for her mother and, Teddy supposed, the whole Whitney family. She'd mentioned talking to her brother, so no doubt they'd discussed the possible inheritance at length.

And for all those reasons, Teddy knew she might be facing one beautiful, bright, and insurmountable brick wall.

Because this young woman had plenty of skin in this game, she wasn't going to be swayed, not easily anyway, by the emotional tug of a hundred-year-old family legacy. She seemed interested and asked lots of questions as they toured the gardens and checked out the cottages that weren't currently rented. But her questions were those that a real estate person might ask, even an investor.

The kinds of questions that the hotel people who came in undercover asked. Her interest was, Teddy believed, in the value of the property. The dollar value, not the sentimental value.

As they walked the property and then settled in at the tea house for something cold, Eliza explained why the geography of Sanibel Island captured so many seashells, but Teddy wasn't listening. She was trying to figure out a way to tap into what appealed to Olivia.

And when she and Eliza made a joke about taking some shells back to her Promenade office, Teddy knew the answer.

"You, sweet Olivia, are a retail expert, am I correct?"

Olivia nodded and then gave in to a shrug. "I don't know everything about everything, but I do know my way around the footprint of a store."

"Would you help me?" Teddy asked, leaning forward.

"Sure. What do you need?"

"A secret assist," she said. "I want to show you Sanibel Treasures, which is at the other end of the property. Maybe pick your marvelous brain about how we can change things up there."

"Isn't it one of your most profitable businesses?" Eliza asked.

"It is, but I think it could be so much more. And," she added, "I truly suspect that Roz and George are going to head up to Ohio while their daughter is having a difficult pregnancy. And once that baby's born..." She made a face. "I worry they may never come back. I want to be ready if I have to bring in someone new, someone who doesn't have their history and shell art knowledge. Will you help me?"

"Of course, but..." Olivia looked from one woman to the other. "You may not be keeping this place, right? Once this whole probate business is resolved, isn't it possible the next owners, whoever they are, would want to put their own stamp on this little shell shop?"

Oh, no. She was not going to be easy.

"Livvie, we have no idea what's going to happen," Eliza said. "And you'll love the store, whether or not you give advice. Let's go."

"I'm always game for shopping."

A few minutes later, the sweet little bell rang as they stepped inside the shell and souvenir shop that had undergone so many iterations over the years. The last facelift Sanibel Treasures had received was back when Roz and George took over the day-to-day management, and Teddy let them have free rein to decorate and cram as much merchandise as possible onto the floor.

And they had.

The walls of the former boathouse were painted bright yellow and decorated with dozens and dozens of "shell art" pieces that Roz made, bought, or commissioned from locals. There were two long aisles lined with baskets of shells, organized by type and color. Of course, there was shell jewelry, shell candles, and shell ornaments. One side of the shop sold T-shirts, visors, sandals, sunglasses, postcards, and all manner of kitschy souvenirs, craft supplies, and books.

But the real change had been around in the back, where the layout turned a corner and opened to what had once been a boat storage area. Now, it was completely redesigned as George's "history section," dedicated top to bottom to the colorful and rich history of Sanibel Island.

Yes, there were museums on Sanibel—a shell museum and a history museum—but none of those places had George, or Teddy Roosevelt's message in a bottle.

"Oh, my goodness," Olivia said as she walked in, pressing her hand to her chest and trying to take it in. "Sensory overload!"

"Exactly what I want." Roz came out from behind the counter, caftan and turban in place, arms extended. "I heard a rumor that Eliza's daughter was coming. You are Olivia, I suppose!"

"I am." She accepted Roz's typically effusive hug

somewhat tentatively. "Um...hello." She laughed as Teddy did a more formal introduction.

"Roz is a creative genius, and George is..." Teddy peeked around the corner. "With a customer, so Roz, give Olivia a tour. She's a merchandising expert."

"Technically, a buyer," Olivia corrected. "But I do know a thing or two about merch." She glanced around. "And you sure have plenty of that."

"Oh, let me show you." Roz slipped her arm into Olivia's and guided her away from the souvenirs and to the high-end displays. "Do you know anything about shell art, darlin'?"

"Less than nothing."

"Well, let me teach you. It's the one kind of art that anyone with a glue gun can do, but the key is to honor the shells, because they *are* alive. Or they were once. Come here..."

As they walked off to the art wall, Teddy got close to Eliza, who was admiring a new selection of tiny shell rings and necklaces.

"Are you happy she's here?" she asked softly. "You two seem very in tune with each other and close."

"As close as two people who live a thousand miles apart can be," Eliza said wistfully, glancing toward Olivia and Roz, deep in conversation. Well, Roz was deep. Olivia was in the middle of a lesson on how to shellac an exotic sea creature. "I do love having her here."

"I can tell," Teddy said. "Your spirit seems lighter."

Eliza smiled as if she were finally getting used to Teddy's comments about such things. "It is."

"But also troubled." Teddy angled her head and put a hand on Eliza's shoulder. "She's worried about you and you're picking up the vibe."

"No, *you're* picking up the vibe," Eliza joked. "How do you *do* that, anyway?"

"Trade secret. But I'm right?"

"It's just the situation," she acknowledged with an uncertain expression. "It's hard and could get harder. It's complicated and I don't want it to be. I don't want to blow in here and take this inheritance, or split it, if we must, knowing that's not what you want. But..."

"But your daughter, a businesswoman, sees dollar signs and common sense. I get that," Teddy said. "I really do. And I don't want you to feel torn. Whatever decision is made, ultimately, you should be happy."

"And you," she said, taking Teddy's hand. "I'm just—"

"Oh, check this out, Mom!" Olivia called. "Have you seen this message in a bottle thing? How awesome is this?"

Teddy and Eliza headed around the corner to George's section of the store, where he was already doing his Teddy Roosevelt spiel for Olivia.

"You just use this special bottle and..." He noticed Eliza and Teddy and nodded to them. "Morning, ladies. Can I interest you in a message in a bottle?"

They laughed, but Olivia gushed. "You can interest *me*. I love this. So very cool. How does it not disintegrate over time?"

"This is a non-corroding cork, and a wax seal," he told her, his eyes bright as he talked about his passion.

"And you just write a message and toss it in the water? Feels environmentally shaky," she said.

"This is specially designed glass that will, over time, turn to sand. Same with the paper that we provide. However, if your bottle is found and returned here? We make a hefty donation to the Sanibel Historical Society and..." He gestured toward a shelf on the wall where at least a half dozen bottles stood side by side. "You become a part of Sanibel Treasures."

"Very cool!"

He leaned in and whispered, "Don't tell anyone, but sometimes I give the person a Benjie or two, if you get my drift. Just out of my pocket to say thanks."

Teddy chuckled as if George thought his generosity was some kind of secret.

"It's so romantic," Olivia said, holding the bottle, her eyes glinting. "I know, I know. I've read one too many Nicholas Sparks books."

So, Teddy mused, the pragmatic businesswoman had a soft spot for...the dreamier side of life. Her grandfather had that quality, too.

"Dutch sent one out," Teddy said, joining them.

"Oh, he did," George agreed, laughing. "Took it right out of here one day and headed to the gazebo with a pen, so hopeful someone would find it before he died." His smile faded. "It's still out there."

Olivia didn't seem that interested in Dutch's message

as she studied one of the bottles, her eyes narrowed in thought.

"I bet people love this," she said. "It's interactive and fun and connects tourists to the island in the most fundamental way."

"Yes and yes," George replied, laughing.

"And you sell all that for an easy ten dollars? Brilliant. I wish I could figure out a way to steal that idea for Promenade."

"Steal our idea?" Roz scoffed. "We should be getting them from you. What would you change in this store to sell more products, Olivia?"

Olivia considered the question and scanned the store, clearly hesitant to answer. "I'm sure you're doing just fine," she said.

"Fine enough," George replied. "I personally think people get so overwhelmed by the shell stuff that they buy less, not more. But my boss here"—he winked at his wife—"disagrees."

"There is something to be said for a minimalist approach." Olivia smiled at Roz, clearly doing her best to be diplomatic.

"Yeah, yeah, yeah," Roz laughed. "If you get repeat customers. Most tourists are here once, on vacation, so I have to snag them with everything on their one and only visit."

"I get that," Olivia said kindly. "And you're selling your heart in those gorgeous shell pieces, plus a one-of-a-kind shopping experience. All that factors into what they spend."

"Plus my message in a bottle history."

"Plus that," Olivia agreed enthusiastically, still holding the bottle he'd given her, closing her eyes for a moment. Teddy could practically feel Olivia's mental wheels turning as she pressed her hands to the bottle. Was she imagining what her note would say?

"You want to buy one and toss it in the water?" George asked.

Olivia's eyes popped open. "I want to buy...a thousand. For starters."

"Wh-what?" George sputtered the question.

"I have the best idea!" she exclaimed. "My brilliant twist for the cruise wear assignment I got stuck with! What better thing to take on a cruise than the message in a bottle you're going to throw over the side? Buy an outfit, get a bottle to take on your cruise! Yes, I will want to put in an order for at least a thousand at the crazy good price of ten bucks a pop."

"Holy moly!" He slammed his hand on his chest and Roz gasped.

"George, your heart!"

"My heart has never felt better, Roz. Did you hear that, Teddy? I want a bonus!"

As they all cheered and chatted about the idea, Teddy put an arm around Olivia, pulling her aside. "I will accept this amazing idea on one condition," she said.

Olivia looked right at her. "You want your resort?"

"I want you to stay for a while. As long as you can. Having you here makes your mother happy."

She thought about it for a minute, glancing at the

group, her gaze lingering on her mother. "Well, now that I can write off this trip as part of the cruise wear rollout? Maybe I can stay through next week. Would that meet your conditions?"

Teddy smiled. "I can't ask for more than that." Well, she could, but Teddy didn't need a lot of time to gather people to her heart, and Shellseeker Beach could work its magic very quickly.

Just look at Eliza, who was laughing with Roz and George like they were, well, family.

Chapter Eighteen

Eliza

With Olivia staying for at least an extra week, the days on Shellseeker Beach started to run together in that lovely way that vacations often do. Eliza forgot, more or less, about the rest of the world, save for one conversation with Nick down in the Keys. He'd offered to bring her belongings up on the ferry, but she told him not to bother.

She'd get back down there eventually, maybe on a day trip with Olivia. For now, her schedule consisted of waking late, walking the beach with Olivia, gardening with Teddy, and taking a few trips around Sanibel or to the mainland.

Some afternoons, like this one, she hung out on the deck with Teddy, sipping iced tea, sharing stories of their lives. When the relaxation got boring for Olivia, who had endless energy, she went down to Deeley's cabana, grabbed a paddleboard, and spent the day on the water.

From the second-story deck, Teddy and Eliza could see her out there, and today, it looked like she had company, with her laughter and Deeley's floating over the beach.

"They make a nice couple," Teddy mused, smiling at the two of them.

"An odd couple, but beautiful."

"Why odd, Eliza? They do seem to laugh a lot together."

"Oh, there's definitely some chemistry," Eliza agreed. "But he's a little laid-back for my go-getter. She likes a man who'll match her rung for rung as she climbs the corporate ladder."

Teddy sighed, clearly not liking that response.

"They're having a vacation flirtation," Eliza said. "That's all."

"You don't know Deeley."

"What don't I know about him?"

"A lot. He's not the Good Time Charlie he appears to be, I'll tell you that much."

Eliza smiled at the term. "What's his story?"

Teddy shook her head. "What I know of it, and I do know a lot, is confidential. I'm sorry."

Eliza inched back, surprised after all they'd shared. "You can't tell me anything?"

Teddy took a long drink of tea, her gaze locked on Olivia and Deeley in the water.

"I can tell you this much," she said. "When Deeley arrived in Shellseeker Beach, he was a broken man, suffering from the effects of things he'd experienced in the Navy."

"Oh." Eliza pressed her fingers to her lips. "How sad."

"It was, and he essentially locked himself in one of

the cottages for almost two weeks, not opening so much as a window. Finally, after trying and trying, he let me in."

Eliza smiled at her, so used to Teddy's healing ways now, and charmed by them. Inspired, even. "I'm going to guess you took him tea and crystals and wrapped him in lemon balm and love."

"Pretty much," Teddy laughed. "And I listened to all he had to say, which is what I can't share. But very slowly, one tender inch at a time, Deeley emerged from the shell around him. And when he's not renting paddleboards, he's...doing remarkable things for other people. He just likes to keep all that off the radar."

Eliza studied the man out on the water, not just admiring his masculine silhouette as he maneuvered his paddleboard like a pro, but also the fact that he'd been that low and climbed out of the hole.

"It's amazing what you do," Eliza whispered.

"Well, the healing's a gift," she said. "I'm just honored that I get to use it to help people."

"It's not just the healing, Teddy. You walk this beach and find the broken shells, the ones that others discard because they aren't perfect, and you gather them to your heart. You don't repair them, exactly, but you make them beautiful as they are. And they are your family."

"Eliza." Teddy whispered her name, clearly choked up. "That's so kind."

"It's true."

"Maybe it is," she conceded. "But still very kind of you to notice and appreciate it. I never quite thought of it that way, but I'm keenly aware that I've created a family, which is ironic, because I couldn't have one of my own."

Eliza reached over and put her hand on Teddy's arm. "I feel like I'm your latest broken shell."

"Oh, honey. If only that were true. If only you'd join my family here on Shellseeker Beach." Teddy squeezed her hand. "Nothing would give me more joy."

Eliza dropped her head back, letting the sun, and the idea, warm her whole body. "How would that work, do you think?" she finally asked.

"I don't know, but it would be fun."

"Everything about Shellseeker Beach is fun," Eliza admitted. "You even make running this place look fun."

"That's because it's June and we're slow," Teddy replied. "For the next two months, we'll border on dead, with several weeks when only one or two of the cottages are rented. But come September? Then October? This place is crazy. I actually don't have a single vacancy in December. We're booked. Tourism is booming on Sanibel."

"That's amazing." Eliza sat up straight, turning to her. "Why do you not sound happy about that?"

"Because I really had hoped to use this summer to make some big improvements that we so need. The landscaping is getting tired, the boardwalks could use refinishing and painting, and if I could put new kitchens and baths in the cottages, I could charge more. But with Dutch gone and this...this threat of the unknown over my head, I haven't scheduled anything. Without the improvements, we're slipping into being one of the less desirable rentals." She slid a look to Eliza. "I don't want to make all these expensive upgrades just for some big hotel company to come in and wreck it all."

"That might not happen, Teddy. We still don't know." Eliza took a sip of tea and asked, "Do you hire extra help in the winter?"

"Oh, yes." Teddy nodded. "Katie can't clean all the cottages alone, so I usually bring on two more housekeepers. Deeley gets a few more hands to run the rentals, too, and Roz and George bring on part-time help." She closed her eyes. "If Roz and George are even here and not in Ohio. I don't even want to think about that." Then she opened her eyes and smiled. "Of course...if I had a partner..."

Eliza looked at her for a long time. "I see where you're going with this, Theodora Blessing."

"Nice idea, though, isn't it?" Teddy grinned. "You and me, running Shellseeker Cottages."

Eliza lifted her brow. "I know nothing about running a place like this."

"I'm a great teacher," Teddy said simply.

Wow. Staying and managing and...

Eliza tried to breathe, but she was suddenly aware of the pressure on her chest. It was a mix of fear and longing and excitement and hot, holy terror. "That would be quite a change for me."

"Well, it's just a dream."

Eliza smiled, closing her eyes again, enjoying that dream for a minute herself, seeing herself living here, although...where, exactly?

"I have a lot of room in my house," Teddy said softly, as if she could read Eliza's mind. Of course, she sometimes could.

"But my whole life is three thousand miles away, Teddy. I know, I know—I don't *have* much of a life," she added quickly, expecting Teddy to remind her of that. "But my kids are on the West Coast and my house and I have friends and..." With each word, her excuses sounded weaker.

"I suppose it's worth thinking about, except..." She opened her eyes and looked at Teddy. "Camille."

Teddy shook her head. "She's hanging over us like a dark, dark cloud. No word from Miles?"

She picked up her phone as if he might have called her, but the screen was blank. "I'm going to call him and push a little. We need closure, Teddy."

"We need to have our dreams, Eliza."

"Yes, we do," Eliza agreed, tapping the screen to find his name in her contacts.

He answered on the first ring, his voice deep and confident as she put him on speaker for Teddy to hear. "Hello, Eliza. Anything new?"

She laughed. "You're the one who should have news."

"Well, I might soon. Not yet. Is that why you're calling? Kick in the ass?"

"Yes," she said, not bothering to hide her impatience. "Teddy and I are kind of in limbo here. Not able to plan anything until we know what's going on."

"I understand. I'm actually meeting with someone tomorrow who might have some concrete news."

"Oh? Can you tell me anything?"

"I really don't want to," he said, his voice full of understanding, but strong enough for her to know she wasn't going to change his mind.

"All right," she said. "I guess I can wait. How's my favorite dog?"

"Tink?" She could swear heard a smile in Miles's voice. "She misses you."

"Well, maybe I'll see her if you get that news."

"Is your daughter here? Because I'm taking the boat out for a sunset spin tonight. Want to join us?"

She sat up a little, smiling and looking at Olivia and Deeley as they brought their paddleboards to shore. "I think we'd both love that."

"There's room if Teddy wants to come."

She glanced at Teddy who shook her head. "Another time for me," she mouthed.

Eliza nodded. "I think it'll just be Olivia and me. What time should we be there?"

"Come at six. I'll have some food and wine, and a great sunset."

"That sounds amazing. Thank you." After she hung up, she looked at Teddy, smiling. "A sunset cruise sounds nice, doesn't it?"

"You know who's nice? That man, Miles."

"Nice, but not working fast enough. You sure you don't want to go?"

"I'm sure. I like his boat but I'm going to rest tonight." She added a lifted brow. "I think Miles likes you."

"You could feel that through the phone, woo-woo woman?"

Teddy chuckled. "I could smell the pheromones when we went to the house and he looked at you, well, kind of like his dog does."

"Now his dog likes me," Eliza agreed, standing up to end the discussion. As if she'd consider a man in her life right now. "I'm going to go tell Olivia we have a sunset cruise tonight." She blew a quick kiss to Teddy and started toward the stairs, then paused, turning. "You keep fantasizing, Theodora Blessing. And not about Miles, but..." She swept a hand toward the cottages. "Realistic dreams."

"You know it's a good idea."

"The resort, not Miles," she quipped as she jogged down the stairs, already knowing that in the last few minutes, her life might have shifted. She was still thinking about that, and smiling, as she crossed the sand and walked toward the cabana.

"Hey, Mom," Olivia called as Eliza got closer. "Want to take my board out? It's absolutely amazing out there."

"I'll pass, but it sure looked like you were having fun. Hi, Deeley."

He gave her a warm smile, pushing up his sunglasses so she could see his eyes. "Hi, Eliza. Your daughter's a natural. Perfect balance."

"You would be, too, Mom. She was a dancer on Broadway," Olivia told Deeley. "I get my balance from her." She came closer to Eliza and gave a quick hug, smelling like sunscreen and sea salt, her face completely free of makeup but utterly beautiful. "Want to take a walk?"

"We can, but I came down to let you know that we've been invited on a boat ride tonight with Miles Anderson."

"Really? That sounds like fun."

"It will be," Deeley said. "I'm a regular on that fishing cruiser and you are in for a treat."

"Why don't you join us?" Eliza asked. "Miles said he has plenty of room."

He thought about that for a moment, looking at Olivia as if he wanted to get her buy-in on the idea.

"You should come," Olivia said. "Although I may push you overboard to get back at you for that last stunt."

He laughed easily at whatever the inside joke was, then lifted Olivia's board to put it back in the rack. "Sounds good. I'll check with Miles in case he needs anything and see you there."

"Thanks for the free rental!" Olivia called as she and Eliza started walking away. "See you tonight."

When she and Olivia were out of hearing distance, Eliza whispered, "You sure seem to be having fun with him."

"He's a fun guy," she said, then lowered her sunglasses to look at Eliza. "That's *all* he is, Mother."

Eliza laughed. "Hey, if it would get you to spend more time here, I'm all for a little summer romance."

"Romance? Please."

"Come on, Livvie. He's a good-looking man, don't you think?"

"Looks aren't everything," she said, glancing over her shoulder as they stepped onto the boardwalk. "Although his are pretty fine, not going to lie. But so not my type. I mean, he's okay for a fling, but I'm not a flinger. I'm looking for solid, grounded, hard-working, and dependable."

Eliza nodded, grateful for that about her daughter. "Teddy says he has quite a story. Has he shared anything with you?"

"We've paddleboarded, joked around, and flirted," she said. "Nothing has been shared and nothing will be." She leaned into Eliza. "Not. My. Type."

"Gotcha."

"Although..." Olivia gave a sly smile. "Somehow our little vacation includes a double date and a sunset cruise."

"Not a double date."

"Semantics, Mommy. I say we're bouncing back like a couple of red rubber balls."

Eliza smiled, thinking of the conversation with Teddy, about the possibility of staying and running the resort. No. She wasn't quite ready to tell Olivia she was considering bouncing that high and that far. Not yet, anyway.

Chapter Nineteen

Olivia

N ot *my type. Not my type. Not my type.*

If she said that often enough, it would be true, Olivia decided shortly after boarding the sizeable fishing boat. There, she met Miles, a good-looking man in his mid-fifties, and his adorably chunkalicious dog, Tinkerbell. As they exchanged greetings and pleasantries and she got a tour of the vessel, Olivia kept the mantra in the back of her mind.

Not my type.

But every time she looked at Connor Deeley, she wondered if she had a type at all.

Especially now, as he stood on the deck of *Miles Away* wearing shorts and a T-shirt, the golden glow of sunset bringing out the natural highlights in his near shoulder-length hair, a beer in one hand, an easy smile in place.

He was literally the last man on Earth she'd ever imagine she could be attracted to. The last man she *should* be attracted to. Because she might be a workaholic committed to her job above all else, but deep down—oh, heck, maybe not so deep—Olivia longed for a rock-solid husband.

And that man right there? The only thing rock solid about him was his abs. He wasn't husband material.

But then he turned from his conversation with Miles and melted her with a smile that made his amber eyes glint, and she kind of forgot about a husband.

"Olivia, how about a glass of wine?" Miles asked from his perch at the helm, gesturing toward an open bottle over ice in a bucket. "Please help yourself."

"I'd love one."

"I got you," Deeley said, filling a plastic cup for her.

Olivia walked over to the white banquette on the bow where her mother was already nursing a glass of her own, her reddish-gold hair blowing in the wind as she gazed out at the water. Next to her, Tinkerbell was curled in a ball with her chin on Mom's thigh, gazing upward with adoration in her big brown eyes.

"You truly have a one-dog admiration society there, Elizabeth Mary."

She laughed and rubbed her hand over the white spot on Tinkerbell's head. "She's a doll, isn't she? And, wow, this view."

"Amazing," Olivia agreed, barely glancing at the stunning orange horizon because she could have sworn her mother was just a little pensive tonight. Friendly and warm, as always, but Olivia knew her well enough to know something was working on Eliza Whitney.

She sat down next to her, thanked Deeley for the wine and lifted her glass in a toast toward Miles at the helm.

"Thank you for the invitation," she said. "I love boating, but most of the time it's too cold to enjoy a cruise in Seattle."

"Not a problem we have here," Miles said over the soft rumble of the inboard engines. "It's warm, calm, and perfect. You'll have to experience letting me open her up when we get further offshore. I usually put Tink below so she doesn't fly out. You might have to go with her, Eliza, or she'll cry."

Mom leaned over and gave the dog a kiss. "No crying on the sunset cruise, Tink."

Smiling at that, Olivia glanced back at Miles, catching him looking at Mom...kind of with the same expression Tink was wearing. Whoa. Hadn't expected that. Maybe this really *was* a double date.

She filed that away and kept up with banter and small talk, enjoying everything about the air and the view —on board and off—and loving it when Miles, true to his word, kicked up the speed and took them way out into the Gulf. Tink didn't have to go below because Mom held that pupper in two loving arms and no dog was ever happier.

The sun was just below the horizon when Miles dropped the anchor and pulled a table for four up from the deck in that clever "secret compartment" style the boats always had. He served them a delicious buffet of seafood and salads that he'd had tucked into a cooler on deck. They ate and laughed and finished one bottle of wine and started another.

"You look more relaxed than I can ever remember, Livvie," Mom said as Miles packed up the food when they finished.

"It's this vacation thing," Olivia joked.

Deeley gave a wry chuckle. "What a concept, huh?"

"I might actually become a believer and try one every few years."

Deeley laughed and pointed his thumb toward the back of the boat. "Fishing off the stern. Wanna try it?"

"Fishing?" Olivia glanced at her mother. "Don't think I've ever done that."

"At camp once," Mom said. "You called it stinky and boring."

"Sounds about right." Deeley reached for her hand to pull her up. "But it's not a real Florida vacation until you do."

His hand was warm and large and she kind of hated to let it go when she got to her feet to follow him.

"Join us, Captain?" Deeley asked Miles.

Miles closed the cooler and shook his head. "You guys reel in a big one. I'll just stay here and see if my dog will ever remember me."

Olivia followed Deeley around the narrow side of the boat, then watched as he produced two fishing rods, a bucket of bait from another cooler, and set them up on the two swivel chairs she assumed were there for the sole purpose of sport fishing.

"Wow, this is a nice setup," she said as he put one of the rods in her hands. "Do you do this often?"

"Miles and I get out a couple times a month," he said,

glancing over his shoulder toward the bow. "He goes a lot more often. In fact, it takes something pretty powerful to keep him from that chair you're in. Guess he found it."

She followed his gaze to see Miles leaning forward, telling Mom a story, but they were too far to hear the subject.

"My mother?" she guessed.

Deeley gave her a look. "I would say, 'Nah, she's a client—'"

"And a very recent widow," Olivia added.

He shrugged. "Well, we're here to chaperone."

"Is that what we're doing?" she asked on a laugh while he put some bait on her hook.

"Just keeping it real, Livvie."

She angled her head. "I don't remember giving you permission to call me that," she teased.

"You said I could if I liked you."

"I said if *I* liked *you*."

He just smiled, enough to send a little unexpected thrill through her, though he was adept at low-grade flirting and even more adept at giving her an unexpected thrill. Good thing he was *not her type.*

"You know how to cast?" he asked, standing up and getting closer. "Lift the rod like this..." He put one arm on her back and one under her casting arm. "Hold that button, draw it over your head about this far and let it go. At the arc of your throw, take your finger off the button."

"Okay. Step away," she said. "I don't want to take your eye out."

He stayed a decent distance while she made her first

cast, which wasn't impressive, but it got the bait in the water.

"Now what?" she asked.

"Now you wait until nothing happens, watch for a dolphin, enjoy the remnants of the sunset. Then we go home."

She laughed. "What about the fish?"

"Oh, I never catch anything. Miles does, but the fish hate me. I just like holding the rod, a beer, and living the good life."

"You actually live on vacation."

"Exactly. And don't try to tell me that's not better than never taking one."

She didn't even bother. "So, the fish hate you? How do you know?"

"I can catch 'em, but never reel 'em in. It's like they get one look at me and think, 'Nah, he's nothing but trouble.'"

She couldn't help smiling. "Smart fish."

He chuckled as they eased into fishing positions next to each other, but he hadn't cast. Instead, he studied her, his gaze so intense that she could feel it, even though she stared at that thin fishing line that disappeared into dark blue water.

"You don't strike me as a woman who avoids trouble."

"Nope. Just vacations."

He finally looked away, lifting his rod to cast it. "What scares you most?"

She inched back at the question, looking at him with surprise. "About vacations? Or life?"

"Both."

She thought about it, then shook her head. "Well, nothing about this vacation scares me so far. And life? Oh, I don't know. The usual. I'd be scared to run into a burning building or jump out of a plane, I guess."

He snorted softly. "Neither one is that scary."

"You've done it?"

He just lifted a shoulder.

"You have?"

His only answer was to cast his own line, a move that was graceful and way more effective than hers.

"What exactly did you do in the Navy, anyway?" she asked.

"You know—"

"I know, this and that," she said, remembering his answer the last time she'd asked him that question. They'd finished swimming back from paddleboarding and she noticed he held his breath a whole lot longer than she could. "But everybody has a job in the Navy. They do something. They cook or work on submarines or...whatever Navy guys do. What did you do?"

"No cooking and no submarines."

"Connor," she pressed.

"Olivia," he echoed in the same voice.

"Come on. Tell me what you did. I'm pretty sure being in the Navy wasn't a year-round vacation."

He grunted under his breath. "No, ma'am, it wasn't."

"Were you stationed overseas? Did you fight in... Afghanistan? Somewhere else? Did you fly planes like *Top Gun*? Dutch would have loved that if you did."

"No, no, can't say, no, and yes, he would have."

"Can't say or won't?" she asked, fully invested and determined to get an answer.

He blew out a breath. "I was part of a team that rescued people."

She frowned, thinking about that. "Like, what kind of team? What kind of people need rescuing?"

"People who get themselves into binds and the only way to get out is with the help of the U.S. government and a special...team."

"Special forces?" she asked, blinking at him, leaning forward. "Were you a SEAL?"

"Ding-ding-ding, we have a winner," he said dryly.

She sucked in a breath. "Why are you ashamed of that?"

His eyes flashed. "I'm not ashamed, not a single bit. It's just that people hear the word SEAL and think it's something...holy. Exalted. It changes opinions, that one word. Like all of a sudden, I'm superhuman."

"Well, a Navy SEAL is kind of impressive."

With another one of his careless shrugs, he shook his head. "It requires disciplined training and some brains and muscles, but we're not, you know, gods. People have such an inflated impression of SEALs from movies and books. We're not all perfect."

"No one is," she said, "but I'd be a little more proud of it if I were you."

"I'm proud enough, but having been a SEAL isn't my whole identity. I was just a...what did you call it? Navy guy. One of the troops. A man who could do some things that others couldn't. Now, I'm just a..." He smiled. "Paddleboard guy."

"Oh, the modesty." She leaned back. "It's an interesting approach."

"Approach to what?"

"Life." She studied him for a long time, trying to wrap her head around this new information. "And, you know, the subtext flirt. It's effective."

"Is it?" Feeling her gaze on him, he slid her a look, his golden-brown gaze rich with humor. "That mean you like me now, Liv?" he asked, the slightest bit of resentment in his tone. "Now that I'm not just a handyman who hangs at the beach, but something a little more, uh, what was the other word you used? *Impressive?*"

A tendril of guilt slid through her, because she *was* impressed. "You don't want me to like you?"

"I don't want you to like me because I was a Navy SEAL," he said. "I sure do want you to like me, but not so you can go back to Seattle and brag to your friends that you hung out with some kind of hero."

"Is that what you think I'd do? I don't—" Suddenly, her rod tugged so hard, she almost dropped it.

"Whoa, you caught one."

"Really?" She grasped the fishing rod, surprised at how much strength it required. "I did?"

"Start reeling it in, Liv."

She grabbed the little wheel and tried to turn it, the echo of her nickname still in the air. She liked that he called her Liv. She liked that there was more to him than met the eye. But, man, she hated that she could be that shallow.

"You're gonna lose him if you don't start spinning, girl," he told her, leaning a little closer.

Something about the way he said that made her sneak a look at him, just long enough to let the fish get the better of her. "Oh!" she cried as the rod slipped.

In an instant, Deeley was up, wrapping his big hands around hers on the fishing rod.

"This is a keeper, Livvie. Do *not* let him go."

"You do it." She opened her hands and relinquished control, even though it went against everything in her nature.

"What have you got there?" Miles called as he and Mom got up to join them.

Suddenly, a huge fish jumped out of the water, leaping high into the air with the hook clearly in his mouth, then dove back down, yanking at the rod.

"That's a grouper!" Miles yelled. "He's a beauty!"

"He's a beast," Deeley shot back, fighting the fish. His whole body moved like it was in a choreographed dance, his muscles bunching, his face clenched in an expression of pure grit. Everyone watched the water for the fish. Well, everyone but Olivia. She watched the fisherman.

Once more, her catch jumped into the air and as it did, it somehow unhooked its lip, dove back in, and swam away, disappearing from sight.

With a groan of frustration, Deeley fell into his chair

like he'd lost his balance and the battle. He looked up at Olivia with something akin to pain in his eyes. "I told you fish hate me."

Fish, maybe. But not Olivia.

❦

"Oh, look at that." When they stepped into the dimly lit cottage after returning from the boat ride, Mom walked toward the living room. "Teddy was here and left us a present."

"What is it?" Olivia asked.

In the middle of the table was a tray with a teapot, two cups, and a metal tin of her loose tea. And next to that, a large purple crystal and a seashell that looked like a spotted giraffe.

"Oh my gosh," Mom said. "It's a junonia." She dropped onto the sofa and reached for the shell.

"Because it's the name of this cottage?" Olivia guessed.

"Because it's the rarest of all shells and..." She smiled and looked up at Olivia. "This one's broken."

"Aww. Too bad. Why would she bring you a broken shell?"

"Because..." Mom whispered with a strange look on her face. "She collects them."

Olivia reached for the handwritten note that Teddy had left with the gift. "'Shells might break, but not dreams. All my love, T.'" She looked at her mother, waiting for the explanation that had to come with that note.

Mom's whole expression had softened and she actually held the shell to her chest. "That's so sweet."

"Not following," Olivia said, falling into the chair across from her. "Inside joke with you two?"

"Not a joke, just..." She shook her head and chuckled. "A full-court press."

"Really?" Olivia leaned forward. "You've been a little strange tonight, Mom. Is everything okay? Did Miles tell you any news?" Although her mother had been quiet even before they'd gone out on the boat.

"No, he didn't. He wouldn't, as a matter of fact, say anything more than that he had a lead he was following up on tomorrow." She blew out a breath and reached for the crystal. "This is an amethyst. Teddy says these are like nature's GPS. They give you directions."

"Why? Are you lost?"

Mom blinked at her, finally seeming to focus. "Livvie, I need to tell you something. It's preliminary and still a little squishy, but I want you to know first."

"Know what?"

"I'm thinking about staying here. For a long time. Maybe...for good."

"Excuse me?"

"I like it here. And, depending on what we find out about the will, I might have a really solid reason to stay if I own the place."

"Mom." She barely breathed the word. "It's so far. It's

not your world. It's not ..." The words faded out because she really couldn't think of any more excuses. "It's a big change," she finished, kind of weakly.

"I haven't made a decision."

"But she's pushing for you to stay?" Of course she was—that was the full-court press. If Mom inherited the place and stayed, then she wouldn't sell and Teddy could stay put.

Mom looked down at the crystal. "She wants us to both find the right path."

"Well, normally you do that with, you know, pros and cons lists, maybe a long talk with your accountant and..." She sighed. "Your kids."

"You think I'll be too far away?"

"Just three thousand miles in the opposite corner of the country," Olivia said. "But are you sure that's what you want? Not what she wants you to want?"

Hurt flashed in her mother's eyes. "I know the difference, Liv."

"I know you do, but this would be a massive life change. Is this where you want to be? Is running a place like this on the beach what you want to do with your life? Is that Eliza Whitney?"

Her mother smiled and gave her that look that usually preceded some amazing advice. "I don't define myself by my job or where I live, honey. There's a high price to pay for that if, say, you lose that job or have to move."

Was that the second person in one night to make a

sideways dig at attaching too much worth to a job? Or was Olivia just hearing that message everywhere she turned?

"Spoken like a woman who got canned in the most unfair and ugly way," Olivia said.

Mom closed her eyes for a moment, obviously choosing her words with care. "Yes, when AAR fired me, it was both of those things. And it hurt, especially because I brought the agency two major stars. But the sum total of my life was—*is*—much more than my job as a talent agent at AAR. So when they let me go, it didn't hurt nearly as much as I thought it would."

"Well, you were already grieving Dad."

"Exactly. I defined myself by my marriage to Dad, by our deep and abiding love. And as a mother to you and Dane. But work? It never held sway over me."

"Like my work does," she said, a little glumly.

"You do...live to work."

"I don't have anything else, Mom."

"You could."

She studied her mother for a long time, thinking, and suddenly realizing that she wasn't being fair. "This is a beautiful place, Mom. One in a million. And Teddy is very cool, and the property is most likely being handed to you, so who am I to fight your change? I get it, I support it, and I love you for taking chances like this." She reached out for her mother's hand, to underscore that she meant every word of that.

"Thanks, Livvie."

Just then, Olivia's cell buzzed, reminding her that it

had been hours since she'd even looked at the thing. Pulling it out of her purse, she curled her lip at the name Marietta O'Neal. "Ugh, it's work. The last thing I want to think about right now."

"Ignore it."

"I want to, but I'm not strong enough." She smiled as she tapped the phone. "Hey, Marietta. What's up?" She stood and walked toward the open slider to take the call outside.

"He did it. He freaking did it."

She shut her eyes to block out the moonlight and sweet smells of Shellseeker Beach, dragging her body and soul back to the cold and impersonal merchandising offices of Promenade. "Who did what?"

"Alex gave the promotion to Jason Bryn. Not you and not me. It's sexism, Olivia. Pure and simple, we were both bypassed for a man."

"I'm not surprised," Olivia said, her heart dropping. "I saw the writing on the wall."

"He's bringing in one of his Saks people to replace Jason, a woman named—"

"Apple. I know." She closed her eyes, so not wanting to deal with this right now.

"Apparently Nadia went freaking nuts over Jason's Jazzberry rollout. I thought you were doing that, but then you left and—"

"*What?*" She choked the word.

"Oh, yeah, there's a color wheel and all these amazing ideas, so Jason is the new golden boy of Promenade."

Her legs literally felt weak. She shouldn't have left.

She shouldn't have sent that proposal to Alex. She shouldn't have trusted him. Hell, she shouldn't trust *anyone.*

"Nadia's scheduled to come here next week for a team meeting and I guess to fawn all over Jason and prep him to do the rollout in New York."

Her rollout? In New York? As a VP? This couldn't be happening.

"I'm so mad, Olivia," Marietta whined. "I've given my life to this company. When are you coming back?"

If she had a brain, she'd be on a red-eye tonight. But the very thought of that pained her. "I'll be back in time to see Nadia in person."

What would she tell the woman who was two levels above her on the org chart? Would she claim the rollout as hers? Alex would just finesse some excuse and say that Jason redid her plan after she left and blah blah *blah.*

After she ended the call, she dropped into the chair and let out a soft moan, closing her eyes and seeing... Deeley. His smile and his arms and his whole...Navy SEAL vibe. Not a beach bum. Not a surfer dude. And... not *not* her type.

"Sounds like you need this more than I do." Mom stood next to her and gently handed her the purple crystal.

"Am I lost?" Olivia asked.

"You tell me."

Olivia looked up at her. "I'm going back to Seattle. If I stay here too much longer, I'll fall under the spell of Shellseeker Beach."

"Worse things could happen."

"They already have, and I have to get home to Seattle and salvage my job." Because as much as she hated to face the truth, that job was her whole life and she needed to get it back on track.

Chapter Twenty

Miles

I t was well after five in the afternoon when Miles and Tinkerbell arrived at their destination, almost ten hours since they'd left Sanibel. As he pulled up in front of the house on Doverdell Drive in an upscale 'burb just outside of Mobile, Alabama, Miles took one more look at his phone to be sure he was at the right place.

He wasn't sure who he'd meet when he knocked on the door, but even getting this far had been a feat.

Ever since he started on the trail that led to a fifty-seven-year-old woman, he'd hit a remarkable number of dead ends. But one path led to this understated brick home with an inviting porch, nestled among tall oaks on a quiet street. All he could do now was knock and ask questions.

He parked in the driveway and left both windows open for Tink, gave her a treat, and some stern instructions. Then he walked to the front door, rang the bell, and hoped the trail ended here.

She wasn't French. She wasn't named Camille. But she did have a surprising connection to Dutch Vanderveen.

"Who are you?" a woman called from behind the windowless wood. "If you have a package, just leave it."

"I'm looking for Roberta...Vanderveen," he said, with no idea if that was still her last name.

"For what reason?"

"I'm trying to find out information about a woman who was once married to Aloysius Vanderveen."

That was met with dead silence, which in and of itself communicated something important: she knew who that was.

"Is he dead?" she finally asked.

"Yes."

"Are you a lawyer?"

Technically, he was. Not practicing, certainly not licensed in this state or any other anymore, but he was an attorney. "Yes, ma'am."

The door whipped open so fast, it ruffled the blond hair of the woman behind it. "Well, hallelujah and thank the good Lord, Dutch has gone to meet his maker." She smiled at him, adjusting gold-rimmed glasses around bright eyes, a petite woman in a polka-dot sweater and blue jeans.

One thing was certain: Roberta Vanderveen was not the woman in the picture Eliza had shown her.

She looked her age, but well put together, her thick Southern accent giving off a Steel Magnolia vibe. "Did you bring my inheritance?"

He inched back at the question. "Ma'am?"

"Dutch is dead, and you're a lawyer. There's only one

reason you'd be here. Are you safe?" She searched his face. "You look like a good man. I suppose I should see ID, but you can come in for a spell. It's hot out there."

"My dog's in the car," he said. "Could we sit out here and talk?"

"Sure, sure." She stepped out and closed the door behind her, gesturing for him to sit on a glider. "Can I get you something? Sweet tea or water? Something stronger?" She lifted her lips. "I do have a bit of sherry, though I never touch the stuff myself."

"I'm fine, ma'am." He extended his hand. "You're Roberta Vanderveen, correct? Do you still go by that name?"

"Depends on who's asking."

"My name is Miles Anderson and I'm here in my capacity as a private investigator."

"Oh, really. I thought you were a lawyer."

"I was," he answered honestly. "But that's not why I'm here."

"Who hired you?"

"I'm not at liberty to say, ma'am."

"Lie of omission," she shot back. "It's a sin, you know? Lying is a sin. Maybe venial, which weakens the soul. Now, it doesn't kill the grace within, but, it's a sin none-theless. So, fine, don't tell me who sent you. Sit down."

He wasn't technically lying or omitting anything, but he sensed that telling her who sent him was a rabbit hole he didn't want to go down with Roberta. He took a seat on the glider, eyeing her as she took a chair and folded her hands on her lap and crossed her ankles, tucking them under the chair. The whole pose was somewhere between schoolgirl and the Queen of England.

"How'd it happen?" she asked. "Plane wreck? I always thought he'd go in a plane crash."

He shook his head. "He had a brain tumor."

"Oh." She closed her eyes and made a very quick sign of the cross. "I do hope he was right with God. The man sure had some mighty big sins on his record. Mighty big."

"I don't know his, uh, spiritual state, ma'am. I'm here because a formal will hasn't yet been filed or found and I'm trying to track down any possible heirs."

"Heir," she mumbled under her breath, leaving him uncertain as to what she said.

"Ma'am?"

She held up her hand and exhaled, closing her eyes, giving him the impression she was thinking, maybe grieving. Or praying. He had no idea, but he waited, giving her time to gather her thoughts.

"Where was he?" she finally asked.

"He lived on Sanibel Island, on the Gulf Coast of Florida."

"Oh, okay. So he still owned that little resort and some other businesses?"

He nodded, not in the habit of giving away information, but getting it. "Have you been in touch with him, then?"

"I followed him, for obvious reasons."

"Followed, like on social media?" he asked. "And I'm

afraid I don't know the obvious reasons. Could you enlighten me?"

She gave him a "get real" look. "At the risk of being crass, I will cut to the chase, Mr. Anderson. How much do I get?"

"I have no way of knowing that without a will, ma'am. Unless you had a prior agreement or it was part of a prenuptial arrangement..."

She stared at him for a long moment, then removed her glasses very slowly, reaching into her pants pocket for a tissue. She used it to wipe the glass very thoroughly, her fingers trembling slightly. Then she very slowly put them back on, looking at him again.

"Is that the way it's going to be, then? A protracted legal battle? I'm prepared for that, Mr. Anderson. I have God on my side. Always have, always will."

He frowned. "There won't be a battle until a will is found and filed. And if it isn't, his daughter—"

"His daughter?" Her voice rose in disbelief as her skin, already so pale it could be described as bone white, grew even more bloodless. "I'll have none of that. None. I have reviewed my rights very carefully and nobody, and I do mean *nobody*, including his daughter, is going to take what's rightly mine."

"I'm afraid as his former wife, you don't have next of kin-type of rights, but perhaps if you have children?" He leaned forward. "Did you and Dutch have children?"

She death-stared him, then stood, walking into the house without saying a word.

What the hell? Was she leaving him out here or...what?

He waited for a minute. Two. Then just as he started to stand, the door opened again. She stepped outside holding a manila envelope.

"I have two documents in here. You are welcome to take pictures of them, and then I don't want to see you again until we're in court."

She snapped open the envelope and pulled out a multi-page, legal-sized document, opening it slowly.

He glanced at the paperwork, already recognizing that it had been filed in a court and looked quite official, though that didn't mean anything.

"So, heir," she said. "No S." She reached into the envelope and pulled out a business card, handing it to him. "My attorney, Leonard Buckells. I'll be calling him when you leave and I'm sure he'll be happy to meet with you and set you straight."

He read the card and the local address, hoping he could get to the guy first thing in the morning. "Thank you...Mrs. Vanderveen."

She gave him a tight smile. "Oh, please, no one calls me that. No one, not even you."

"Then, thank you, Roberta."

"Or that." She crossed her arms. "If Dutch ever talked about me, which I doubt he did, he'd never call me that, either. My name is Birdie, short for Roberta, spelled like the animal. Birdie Vanderveen. Good day now."

She pivoted and closed the door, and this time he heard the latch.

He headed back to the car, where Tink was whining, opening the door and folding into the seat with a long, slow sigh.

The last thing he wanted to do was break Eliza Whitney's heart, but he had a feeling he was about to.

Chapter Twenty-one

Teddy

When she heard the news that Olivia was going back to Seattle the next day, Teddy decided to throw her very best going-away party. Roz and George picked up pizza and a platter of lasagna, meatballs, and salad from Marco's, everyone's favorite. Katie baked a few cakes, but Teddy snagged some back-up Key Lime pie from a great island bakery, just in case of a cake disaster.

Deeley set up a big tent on the beach, and strung vineyard lights from end to end. Teddy used her favorite crystals to hold down the tablecloths, and Harper collected shells to scatter over the tables to create a festive beach atmosphere.

She even had Deeley bring over his sound system and drag a platform from the back of his cabana to use as a stage so Harper could perform the dance that Eliza had taught her. Everything was perfect.

As she stood at the bottom of the boardwalk admiring her hard work and waiting for her guests, Eliza joined her, looking around in amazement.

"Pulling out all the stops, huh?" Eliza asked on a laugh. "The big tent? A stage? Next you'll tell me there are elephants and an aerial act."

"Don't give me any ideas." She drew back and looked at the gorgeous dress draped over Eliza's trim figure, the bright hibiscus flowers perfectly festive and beachy. "And you wore the dress from your dream!"

"Just for you." She glanced around. "Um, Teddy? There are enough tables and chairs for twenty-five people. Who's coming?"

Teddy laughed and threw up her hands. "What can I say? I love a party. When I do one on the beach, I invite anyone staying at the Cottages, friends, and, oh, you know. I want Olivia to know how much we've enjoyed having her here, however brief her stay was." She leaned in to add in a conspiratorial whisper, "Sometimes it's the going-away party that gets them to come back."

"You're a grand schemer, Theodora. I do believe she's enjoyed herself enough to come back to Shellseeker Beach someday. In fact, she's torn about leaving, but so worried about things at work that she feels she has no choice." She sighed, shaking her head. "Sad, because I could use a good long time with her here. Months, even."

Teddy inched back and looked at Eliza. "Are *you* staying months?"

Eliza smiled, then took each of Teddy's hands in hers. "I was going to save this for a big toast or something tonight, but I might as well tell you now while it's only the two of us."

"Oh?" Teddy's heart jumped a little as they squeezed hands, the warmth and love rolling off Eliza already giving her a clue about what announcement she was going to make.

"This probably isn't going to be a surprise to anyone, but especially not to you, who seems to know everything that I'm feeling and thinking."

Hope and a familiar joy clutched at Teddy's chest. That same feeling she had when Roz and George accepted the job to run Treasures. When Katie dropped her backpack in the guest room and hugged Teddy with her little baby bump. When Deeley stood at the old, decrepit cabana and announced he could turn it into a business, if she'd let him stay. And, of course, the day Dutch took her hand in that gazebo and announced they were connected forever.

She lived for this feeling, for finding her treasured people, adding to her family. It made up for the miscarriages and losses over the years. It made life worth living.

"Teddy!" Eliza exclaimed. "You're crying and I haven't even told you anything."

"You're going to say that you're staying in Shellseeker Beach," she guessed.

Eliza sighed. "Like I said, you know all before it's official."

"You *are* staying?" She barely whispered the words that were just too good to be true.

"I am."

Teddy gasped. "Really? For...good? Forever, Eliza?"

"For as long as it makes sense, Teddy. And right now, it makes a whole lot of sense. Until we know anything about Dutch's will, and the woman in that picture, or Miles produces something that gives us an answer, I'm staying."

"Then I almost hope we don't get any answers," Teddy admitted. "I left Miles a message to invite him tonight but haven't heard back."

"He said he was going on a trip to follow a lead, and that's all he'd say. Fingers crossed he'll return with news or information."

Crossed, but not too tight. Teddy didn't want anything to change Eliza's mind.

"You cannot imagine how happy you've made me, Eliza." Teddy wrapped her in a hug, burying her face in the sweet-smelling strawberry-blond hair.

Eliza drew back. "You're sure? I mean, I'm not a constant reminder of Dutch or a complete stranger who blew in to upset your life or just...a problem of any kind?"

Teddy pressed her hands on Eliza's cheeks, looking into her eyes. "Roz is like a sister to me. Katie is like a granddaughter. You know what I've been missing in my made-up little family tree, don't you?"

"A daughter?" Eliza guessed, her eyes filling a little.

"Will you be mine?" Teddy asked. "My not-real-but-very-dear daughter to stand by my side and help me and love me and—"

"Yes!" Eliza cut her off and squeezed her again. "Now tonight, we will celebrate! Come and show me your over-the-top party."

"Absolutely." They walked arm-in-arm to the tent, waving to Deeley, who was putting the finishing touches on the sound system.

"Maybe Deeley can do what we can't," Teddy whispered before they reached him.

"Make the music play?"

"Make your daughter stay."

Eliza looked at him for a long time. "No denying they have chemistry, but her heart's pretty guarded."

"But they belong together," Teddy said.

Eliza gave a quick laugh. "You sound so matter-of-fact, Teddy."

"Because this matter is a fact. They belong together. I feel it."

"That, my dear Teddy, is the most wishful of wishful thinking. He's not her type, as she has told me quite a few times."

"Doesn't she have eyes? And hormones? And a beating heart?"

"She has...expectations," Eliza said. "And high hopes for a husband, I think, or at least that's what I pick up between the lines. I like the way you think, but I don't share your assessment that they belong together. Deeley's not husband material."

Teddy just smiled, because sometimes she knew in her heart when she was right, and it didn't make sense to try and convince someone otherwise.

"Will you sing tonight?" she asked Eliza as they walked around the little tables and straightened chairs.

"Sing?" Eliza's eyes popped. "I can't...no. Thank you for thinking of me, but the only person on that stage will be Harper Bettencourt, superstar."

"Did someone say my daughter's name?" Katie floated in carrying her cakes while Harper followed, wearing bright pink from tiny head to toe, carrying some bags. "I think you mean the better half of the...what does Deeley call us? The Bad Baking Sisters?"

"We're not sisters!" Harper insisted.

"No, but you are a star!" Eliza said, heading straight for the child. "Come and see the stage. I hear you're our entertainment tonight."

As Eliza took Harper to the little platform "stage," Teddy took the bags and helped Katie get everything to the table they were using for the buffet.

"This looks amazing, Teddy," she said. "And you look so happy. Are we allowed to be that happy for a going-away party?"

"It's also a staying-here party."

Katie frowned, and followed Teddy's finger as she pointed to Eliza. "She's not leaving?"

"Not for a while, and I couldn't be happier."

"I really like her, Teddy," Katie said. "And Harper adores her. This is just wonderful news."

Roz and George arrived with mountains of food, announcing that they had just closed the deal with Olivia for Promenade to buy a thousand bottles and blank messages to be shipped to Seattle.

With that sealed, the mood was festive and lively, with music playing and quite a few of the Cottages guests already drinking and eating when Olivia came down the boardwalk. She wore a blush-colored dress, with her dark waves cascading over shoulders that had gotten tanned from quite a few hours spent on the paddleboard with Deeley.

And speaking of him, Teddy sneaked a glance in

time to see him pause in his conversation with George and shift his attention to the beauty on the beach. His eyes flickered, a smile teased his lips, and his whole body seemed to lean an inch forward as he drank her in.

Yep. She knew it.

"Holy heck," Eliza sidled up next to her, her gaze in the same direction. "You might be right."

"Oh, I usually am." She tugged Eliza closer. "You know, I think old Dutch might be up there in heaven pulling some strings for his granddaughter and the young man who was like a grandson to him."

She could feel the chills rise on Eliza's arms.

"Of course, that's assuming he went to heaven," Teddy added with a rueful smile.

"I'm sure he did," Eliza said. "You made him a changed man and I'm sure that counted for something in the end."

"I hope so," Teddy whispered. "Now come on and get some food. It's a party."

"Rumor has it you have a show-tune playlist." Deeley leaned on the table where Teddy sat with Eliza and Olivia. "Can you share it with me?"

"I do, but it's only instrumental. No vocals."

"Exactly what we want. Can I transfer it into the sound system?"

"I hope you can, because I sure as heck have no idea

how to do that." She picked up her phone and frowned. "And the playlist is on shuffle, so..."

Olivia smiled and put her hand over the phone. "I got this, Mom." She added a wink as she stood. "I'm a millennial."

They took off and Eliza and Teddy shared a look.

"A millennial who wasted no time taking off with Deeley," Teddy teased.

Roz drifted over from the next table. "Are you in a good enough mood to take some news?" she asked Teddy.

"Only if the news is that you're going up to Ohio to help Asia." Teddy crossed her arms and stared back at her friend, aware of George coming closer to join them, holding a paper plate.

"She knows already," Roz said to him. "Just like I know without looking that there's a slice of cake on that plate, George."

"Of course she does," George said, sitting down. "And I'm eating this cake, Roz."

Roz looked at it and raised one brow, then flicked her hands. "Never mind. It's a party and you've been good all week." Then, back to Teddy, she looked contrite. "Can you handle it for a few weeks?"

"We will manage," Teddy assured her. "Take care of your daughter."

"Maybe Olivia would stay and help," George suggested.

"Oh, that would be nice," Teddy agreed. "But this is her going-away party, so don't get your hopes up."

"But..." Roz looked over her shoulder to where Olivia

and Deeley had their heads close together as they worked on the sound system. "There's a very good reason for her to stay, don't you think?"

"Seriously," George added. "Deeley hasn't wiped the smile off his puss since Olivia floated down here like a pink cloud of temptation."

Eliza laughed. "So poetic, George!"

"See? It's not just me," Teddy said.

"We all see it," Eliza agreed. "My daughter is gorgeous and brilliant. Deeley is kind and..."

"Smoking hot," Roz added. At George's look of dismay, she flicked her fingers. "What? You just called Olivia a 'cloud of temptation.' Please."

Eliza laughed at them. "That cloud is leaving on a jet plane tomorrow and once she gets back on the ladder to climb to the top, she's going to forget all of us."

"Shame," Roz said. "Because she's a retail natural."

George nodded. "When we were doing the paperwork for the bottles with her? She had so many good ideas. She could really make a difference at Sanibel Treasures."

"Well, why don't you ask Olivia?" Teddy looked from one to the other. "What if she didn't say no?"

"Do you think..." Roz's voice trailed off as Olivia slipped into her chair and looked around the table. "Whoa, guilty faces. Am I the subject du jour?"

Teddy smiled. "In a good way, dear."

"No, I didn't make a date with Deeley," she said with an exasperated laugh.

"That's not it," Roz said.

"Although Deeley would like it," George added.

"Forget it." Roz cracked. "He's mine. Unless...we work out an arrangement." She leaned closer to Olivia. "I have a proposal for you. Not the kind with a ring, although if we're gone long enough, who knows?"

Olivia looked incredulous, then glanced at Eliza and Teddy. "Are you two in on this?"

"Hear her out," Teddy said. "Roz has a question for you."

"George and I have decided we have to head up to Ohio to help our daughter, and we were just wondering if there is anything at all that would change your mind about staying, so you could run Sanibel Treasures? I know it's crazy to ask and you have bigger fish to fry, but..."

For a moment, Olivia almost looked...interested. Enough that Teddy's heart jumped in her chest.

"Wow, that's so sweet of you," Olivia said. "And I have to say, I'm utterly charmed by that place and would have a blast. And it's not that I have bigger fish to fry, 'cause your fish is really, really special, Roz. But I have made a commitment to my company and..." She smiled and sighed. "I'm touched, Roz. And George. Really. I know how protective you are of your store and I'm honored that you'd even consider me."

Teddy put her hand on Eliza's arm and leaned closer. "Classy young lady you raised."

Eliza beamed at her daughter, obviously thinking the same thing. "She's a keeper."

All of a sudden, the speakers crackled and some rich orchestral notes filled the little tent.

"Oh." Eliza sat up with a smile. "The overture to *State Fair.* Where's our little dancer?"

"Miss Eliza!" Harper came running over with her blond locks flying. "I'm going to do our dance. I'm going to sing! Will you help me?"

"I'll cheer you on," she said. "I'll be right here, if you forget a word or a step."

"But I need you! I can't do it right without you."

"I feel you, kid," Olivia teased. "She's had that same effect on me my whole life."

They all laughed but Eliza got up, reaching her hand out. "I'll stand next to the stage, if that will make you feel better."

She slipped her little hand in Eliza's and they walked off, making Teddy smile.

"She's the granddaughter she may never get from me," Olivia said softly, leaning into Teddy. "Thank you for that."

"Because the pressure's off you?"

"No, because my mom is happy. It's all I want. For her to be happy again. And she is that."

"Ladies and gentlemen," Katie said to the group, clapping a few times for quiet. "I give you Harper Bettencourt, singing and dancing to *State Fair!*"

There was a round of applause, then Harper took one slow step up onto the stage.

"Wait," Olivia whispered. "Isn't she, like, paralyzed with shyness?"

"Not on stage," Roz said. "Wait until you hear her sing."

And the minute the little girl opened her mouth, Harper proved the point. She sang remarkably well for her age, and danced the simple steps Eliza had taught her with her shoulders square and her head held high.

"Oh, man, does anything make my mother happier?" Olivia laughed, her hands pressed together as she watched. "She loves kids and the stage and finding talent. This is perfect for her."

"She loves singing, too, right?" Teddy asked.

"More than anything, but it's been a struggle since my dad died."

Teddy nodded. "She told me."

They stayed quiet to enjoy the dance, which ended on a big flourish and got huge applause. George started a standing ovation and at that, Harper pressed her face into the closest legs she could find, which happened to be Eliza's.

She put her hands on Harper's shoulders, leaning over to say something, helping her turn around and make a little curtsy to the crowd. As the applause died down, the next song started with haunting strings and a melody that was far more familiar to Teddy.

"Is this from *West Side Story*?" she asked Olivia.

"Yes. It's called 'Somewhere,' and this is the music-only version," Olivia said, staying standing while everyone sat down. "Sing it, Mom!" she called out. "You love this song!"

For a moment, Eliza looked flat-out horrified,

blinking at Olivia with that, "I'm definitely going to kill you," look most mothers had perfected.

"Eliza!" George hollered.

"We want Eliza!" Roz added.

They started clapping, the music continued, and Harper, bless her sweet soul, gave Eliza a slight push toward the front of the platform.

"I...can't..." But Eliza's protests were lost in the music. It played what had to be the first stanza, but Eliza still didn't sing.

"Come on, Mommy," Olivia breathed the words, taking Teddy's hand. "Sing again. Please. Dad would want you to."

Teddy felt her eyes fill as Eliza took a deep, slow breath, closed her eyes, and opened her mouth and...

"There's a place for us," she sang, a little raspy, a little uncertain. She smiled and put her hands on her chest, committing to the words. With every line, her voice grew stronger as she reached the emotional, plaintive title word of the song.

"Oh." Teddy covered her mouth as a wave of love nearly drowned her. "Her voice is beautiful."

"So beautiful," Olivia agreed, fighting her own tears. "My mother is an angel."

The lyrics touched her heart and Teddy felt a tear trickle down her cheek, and the pressure of Olivia's hand on hers. They listened as Eliza sang the whole song with a clear, glorious voice.

Teddy took one second to look around the party as

the guests listened, rapt, to the music. Until her gaze landed on a new arrival at the back of the tent.

Miles made it!

He watched Eliza, too, his gaze locked on her, his broad chest rising and falling with a sigh, his whole face looking...worried. Sad, even.

Oh, dear. Miles had news, Teddy realized. And just looking at him, she knew none of them were going to like it.

Chapter Twenty-two

Miles

As Eliza reached the crescendo of the song, Miles felt his whole body react, rising up there with her, lost in the clarity and beauty of her voice.

Oh, man. He did not want to like her any more than he already did. Too late for that.

As she finished, she clutched her hands to her chest, her eyes alive with joy over the performance and the words that had touched everyone in the room. She looked surprised that she'd sung the song, but so happy as she reached out both arms to Teddy and Olivia when they came toward the stage to hug her.

Man, he didn't want to ruin this night. He wanted to wait until tomorrow. With any other client, he most certainly would have postponed this news, but he'd made Eliza one promise while they were out on his boat and that was to tell her what he knew, when he knew it.

And not just Eliza, but Teddy. They all needed to know that a tsunami waited out there and Shellseeker Beach, at least as they knew it, was about to get wiped out.

He walked slowly toward the center of the party,

holding back while Eliza accepted hugs, her laugh, as pretty as her singing, floating over the little crowd.

"I can't believe it," she cooed to them. "I did it! I sang!" She hugged Olivia again, and kissed Teddy on her cheek. "Officially the best day ever!"

And here he was to destroy all of that. For one second he thought about bolting to let them have their party, but as he took one step backwards, she saw him.

"Miles! You're here!" Eliza broke away from the group, going toward him and waving him closer at the same time. "Let's get you a drink and..." Her voice faded as she searched his face.

"No, no drink." He never was very good at hiding things, not when he liked the person he was talking to.

"Is everything okay? Do you have news?"

He sure did. But he had no desire to be the one who took the light from her eyes, so he tipped his head and tried to buy a few minutes. "I wondered if I could..." He hated himself for this. Just didn't want to do it to her. "Set up a time to talk to you tomorrow?"

But Eliza gave her head the slightest shake, looking hard at him. "You found something, didn't you?"

He nodded. "I did."

"Let's talk," she said, gesturing toward a table.

"Maybe somewhere private, Eliza." She might have a reaction to this news. Or Teddy might. "With Teddy. Can we go..." He glanced at the beach.

"Let's walk to the gazebo," Teddy said, coming closer.

"And Olivia," Eliza said, putting her hand on her

daughter's shoulder as if she drew strength from the young woman.

"Right now?" he asked, because this was going to end their party fun.

"Right now," Eliza answered. "I have to know."

He nodded and they all moved to the side of the tent, leaving the covered area to walk across the beach toward a pretty gazebo he'd seen but had never been in.

"Quite a set of pipes you have, Eliza," he said, trying for small talk even though he could sense his arrival had tensed her up a bit.

"Rusty pipes," she answered self-consciously. "It's been a while since I...did that." Her cheeks were still a little flushed from the performance, giving her a pretty glow. And he knew he was about to erase that, too. She looked up at him. "How bad?"

"Your singing? It was fantastic."

"The news," she corrected. "How bad is the news you're about to tell us?"

He swallowed and huffed out a breath. "Bad," he said softly. "But it can wait until tomorrow."

"Oh, no it can't," Teddy said. "I don't want to wait."

They crossed the sand, leaving the chatter of the party behind, stepping into the gazebo, taking seats on the benches tucked into the perimeter of the place. The three women looked at him expectantly.

"So, you found Camille?" Eliza guessed. "She has a daughter and..." She grimaced. "The suspense is killing me, Miles."

He gave a tight smile. "The French connection led

nowhere, I'm sorry to say. I simply couldn't find anyone, at least anyone living, who'd qualify as your half-sister, Eliza. I left a detailed message with the French lawyer, but never heard a word back. I simply hit nothing but dead ends."

"Oh." Her disappointment was palpable. "Okay. Maybe they're gone. Maybe they didn't ever exist. Maybe that picture was a friend and when he told Teddy it was his wife, he didn't mean that picture. Or maybe she's another woman we have to find. Or maybe there was no wife."

"Yes, there was." He shifted in his seat. "Actually, to be more accurate, there *is* a wife."

The three of them stared at him, silent and slack-jawed.

"Did you say…" Teddy couldn't finish the sentence, but Eliza put a hand on her friend's arm.

"Please explain, Miles," she said.

"I don't know how else to put this," he said, reaching for his phone, where he had notes and images of the documents he'd seen and scanned in Mobile. Also, all the notes he'd taken from an in-depth conversation with a local attorney, Lenny Buckells, who'd been waiting for him, ready and raring to put up a true legal fight.

"Just tell us," Eliza said.

"In 1990, Dutch married a woman by the name of Roberta Jean Milton…Vanderveen."

"What?" Eliza breathed.

"But you said, 'There *is* a wife'?" Teddy whispered.

"Because Dutch and Roberta never divorced," he said

softly, trying to ease the blow of all he had to say. "It stunned me, too, since I assumed they had ended the marriage. But, no. They were married, or at least lived in the same town, very briefly. She is a practicing Catholic, quite devout, and refused him a divorce. In exchange for letting him go to live his life as he pleased, without an official divorce, she had him draw up and sign a will that clearly states that, upon his death, she gets everything. Every dollar, every asset, every...thing."

"Where has she been all these years?" Eliza asked.

"In Mobile, Alabama." He watched all the blood drain from Teddy's cheeks, but he continued, as gently as he could. "She didn't know Dutch had died. Her attorney periodically checks filed death certificates, ready to pounce. The last time he looked, Dutch's hadn't been filed, so I brought him the news."

Eliza leaned forward, visibly shaken. "How did you find her?"

"I found an old marriage announcement in an Alabama paper, but it took a little bit of work to find her. But she's alive and well, and..."

"And inheriting all of this," Teddy said, gesturing to the world around her. "So that's who Dutch meant when he said his 'only living heir.' I thought he meant you, Eliza."

"Well, she isn't his only living heir," Eliza said.

"In that will, she is," Miles said.

Teddy groaned and reached for Eliza's hand. "Maybe...maybe she has a heart. Maybe we can meet her and..."

Miles shook his head, hating what he had to say next. "Please don't get your hopes up. She's never coming here. Once the final paperwork is signed, she has buyers lined up. Her attorney has a list of contacts at the major hotels and is already setting up meetings. Birdie has no interest in protecting the land, or you."

"What?" Teddy demanded on a gasp. "What did you say her name is?"

"Roberta, but she goes by Birdie."

"Birdie," she whispered. "It was the last thing he ever said."

The three women all sort of sunk with a sigh of sadness and shock, but then Eliza's eyes focused. "Wait. Was she the woman in the picture? Does she have a daughter?"

"No, not a chance that she's that woman. And she made no mention of children, none at all. She's only fifty-seven, so she was quite a bit younger than Dutch, more than twenty years his junior."

Teddy dropped her head into her hands, groaning as all of it hit her. Eliza put her arm around her, shoulders square.

"Miles, please. There has to be some way to fight this. A woman he was married to briefly more than thirty years ago? She can't claim this property. Do you think there's any chance, any chance at all, we could take her to court and win?"

Oh, he wished he could say yes. "You could try, but it would be long and expensive. In the end, you might end up spending hundreds of thousands of dollars and losing."

"A settlement?" she pressed. "Maybe pay her off? I have money. Not what she'd get for this place, but maybe we could work out an arrangement—"

"No," Teddy said, lifting her face to show teary eyes. "I can't let you do that, Eliza. You need your money to live."

"And what about you? And everyone here? And Shellseeker?" Eliza stood, fisting her hands. "This can't be it. We can't hand this over to some stranger who refused to divorce him and held him hostage!"

Fire lit Eliza's eyes, and as beautiful a thing as that was to watch, Miles knew he had nothing but cold water to throw on her arguments. Without a physical will, it was beyond an uphill battle, one that could cost her life savings.

"I wish I had better news," he said softly, pushing up. "Eliza, I have good attorneys who know Florida law, and I have copies of all the documents for you to look at, but I do really want you to keep your expectations low."

She nodded and walked toward him, reaching for his hand. "Thank you, Miles. I promise I'll be in touch. Give Tink my love."

He just looked at her for a long time, ignoring the warm feeling in his chest, but knowing it would all be moot when he left.

With a nod to all of them, he turned and crossed the beach, not liking this part of his job at all.

Chapter Twenty-three

Eliza

Deeley, Roz, and George cleaned up the entire event, with the help of some friends, while Eliza and Olivia stayed with Teddy in her house. After a while, she wanted to go upstairs, so Eliza went with her to draw a crystal bath.

When Eliza came downstairs, she found Katie and Roz and George sitting at the kitchen counter, quiet.

"Did Olivia leave?" she asked.

"She's helping Deeley finish the last of the cleanup," Roz said with a vague smile. "Either that or they're walking in the moonlight, holding hands. That lucky girl."

They all smiled at her expected humor, but no one actually laughed.

Katie came closer and reached for Eliza's hand. "I put Harper in the guest room. She's crashed from all the performing and wonderfully oblivious to the drama. I can stay here tonight, so you guys don't have to worry about Teddy being alone."

Eliza put a hand on Katie's shoulder and gave it a squeeze. "That's so sweet, and it's a good idea, Katie.

Even though she is probably the strongest woman I've ever met."

"She's been through a lot," Roz said. "And she's our matriarch. We are all strong because she is."

On a sigh, Eliza slipped onto one of the barstools next to them. "I was going to stay and become one of you," she told them.

"I know." Katie dropped her chin into her palm, giving Eliza a sad look. "Teddy was so happy when she told me. She has a wonderful connection with you, Eliza. I guess your staying doesn't make sense now."

"Who knows what makes sense?" Eliza lamented. "We can't just give up without a fight."

"Oh yes we can." Teddy's voice floated in from the stairs as she came down, wrapped in a comfy robe, her silver curls wet and falling around her face. She suddenly looked much older and more vulnerable than any other time Eliza had seen her, and it twisted her heart.

"There you are," Roz said, getting up. "Some chamomile, Teddy?"

She shook her head, taking a breath. As she did, the sliders opened and Deeley and Olivia walked in, slowing their steps when they saw Teddy and everyone looking at her.

"You okay, Mama T?" Deeley asked, searching her face.

"I'm fine," Teddy said. "I've made a decision."

They all waited, no one breathing.

"For starters, I'm going with Eliza tomorrow to the

Keys. She has some things to pick up and I need a change of scenery." She came a little closer to the group, tightening the belt of her robe. "Roz and George are going—as they should—to Ohio for Asia, so we'll close Sanibel Treasures for the moment. Katie, we're going to cancel all the reservations going forward, but you can close out the guests we have, clean the cottages, and lock them. Turn away any walk-ins. I will pay you indefinitely until you have a job, but if you need to stay here to lower your bills, you can."

"Teddy—"

She held her hand up to stop the arguments, which were about to come from a number of people.

"My decision is made. Deeley, you keep that cabana running and take every dime for yourself, rent free. Dutch has it off the books, so that is the one thing that Birdie can't take from us. In the meantime, I'm not going to build up the property value at all."

"What are you going to do after you go to the Keys?" George asked her.

"Eliza said I could go to California with her," she said. "I bet I could find my people out there. Lots of crystal lovers."

Eliza sighed with a smile. "I'd love for you to come and stay with me, Teddy. I just want you to be happy." She stepped closer. "We don't have to give up yet."

"Eliza. Birdie was the last word that crossed his lips. He knew." She bit her lip, her voice taut with pain. "For two years we were together, and he knew he was still married. Now I know why he wouldn't marry me, why we had to have a unification ceremony instead of a wedding." Her voice cracked as she gathered herself, and no one said a word.

"Why wouldn't he trust me?" she asked. "Why wouldn't he do something, anything at all, to fix the problem he was leaving me with? Why would he be so selfish?"

Eliza swallowed any comment, because it wasn't the time to tell them all she always knew *selfish* was exactly what Dutch Vanderveen was. Heck, she'd almost forgotten while she was here, falling under the spell of his nice-guy image.

"He was obviously struggling with the truth," Roz said. "He was dying and had to face that and what he left behind."

"I know he loved you," George said.

"But he had demons," Deeley added. "Deep ones that he never let out."

Teddy sighed and nodded. "Anyway, I'm going to gather my strength and wits and not stay here and suffer. I simply don't know what to do about...all of you."

"We'll be fine."

"Worry about yourself, Ted."

"We're all adults."

She gave a sad smile at the litany, then reached for Eliza. "You and I are two widows looking for a new life. And we'll find it...somewhere, just like your song. We'll find it. Like, you know, Thelma and Louise."

"God, I hope not," Olivia cracked, breaking the tension in the room. "But I'm really glad you have each other."

"So am I." Eliza folded Teddy into a hug, hoping that time might change her mind. But if it didn't? Teddy was always welcome with her.

"I don't know what I'd do without you, Eliza," Teddy whispered.

"You don't have to find out, because now..." She put her lips near Teddy's ear and whispered, "You have a daughter."

Teddy squeezed her tighter as a soft whimper escaped her throat.

"You PRACTICE your singing and dancing while I'm gone, okay, Miss Harper of Broadway?" Eliza tapped the child on the nose, getting a huge smile and a leg hug in return. "When I come back, we're going to work on a whole bunch of fun stuff."

"*Frozen?*"

She laughed. "Yes, *Frozen!*"

Just then, George and Roz stepped out of Teddy's house, with Deeley behind them, and headed toward the stairs.

"She's on her way down," Roz told them. "We've said our teary goodbyes."

"Then let me say mine." Eliza reached out to Roz, gathering her and George in a hug. "Good luck in Ohio, you two. Please give our love to Asia."

George turned to Olivia, holding his hands out. "We came so close to making history together."

"I know," she said. "I'm sad I can't use your bottles in my promotion. In fact, I think I'm going to just can the whole idea. I don't want anyone else to profit off your genius."

He gave her a kiss on the cheek. "You're a good girl, Livvie."

They all looked up at the sound of Teddy closing and locking her sliding glass door with a firm click.

No one said a word as she came down the steps and joined them, but then there was a flurry of goodbyes and hugs and some tears and promises to call and text and more hugs.

One particularly long one between Deeley and Olivia that no one even teased her about. Without hope, it wasn't fun to tease.

Eliza skipped the convertible option, not in the mood to cruise with the top down. But she honked at the crew as she drove off, glancing at the glorious vista in her rearview mirror, praying it wasn't the last time she'd see Shellseeker Beach.

"You okay?" she asked Teddy, who sat with her hands on her lap, staring straight ahead.

"I never knew him," she said on a whisper, proving she was so not okay. "Me. The great 'reader of people's vibes.' Hah! He lied to me, and I had no idea."

"And we still don't know about Camille and the kid in the picture," Eliza said sadly, already haunted by the possibility that she had a sister out there *somewhere*. Would she ever give up trying to find her? Would she spend the rest of her life thinking about her?

Teddy grunted softly. "Who knows? Certainly not me. All I know is he was a liar, and a cheat."

Eliza looked up and caught Olivia's gaze in the rearview mirror, both of them sharing a knowing look. Yep. That was the Dutch they knew. Now, Teddy sounded so much like her mother, her words an echo of Mary Ann's.

Eliza knew better than to try and talk her out of this anger now. Instead, she put her hand over Teddy's and gave her a comforting squeeze. "I'm sorry, hon."

"And *she* gets everything," Teddy lamented. "My life, my land, my legacy. All turned over to Hilton or Marriott or Baldwin and everything I know and love will be gone."

"Corporations are the worst." Olivia's comment, her first since they'd left, made Eliza look in the rearview mirror again to see the look of pure misery on her daughter's face as she tossed her phone on her lap.

"Did something happen at work?" Eliza asked.

"Nadia's called me three times and I'm actually letting her go to voice mail." She leaned forward and put her hand on Teddy's shoulder. "Oh, man, Teddy, I feel you. Stinging betrayal. Lost trust. Dashed hopes. Why did I ever say I loved my job?"

"For the same reason I said I loved Dutch," Teddy said, sliding out of her own pain to focus on Olivia's. "Because, at the time, you did. But, honey, are you sure you don't want to tell them to put that job where the sun don't shine? You're better than them."

Olivia snorted but Eliza chimed in with her agreement.

"I wish I had the nerve to call Nadia back and tell her what's what...and that I'm staying here because..." She read a sign on the road. "I haven't even been to Ding Darling yet!"

"Then you haven't really been to Sanibel," Teddy said.

"You can get a book about it," Eliza told her.

"Right there." Teddy pointed at the welcome center. "They have a whole Ding Darling section and there's a free magazine about Sanibel. Take one home and you can read it when you feel down."

"Shall I pull into the unwelcome center?" Eliza joked. "Nothing like a little comedy from Patty and Penny on your way out."

"Yes," Olivia said, surprising her. "I may never get back here in my whole life."

That made Teddy release a soft moan of sadness, but Eliza flipped her turn signal on and slid into the parking lot. "Here we come, Penny and Patty." She unlatched her seatbelt and glanced at Teddy. "Do you want to come in?"

Teddy shook her head. "I'm not in the mood for those two to sniff out the truth. Don't tell them."

"Promise." Eliza leaned over and gave Teddy's cheek an impetuous kiss. "Be right back."

She climbed out and joined Olivia in the parking lot, and together they walked toward the door, which swung open right before they got there. Two women stepped out and gave tight, quick smiles, the older one holding the door for Eliza and Olivia.

"Thanks," Eliza murmured as they passed, getting a whiff of a floral perfume that was utterly unusual and compelling.

And weirdly familiar.

She glanced over her shoulder, trying to get one more sniff of the perfume because it smelled like—

"Eliza!" From behind her desk, Penny gave a friendly wave. "Good to see you again. I heard Teddy had a party last night. Where was my invitation?"

"Oh, I don't know, Penny. It was pretty spontaneous. This is my daughter, who wanted to grab...that?" She pointed at a glossy magazine with a picture of the entrance to the Ding Darling Wildlife Refuge on the front. "May we?"

Patty poked her head out from the side-office door. "It must be Shellseeker Beach day," she said. "We just sent those two ladies there."

"To stay at the Cottages?" Eliza asked.

"That's what they were looking for."

"Oh, dear," Eliza said. "The Cottages are closed for a while."

"What?" Penny's eyes widened. "Why?"

"Teddy's going to take a short trip with me," Eliza told her without hesitation. And that was *all* she'd tell her.

But Penny frowned as if she smelled more to the story. "Why would she close? She has guests right now, doesn't she?"

"Not many, and she's doing me a favor and taking a short trip with me."

"Oh, dear, those ladies are going to be mighty unhappy," Patty said. "They came all the way from Canada to stay there."

"Not both of them," Penny corrected. "Weren't you listening? The daughter was from New York, and the mother..."

Sensing an onslaught of Penny and Patty, Eliza gave a nudge to Olivia, who'd gathered a handful of brochures. "Let's go before we miss your plane. Bye!" They headed toward the door as Penny nattered on to her sister.

"She was from France originally, that's what the one named Camille said. So—"

"What?" Eliza and Olivia whipped around so fast they nearly collided.

"Did you say *Camille*? From *France*?" Eliza practically crawled over the counter and Olivia was right there with her.

"Those two women?" Olivia demanded. "The ones we just passed?"

"They were going to Shellseeker Beach?" Eliza's voice rose with tension and shock and a weird amount of hope.

"They were looking for Teddy," Penny said. "And just like you, they couldn't find the place on GPS."

Olivia and Eliza stared at each other, speechless.

"That's what I smelled," Eliza whispered, rubbing the chills that blossomed on her arms. That perfume. That scent. It was from her dream. "Olivia! That was my sister!"

"*What?*" Penny and Patty cried in unison.

"Let's go!" Olivia grabbed her arm. "Fast! Katie might send them away!"

They shot out the door, both of them staring at the parking lot, empty but for the red Mustang. They ran to it, and Teddy sat up straight when they yanked the doors and leaped in.

"What's wrong?" she asked.

"We're going back to Shellseeker Beach." Eliza yanked her seatbelt with a shaky hand.

"What? Why?"

She opened her mouth to respond, but something made her close it again. Something in her gut told her Teddy would say no, she didn't want to meet Dutch's mistress—it was bad enough she had to suffer knowing the man had been married to someone else while he was with her.

But Eliza *had* to meet her sister. She had to.

"We're really going back?" Teddy asked as Eliza peeled out of the lot and turned right.

"I left my phone charger!" Olivia announced, meeting Eliza's gaze in the rearview mirror, obviously in agreement about not telling Teddy.

"You can buy one," Teddy said. "You'll miss your flight."

"There'll be another one," Olivia said.

"We'll make it," Eliza said, but she didn't mean the airport.

"We will if you keep running stop signs!" Teddy exclaimed in shock.

"Just...brace yourself, Teddy."

"For death?" She clung to her seatbelt and threw her head back, her expression horrified when Eliza whipped the car around a truck and got a long, hard honk in response.

"For..." She looked at Olivia again. "Something."

She shot down the main drag, barely slowed at a stop sign, and broke all the speed laws on the island until she whipped onto Roosevelt Road, letting out a noisy exhale when she saw the car that had been parked at the welcome center.

Teddy finally exhaled and put her hands on her chest when Eliza slammed on the brakes, parking askew. "I'll wait—"

"Suit yourself," Olivia said. "But I want to meet this woman."

"What woman? What are you talking about? What's going on, you two?" she demanded as she pulled herself out of the low-slung car.

Eliza was already out, peering at the beach and the gardens, and halting mid-step when she spotted the two women leaving the tea house. The older woman had black hair, shiny and cut in a bob. She was lean and elegant and...familiar.

She was definitely the woman from the photo.

And next to her, a younger woman. Eliza just knew who it was. Who it *had* to be.

"Who is that?" Teddy asked again.

Eliza put a gentle hand on her shoulder. "It's Camille."

Teddy gasped. "What is she doing here?"

"I don't know. But I want to find out. And I want to meet my sister."

Eliza walked a few steps ahead, then lifted her hand toward them, not surprised it was trembling. "Hello? Camille?"

The older woman stopped and turned, looking right at Eliza. From here it was easy to see that even at her age, which could be anywhere over sixty, she was stunning. She had prominent cheekbones like the beauty in that picture, dark eyes and a wide mouth. Dressed in a bright pink sheath, she looked like a classic Parisienne woman strolling down the Seine, not Shellseeker Beach.

And beside her, holding back a luxurious mane of chocolate brown hair that fluttered in the breeze, was a woman who looked to be in her forties, also attractive. Beautiful, actually.

"We're looking for Theodora Blessing," the younger woman said, coming closer. "My name's Claire."

"Claire." Eliza whispered the name, aware that Olivia was next to her, and Teddy right behind, but all of the other women on the beach faded as Eliza looked into eyes that were golden brown but had the same familiar shape as Eliza's. Her nose, too, looked like Eliza's, and maybe that tentative smile.

"I don't think we know each other," Claire said, reaching her hand out to shake the one Eliza offered. "Claire Sutherland. And you are..."

But a handshake wasn't enough. Eliza took one step closer and put her arms around the woman, who stiffened and gave an awkward laugh.

"Um, okay. Hello." She eased back, humor in her gold-flecked brown eyes. "Local custom?"

Only for sisters, Eliza thought. "I'm Eliza Vanderveen Whitney. And I hope I'm not blowing your mind, but I'm your—"

"Sister!" Claire gasped the word, yanking Eliza in for a re-do and a much warmer embrace. "Finally! I finally get to meet you!"

Finally? *Wait...what?*

"You knew about me?" Eliza asked, easing away. "How is that possible? Why...how?" She looked from one woman to the other, the new arrivals looking kind of... well, not really that surprised about all of this. "I don't get it."

Camille smiled and extended her hand. "Eliza," she said. "You are as beautiful as your father said. And you? Teddy?" She stepped closer and extended both hands this time. "He said your hair made you look like an angel, and I see that now."

"Excuse me?" Teddy barely croaked the words.

Without answering, Camille shifted her attention to Olivia. "And you must be Olivia. How wonderful to meet you. But, as I always knew, it would be sad when this day came. We couldn't meet until he was gone, and now he is." She spoke with the faintest hint of a French accent, as hard to capture as the perfume she wore. They both wore it, actually, and Eliza recognized it as the very scent from her dreams.

This was the woman she walked with, she thought with a start. Claire. Her sister...her family.

But how did Claire know who she was? "Okay," Eliza said. "I am utterly and totally confused. How do you know us, and we don't know you?"

Camille let out a dramatic sigh and looked around. "Such a long story to tell you, but this place is beautiful! Everything my husband told me it was."

Eliza and Olivia both startled at the words, looking at each other.

"Did she say..." Eliza managed.

"Yes, husband," Claire replied. "But relax. It's not as bad as you think." She added a smile. "Sister."

Eliza put her hand to her lips, reeling. Sister. Yes, that was good. But another wife? Oh, that was so, so bad.

As they took a few steps toward the house, Eliza suddenly remembered the time. "Olivia! Your plane."

"Can take off without me. I wouldn't miss this for the world."

Chapter Twenty-four

Teddy

Teddy was so rattled she didn't even offer tea. Why couldn't she get a vibe from this woman, Camille?

They gathered in the eat-in kitchen, starving for an explanation, making some meaningless small talk, letting the awkward moment of meeting slide into something else. The whole time, Teddy tried to sense something from Camille...fear, joy, worry, satisfaction, revenge, concern. *Anything.*

But Camille had an emotional force-field around her. Claire, her beautiful daughter, on the other hand, was vibrating with something good and that, at least, helped ease Teddy's tension.

"So, ladies," Camille started, putting manicured hands draped in gold and diamonds on the table. "Let me tell you everything you need to know."

Across the table, Eliza seemed to soften, unable to take her attention off Claire, who had an equally hard time keeping her gaze off Eliza. Both of them exuded warmth and curiosity toward the other. Olivia, on the other hand, stared at Camille with hardened skepticism.

"Dutch Vanderveen and I had a long, colorful, and,

oh, I guess you'd call it unorthodox, marriage," Camille said with a raised brow. "Is that fair, Claire?"

She glanced at her daughter, who rolled her eyes.

"Let's just say if you want a reason why I had one brief and failed marriage, and remain steadfastly single at forty-five?" Claire gave a humorless laugh. "Look no further than my wacky and weird parents."

Camille gave a shrug. "Whatever. It worked for us, two terribly flawed people."

Teddy heard those very words from Dutch so many times. People are flawed, he would say, in exactly the same unapologetic tone. She leaned forward to ask the next question, the one burning in her heart, the one she had to know.

"When did you divorce?" Teddy whispered.

Camille met Teddy's gaze, unapologetic. "We never did."

Eliza and Olivia sucked in soft, surprised breaths.

"It was just too complicated," Camille insisted. "We were married in France," she continued, as if that explained anything. "And he was American and the idea of divorce, the few times we thought we should get one, was a big, wretched jumble of legal roadblocks and too much time and money. However, Theo..." She smiled as if she knew no one but Dutch called Teddy by that name. "This is now to your most distinct advantage."

Advantage? Nothing was to her advantage.

Teddy reached for a quartz crystal in the middle of her table, holding it between her hands and hoping it would take away the agony that came with knowing she'd spent two years loving, and living with, a man who had apparently been married *to two other women at the same time.*

"After Dutch and Mary Ann divorced, we were married because I was pregnant with my angel, Claire." Camille put her hand on the arm of her daughter, who, Teddy noticed, didn't exactly return the affection. "Honestly, I didn't care if we were married or not. I didn't even change my name. I'm French and we do not live by... American society's rules."

She leaned back to drop a dramatic pause and keep all their attention riveted on her.

"But Pan American airlines?" She looked skyward. "Rules abound and they cared that I was married. They cared very, very much. So, for practical reasons, like health insurance and maternity leave and keeping my beloved job as a stewardess, Dutch and I walked into the council office in Paris and signed the necessary papers to be married legally."

"But never made it un-legal," Olivia said slowly.

Camille spared her a look. "I moved to Canada when Claire was a baby to work. Quebecair had excellent benefits for women with children. So a divorce became impossible then, and...and..." She swallowed hard. "The details don't matter. He took off, made a big fat mistake, and..."

"Married Birdie," Teddy surmised.

She flinched as if the name caused her physical pain.

"Yes," Camille said. "Which was incredibly stupid because he was already married, so their union is null and void."

"It is?" Teddy and Eliza asked in perfect unison.

"Oh, yes. Birdie's in for the surprise of her life. Her beloved marriage that she clung to with both hands isn't a marriage at all, but she doesn't know that yet." Camille smiled as if she couldn't wait to bring that hammer down.

"Wait a second," Olivia said. "All he had to do was tell her he was already married. Boom. He was free and clear."

"That would have ruined his career and life," Camille said simply. "If it came out that he had committed bigamy, he'd have never flown a plane again, lost his Pan Am pension and stock, and been blackballed by all the airlines."

Teddy looked down, thinking of Dutch and how all of that mattered so much to him, more than anything, really. While conventions and legalities and other people's feelings came in a far second, third, and fourth place.

"He liked to ignore things and fly away from his problems," Teddy mused.

"Precisely." Camille gave her a smile that didn't quite reach her eyes. "Anyway, he finally left her, but not without signing her precious 'iron-clad' will. He knew that when the time came, my marriage would have precedence over hers, legally. So, for that reason, and the fact that it was such a monumental bother, we never divorced. And he wrote another will, the one Claire has."

"My father, the bigamist," Eliza muttered as she dropped back into her seat, looking at Claire. "Are you... okay with that?"

The other woman tipped her head. "I've had more time than you to process this," she said.

Eliza smiled at her, the connection between them already palpable.

Camille tapped her finger in Eliza's direction. "But now you know why he avoided you," she said. "He was certain you'd find out, or ask the wrong question, or even dig into his life. Or that your mother would, since she hated him so profoundly."

"He knew he was dying," Eliza said, her voice strained. "He should have undone his mess. He should have contacted me."

"Dutch should have done a lot of things," Camille agreed, a little too carelessly, in Teddy's opinion. "But he was who he was, and all of us, in our own screwed-up ways, loved him."

Olivia curled a lip. "Speak for yourself. The more I hear, the less I love."

"So, after he left Birdie, did you two get back together?" Teddy asked.

"On and off," Camille said. "Mostly off, but we remained very, very good friends. He traveled mostly, visited occasionally, and he just...flew around the world." She closed her eyes. "And then he was diagnosed with an inoperable brain tumor and came here, to his investment property."

Investment property. The words smacked at Teddy's heart, so cold and heartless and not what Shellseeker Beach was at all.

"Months and months went by and I didn't hear much

from him," Camille continued, "but then he called and told me everything. And told me that you, Teddy, had given him hundreds of 'extra days,' as he called it. And he asked that I help you when he died."

"Help...me?" Teddy sat up straighter. "How?"

Camille held her hand out to Claire, who had opened a file folder and produced a legal-sized document. "This is Dutch's *real* will. This document is unassailable and leaves everything to me, his only legal wife."

"Oh." Teddy's heart dropped so hard, she could have sworn she heard it hit the floor. So now *two* women were going to fight for her family's legacy?

"And once it's in my name, I'm selling it to you for one dollar."

Teddy gasped again. And blinked. And nearly fainted. "To me? A dollar?"

"Too much?" Camille asked on a dry laugh.

Around the table, there was stunned silence. Teddy couldn't contain her racing heart. Eliza was beaming at Claire. And Olivia looked from one to the other like...she didn't buy any of it.

"Why didn't you come sooner?" Olivia asked, not making much effort to hide her distrust.

"I didn't know he died," Camille replied. "Not until my attorney in Paris told me your man had contacted him."

"Birdie's going to fight you," Eliza said. "That same investigator met with her lawyer, and she is—"

"Let her fight." Camille swiped her bejeweled hand through the air like she'd use it to slice Birdie off at the knees. "She married a man who was already married, and she doesn't have a leg to stand on."

Teddy pressed her hands harder against her lips, nothing making enough sense to suit her. "Why...would you do this?" she asked. "Why wouldn't you just keep your inheritance?"

Camille's face, the angles and bones and silky-smooth skin so beautiful it hurt to look at it, finally softened. "I owe it to him."

"You owe *him?*" Olivia scoffed. "He literally married another woman while he was married to you."

She slid a cold gaze to Olivia, a sudden tension arcing between them. "I made a deathbed promise, dear. I won't break that."

Olivia's eyes flickered, but she didn't respond.

"Now." Camille held one hand toward Eliza and one toward Claire. "Someone go get Dutch's secret bottle of Chivas next to his bed. We're only here until tomorrow, so let's make the most of it."

Moving as if in a fog of disbelief and shock, Teddy stood, as ready for that Chivas as anyone. As she did, she tried to sense some kind of feeling again, placing a hand on Camille's narrow shoulder.

But, still, she felt absolutely nothing. As much as she wanted to cling to this hope and new possibility, feeling nothing from Camille worried her.

THE SUNSET WAS perfect that evening as Teddy walked down the boardwalk to the beach, stopping at the end to take it in. Streaks of peach and pink across puffy clouds, spilling a river of gold over the indigo waters of the Gulf. Dutch would have called it chasing the light, and told Teddy a story of flying west at just the right speed to see how long he could follow the sunset.

And she'd have listened, fascinated.

Whatever Dutch Vanderveen had been—good, bad, impossible, and delightful—he had a magnetic quality. That was his greatest strength, and his biggest weakness.

Teddy put her hand on the railing, remembering that last morning when she sat right here with Dutch, moments before he died. Closing her eyes, she sank to the wood, squeezing her eyes shut to block out the gorgeous sunset and see, instead, the face of the complicated man who had, in his own messy way, loved her.

A man she'd healed, but hadn't ever really known. A man with so many secrets, it took at least four different women to keep them all. A man who had, even in death, figured out a way to take care of her. Maybe. That is, if Camille was to be believed.

And at that thought, which had plagued her for hours, Teddy's heart gripped and hurt.

"Hey, there."

She opened her eyes at the sound of Eliza's voice, turning to see her making her way down the boardwalk.

"Are they all settled in?" Teddy asked.

"They are, thanks to Katie's amazing assistance. I know they're leaving tomorrow, but I think it was a good idea to give them Junonia. I'm all set up in the guest suite in your house, which was a breeze, since I travel so light. Olivia's in Sunray Venus for the moment. Thank you for making it so easy."

Teddy gave a soft laugh. "Thank you for..." She shook her head. "I don't know where to begin. For finding Camille and chasing her down, standing so strong next to me, and helping me process all of this."

"Not too much to process, I hope. I mean, they came bearing *great* news." Eliza eased herself down to sit next to Teddy at the end of the boardwalk. "It *is* great, Teddy. Hard to wrap your head around, but Claire insists this is what her mother wants, so that's fantastic."

"It is," Teddy agreed.

"Then what's wrong?"

"I guess I'm just shaken by how little I knew Dutch. He fooled me, and not many people do that."

"Maybe you wanted to be fooled," she suggested. "Maybe he just came into your life at the right time, and it was easier not to dig too deeply into his past. After all, he needed to be healed and you need to heal. It was kind of a match made in heaven."

"Maybe," Teddy said, not sure if she agreed, but Eliza was wise and her assessment made sense. At least it helped her rationalize how she could fall so hard for a man who already had two wives.

"And you know what else was made in heaven?" Teddy put her head on Eliza's shoulder. "You."

Eliza chuckled and patted Teddy's head, keeping it close to her. "Thanks. I know things are up in the air,

Teddy, but if you don't mind, I'd still like to stay here for a while. Until everything shakes out."

"Really?" Teddy sat straight as a new emotion shot through her. A happy, joyful one. "I'd love that, Eliza."

"I was thinking maybe we can do some of that renovation work you wanted to do, and get ready for your big season. There's no reason to shutter Shellseeker Cottages now. We're just in a bit of legal limbo, but you're not going to lose this, Teddy."

"Oh." She pressed her hand to her chest, wanting to believe that with every cell in her body. "Yes, please. You can live right in the house with me, unless you want one of the cottages."

"I like your house, but I'd love to unload that rental car. Could get expensive long-term."

"Dutch's car is parked behind Sanibel Treasures," Teddy said. "It's sporty, but if you can drive a stick, it's yours. Well, I guess it's technically part of Dutch's estate."

"Which is going to be yours," Eliza insisted, putting a reassuring arm around Teddy's shoulders. "That's a perfect solution. I'll borrow the car and stay at least through the hearing, which Claire thinks will be held here, at the courthouse in Lee County."

"Oh?" Teddy blinked in surprise. "Even though the wills are in Alabama and New York?"

"Yep. She said because Dutch's last known address was here and the majority of his estate is property in this county, she can legally wrangle a…I don't remember the Latin word, but the hearing would be local."

"And will Claire be Camille's official attorney?"

"No, she's the executor of the will."

"But not named as an heir, I noticed."

"Nope. Everything was left to Camille. Claire said it was because they both knew this day would come and Dutch knew that Camille was strong enough to withstand Birdie. Obviously, when he wrote the will, he didn't know about you, but..."

Teddy nodded. "Do we have to find a local lawyer for her?"

"No, Claire works for a large law firm, and there's an attorney in their Miami branch who specializes in probate law." Eliza tightened her grip, no doubt still seeing the worry in Teddy's eyes. "She's sure they'll beat any argument Birdie has. What do you think of that?"

"Like it's too good to be true," Teddy admitted.

"Now you sound like my cynical daughter."

"I don't want to be cynical," Teddy said. "I want to believe this will happen. It gives us so much hope and happiness. And you seem happy about it."

"I am." A smile lifted Eliza's lips and she let go of Teddy long enough to give a happy clap. "I have a sister! How can I not be thrilled?"

Teddy nodded. "Then I'm going to be happy with you. Deciding to be happy is half the battle, I always say."

They sat quietly for a moment, letting it all sink in. Then Eliza said, "You know, on the way up here, on the ferry, I was thinking of how I never felt like I belonged anywhere. I've always felt like I was one step out of place. But now? Here?"

"You belong here?" Teddy guessed.

"For now, I do. And I love that feeling, Teddy."

"Now *that* makes me happy." Teddy dropped her head on Eliza's shoulder. "You're truly the daughter I never had but always wanted. So, I guess Dutch left me the best gift of all."

"He left us each other," Eliza said softly. "We can't hate him for that."

"I don't hate him at all. I just didn't know him at all, and that kind of frightens me."

"And Camille?"

Teddy gave a wry chuckle. "She kind of frightens me, too."

"Hey, you two!" They both turned to see Olivia striding down the boardwalk.

"How did the call go?" Eliza asked.

"Very well." Olivia stepped around them and hopped on the sand, dramatically throwing her hands in the air. "Better than I expected, actually."

Teddy frowned. "What call?"

"I returned the call to the head honcho in my department, Nadia, and we had a very nice chat about the rollout that she credited to someone other than the true author...*me*." She lifted a brow. "She strongly suspected that it was my work, but since I wasn't there..."

"So you're headed back now?" Teddy asked, her heart dropping at the thought of her leaving now.

"Not exactly." A smile pulled. "Nadia felt awful, of course, and she said she's not going to let Alex and Jason get away with this, but..." That smile grew bigger.

"Instead corporate headbashing, which will change nothing, I asked for a different favor, which will change everything. For me, anyway."

Next to her, Eliza sucked in a breath. "What we talked about, Liv?"

She nodded. "Yep. I requested a sabbatical to further my career with an opportunity to manage an independent retail operation that caters to a constantly changing demographic, and gives me much-needed merchandising and buying experience on the local level."

Teddy leaned forward, lost. "Excuse me?"

Olivia laughed. "I'm going to run Sanibel Treasures this summer while Roz and George are up in Ohio! I just made it sound like a resume builder so I can stay on the Promenade payroll while I'm here. Nadia was so furious about being snookered on the rollout that she said one hundred percent yes."

"Livvie!" Teddy pushed up to a stand, arms out. "Are you serious? Are you sure?"

Olivia met her for a hug. "Never been more certain of anything. Plus, I can't let you two navigate the Frenchies alone."

"The Frenchies?" Teddy laughed, but her smile quickly faded. "What do you mean, *navigate*?"

"Oh, come on now. They blow in here with a new will, a big story, and an offer to sell the place for a dollar?" Olivia shook her head. "Sorry, I'm not quite that gullible."

Teddy inched back, then looked at Eliza.

"Don't ask her," Olivia added. "Mom's in a happy

haze over a new sister. And they might be legit, Teddy. But they might not. Someone has to be the voice of reason when dealing with the French invasion. That someone is me, the family skeptic."

Teddy felt a smile pull, focusing on one word, not the other. "Family," she whispered.

"That's what we are," Eliza assured her, standing up to join them.

"Yes, you are," Teddy agreed. "And come hell, high-water, or the Frenchies, that's what matters."

"We have strength in numbers," Eliza said with a little fist pump. "Even with Roz and George in Ohio, there are three of us plus Katie and Deeley."

"Oh, yeah, Deeley." Olivia slid into a grin. "Forgot about him."

"*Riiight,*" Eliza and Teddy teased in unison.

Laughing from her heart for the first time in days, Teddy draped an arm around each of them, comforted by their warmth and love and that beautiful sensation of connection.

"Come on, girls," she said. "Let's go make sure they didn't sell the place out from under us while we were gabbing in the gazebo."

They stepped onto the boardwalk, walking arm-in-arm while they watched the sun dip into the Gulf of Mexico.

Eliza started humming and Olivia picked up the tune, and soon, the two of them were singing the prettiest words Teddy had ever heard.

"We'll find a new way of living...we'll find a way of forgiving."

Teddy opened her mouth and chimed in. "Someday...somewhere."

As they walked, she held tight to the newest broken shells she'd found on the beach, tenderly adding them to her family. With them, she could face whatever happened next.

Don't miss the next heartwarming adventure! The story continues with *Sanibel Treasures*, book 2 in the series, chock full of family, friends, heartache, hope, and some unexpected surprises in Shellseeker Beach.
Sign up for the newsletter to get an email every time Hope Holloway releases a new book!

The Shellseeker Beach Series

Come to Shellseeker Beach and fall in love with a cast of unforgettable characters who face life's challenges with humor, heart, and hope. For lovers of riveting and inspirational sagas about sisters, secrets, romance, mothers, and daughters...and the moments that make life worth living.

Sanibel Dreams - Book 1
Sanibel Treasures - Book 2
Sanibel Mornings – Book 3
Sanibel Sisters – Book 4
Sanibel Tides – Book 5
Sanibel Sunsets – Book 6
Sanibel Moonlight – Book 7

The Coconut Key Series

If you're longing for an escape to paradise, step on to the gorgeous, sun-kissed sands of Coconut Key. With a cast of unforgettable characters and stories that touch every woman's heart, these delightful novels will make you laugh out loud, fall in love, and stand up and cheer... you'll want to read the entire series!

A Secret in the Keys – Book 1
A Reunion in the Keys – Book 2
A Season in the Keys – Book 3
A Haven in the Keys – Book 4
A Return to the Keys – Book 5
A Wedding in the Keys – Book 6
A Promise in the Keys – Book 7

About the Author

Hope Holloway is the author of charming, heartwarming women's fiction featuring unforgettable families and friends and the emotional challenges they conquer. After a long career in marketing, she gave up writing ad copy to launch a writing career with her first series, Coconut Key, set on the sun-washed beaches of the Florida Keys. A mother of two adult children, Hope and her husband of thirty years live in Florida. When not writing, she can be found walking the beach with her two rescue dogs, who beg her to include animals in every book. Visit her site at www.hopeholloway.com.

Made in the USA
Columbia, SC
23 April 2023

15695446R00183